The Invisible Boarder

The Invisible Boarder

Mildred Davis

Random House: New York

Library of Congress Cataloging in Publication Data

Davis, Mildred B.
    The invisible boarder.

    I. Title.
PZ3.D2963In [PS3507.A7424]   813'.5'4   74-4316
ISBN 0-394-49022-3

Manufactured in the United States of America
9 8 7 6 5 4 3 2
First Edition

To
Lee Wright

With thanks to
Dr. John Lambert

The Invisible Boarder

One

Arriving at a railroad station in a strange town in January is like being dropped in purgatory to await judgment. I felt abandoned, more alone than I had ever been in my life. I examined the street I had been seeing in my dreams for four years, and I wasn't sure I wouldn't wake up this time also, lying in bed at home, back covered with sweat, face streaming with tears, while I begged God to allow me to reweave those few short hours of my life when the whole pattern had been destroyed.

It was the freezing cold which told me it wasn't a dream. A wind tore down the tunnel of the street, howling like a dog. I shivered and drew back into the protection of the building, wishing someone else had gotten off the train here.

At nine-thirty at night, Freetown was nearly deserted. There were few pedestrians, and when a car went by, it darted like a water bug past a predatory fish. The stores facing the railroad station—cleaning establishment, stationer, bakery, gift shop, haberdashery, tobacconist, cheese shop—were like cardboard props with nothing behind their façades. Any minute the director would emerge and start shooting the scene.

I was hesitating, not sure whether or not the Barkers planned on picking me up, when I noticed the man and the small boy disappearing up the street. There was something familiar about the set of the boy's shoulders, and without stopping to think, I shouted, "Teddy! Teddy!" and started to run after them. They turned, and of course there was no resemblance. In spite of the fact that I had known all along that no power on earth could ever bring him back to me, the shock was so great, I lost my breath and nearly stumbled.

They hurried on, avoiding involvement with what the train had brought out of the night, and I went back to the station and sat down. For a long time I stared at the damp muck that had been deposited over the years. Opposite me was a line of benches, littered with abandoned newspapers, gum wrappers and train schedules. Both the ticket office and the newspaper stand were shuttered, and even the washrooms were locked. Only the door to the battered telephone booth hung open laxly. The walls were plastered with ancient campaign literature, names and messages penciled around the edges. There was no sound and no movement, except for the half-imagined disappearing rumble of the train, and something small and black scurrying into a hole. I thought of H. G. Wells' twilight of the world with nothing left but the monster crabs.

"Taxi, miss?"

I hadn't registered the sound of a car driving up, and I turned numbly. He was young, at least five years my junior, with a long beard and shoulder-length hair, and he sounded impatient, as though he'd been trying to attract my attention for some time.

"Yes." I got up and looked around vaguely for my belongings. He took the suitcase and I the duffel bag, and we went out to the dented, dusty-looking cab. Tossing my luggage in back, he motioned me companionably to the seat beside him.

"Barker," I said, getting in. "Circle Drive."

"Sure thing." He was chewing gum, a large wad of it; it made his speech indistinct.

Inside the cab it was so hot I took off my fur-lined jacket and put it across my lap. In addition to the heat, there was a strong smell of sweat, and furtively, I let down the window slightly.

Racing the engine with no regard for the longevity of the machine, he backed up, and then tore around in a wide circle. "You gonna board at the Barkers'?"

I studied his profile. He was good-looking under all the hair. "Do you know the Barkers?" I asked.

"Sure. I know everybody. Not to speak to, but who they are. Driving a taxi around, you listen and you hear things."

You listen and you hear things. The words echoed unpleasantly. Maybe some day he'd listen and hear things about me. Folding my hands, I looked out of the window. The street lights formed glowing islands in the dark, and in the yellowed orbs could be seen the moths of dead summers. All the store doors were bolted, looking tight-lipped and guarded in the night. We passed the Freetown Boys' Club, red-brick office buildings, shabby groceries, a huge supermarket, a gas station, and then a travel agency, windows ablaze with the glories of tropical islands. The dinginess of the street was a melancholy contrast to the glories of the posters. From far off a siren wailed, lonely and sad in the night, evoking images of a fire raging in a tenement, a car filled with crushed teenagers, or a woman in labor being rushed to the hospital.

"What do you *hear* about the Barkers?" I asked, faintly emphasizing the "hear."

"The Barkers? Like I said. They take in boarders. He don't make much money, being a reporter. And anyway, who could keep up a house like they got? It beats me what they need it for. I guess you must of heard about that murder on their property four years ago. It was in all the papers. They never found out who did it. The police—"

"I read about it." The tone of my voice brought his head around sharply, but I turned away.

After we'd driven in silence for three minutes, he said, "You gonna go to the community college?"

"No."

"You a nurse? A teacher?"

"No."

"What *do* you do?"

No wonder he knew so much. "I have a job on the *Gazette*." I wasn't sure why I was so reluctant to say it.

Again his head swiveled. "You a reporter? Like Barker?"

"Yes."

"I once figured I'd be a reporter. I worked for my high school paper. Sports, you know? I was good too. Everyone said.

5

But I didn't have the dough for college, and those lousy editors, they want college grads. You a college grad?"

"Yes."

Flickering light, brilliance and shadows, alternated across his face as we sped through the deserted streets. Then, abruptly, we came upon a solid block of illumination. It was the county hospital, red brick and gray stone. The whole area had a curious air of expectation, as though it were a courtyard in which an execution was about to take place. As we went by, an ambulance burst from the driveway, and with a shriek of the siren, skidded past us, disappearing in a moment.

"—ain't my bag. I can't work all day and study at night, you know? Look at that guy go. The way he's driving, he'll make his own accidents."

We passed a church, and then we were in the older residential area: high, narrow Victorian houses, mean and pinched-looking with their dwarfed porches, filmy yellowed curtains, Lilliputian lawns filled with skeletal hydrangea, broken, gut-spilling furniture peering out from behind the protective bushes. I caught a glimpse of a face at one of the windows. Thin, delicate-boned, sexless, ancient, it stared at the street from a background, I imagined, of stale odors, unmended furniture, cracked china, inadequate food and poor medical attention.

Just beyond was the new recreational park. It was an archipelago of peace, with a lake for skating, and a Japanese-style pagoda filled with the warm radiance of lanterns. Close in physical proximity to the face in the window, it was worlds away in terms of availability.

And then we were in what had been country only four years ago. Now, instead of an occasional farmhouse, there were myriads of well-spaced white frame houses, each with an attached garage, neat lawn and set number of rhododendrons, yews and junipers. Here, too, it was easy for me to sense what was behind the pink, yellow and blue doors: L-shaped living-dining rooms, wall-to-wall carpeting, well-framed reproductions, unused fireplaces, modern kitchens, pine-paneled playrooms.

A six-lane highway, elevated above the road, slashed the fields in both directions with deep, unmendable gashes. The lights of all-night trucks lumbered past, tires humming on asphalt. And then, past the sign reading "Freetown Country Club," we began to reach real country. Except that even here, the woods seemed to wait in their own death row for the bulldozer. The road alternated between macadam and dirt, pulled by contending forces.

We began to climb. Underneath, the ground was hard and gutted, and on either side, the woods slept under a quilt of leaves. An occasional ghostly birch caught the reflection of the headlights amid the welter of darker trees. A startled deer, frozen into immobility, blocked the road until the boy honked the horn at it. I drew in a breath of the icy air and shut my eyes as bitter-sweet memories stung at my mind.

It was a plane passing overhead that brought it back. As I stared at the infinitesimal lights, distinguishable from the stars only in that they could be detected moving, I remembered the JAL flight to Hawaii, our first holiday in three years of marriage.

The stewardess, wearing a long Japanese ceremonial robe, offered us hot scented towels and paper slippers. When we were comfortable, she came back with porcelain dishes holding rice and fish. The drinks were in exotic pottery bowls. Combined with my excitement, the liquor had gone to my head, and Lawford had been faintly embarrassed at my giggling and conviviality.

"Isn't it exciting? I've never been so thrilled in my life. I wish we'd brought Teddy along. He'd have loved it."

"A two-year-old? He'd have driven us crazy."

"But I leave him every day while I'm working, and now I've gone off on vacation without him. The sun would have been good for him."

"Listen, if you're going to start that breast-beating routine again—"

"No, it's just that I'm all hipped up. I can't make up my mind whether to read about the islands or watch the Pacific or sleep so I'll feel good when we arrive. I'm so afraid of missing something. Do you think it'll be the way it is in the movies? You know, a huge orange moon and a deserted beach and guitar music in the background—"

"If the beach is deserted, who's playing the guitar?"

7

Below, I caught sight of a diamond-studded cruise ship on the luminous sea. Every inch of it shimmered and sparkled in the moonlight.

The car turned off the main road and I could hear pebbles crunching beneath the tires. I tried to peer past the trees, but I couldn't detect a light. Hemlocks, pines and spruces lined the driveway, choking off the sky, and straggly trees fought with tangles of underbrush for room to exist. In the swatch of visibility cut by the headlights, I could see an occasional rusted can or a scrap of paper. A large, half-dead maple, weakened by summer storms and winter blizzards, trailed naked branches to the earth. Remains of the last snowfall patched the woods, and I caught a glimpse of a discarded Christmas tree, a few silver icicles still clinging to the needles.

Making a turn, we came upon a large old oak tree which took up over a quarter of an acre of lawn, dwarfing lesser sycamores, dogwoods, sassafras, cypress, chestnut, aspen, apple and wild cherry trees. Almost lost in the tangle of underbrush, a rickety shed with a gaping door revealed stacked garden furniture and a rusted outdoor cooker.

And then, around the next turn, we finally came within sight of the house. Although there were only a few lights on, I could tell it was neither a modern cliché nor a Victorian disaster. A fit termination for the long driveway, it was large, rectangular, and belonged to no recognizable school of architecture. It could have been grand once, but it had never been first-rate, and now it had the look of the demimonde sunk into hard times.

It was a green stucco house, the paint faded and streaked, the trim corroded, several broken windows replaced by cardboard. There was a huge central section, flanked by two narrower wings, and an attempt had been made to soften the stucco with pachysandra, myrtle and azalea bushes. The front door had been painted an odd pink, like an aging woman with a ribbon in her hair, the last despairing effort to redeem the unredeemable.

Then the door opened. It had taken me four years to get here and all my attention was fixed on the woman framed by the light behind her.

She had been watching the driveway, I knew, because she appeared the minute the cab drove up. I had a blurred impression of smallness before I turned away to pay the driver. It gave me a chance to calm down. As though I were losing an old friend, I watched him disappear down the driveway.

There was a moment of cold quiet before I picked up the suitcase and duffel bag and made the final step of my journey.

Blinking in the light, I saw that she was at least six inches shorter than I was, and so delicately made I felt bulky and awkward. She had silky blond hair pulled into two pigtails which were not only anachronistic as far as her own age was concerned, but out of keeping with the current fashion. Her complexion was pink and flawless. The first impression she made was of gossamer fragility, the second of constant movement. I had never seen such mobility in anyone. She fluttered, vibrated and palpitated, all except for her face, which was unusually still. The third impression was more difficult to define. There was a vaguely disturbing lack of balance or symmetry in her which spoiled what should have been prettiness.

She had begun to talk from the first moment she saw me. She had a light, pleasant, regionless voice, slightly marred by a head cold. "You're Norma. I'm *so* glad to meet you at last. I'm Daisy Barker. I've been sitting here on the edge of my chair for *ages* waiting to catch my first glimpse of you. I would have met the train, but they're so often late, I was afraid I would have to wait for hours. I adore seeing my boarders before they even know I'm watching them. I'm simply fabulous on first impressions, and I can tell that *you're* going to be divine. The others will be so sorry they didn't wait to meet you, but they all went off on their usual activities. Mrs. Webster and Johnny—my husband—are in bed—not together, of course—" Her laugh was a high, piercing peal that was too prolonged. "And Wesley, Strandy and Verity are all out on the town. They lead gay, mad, dashing lives. Johnny and I are stay-at-homes. Not from choice, I *assure* you, but from being poverty-stricken. A reporter's salary is fine for you—a girl on her own—but it's terrible for Johnny with a wife to support."

All this time I had been standing at the door holding my suitcase and duffel bag. My arms ached, my head throbbed, and what I wanted most was to go to bed. But she showed no sign of stopping, and I began edging around her toward the stairs. Immediately she was contrite. Relieving me of the duffel bag, she chirped, "How inconsiderate of me! You must be *simply* exhausted! Would you like a cup of tea or coffee? I can whip up—"

"Nothing, thank you."

"It wouldn't be any trouble. All I have to do is boil the water, and while we waited, I could show you around. Then we could sit down cozily in the kitchen and get acquainted. And maybe the boys will get home early and see what they missed. I'll bet Verity'll be green with envy when she sees she has competition at last—she doesn't count me, of course, since I'm married and in my late thirties—"

I shifted the suitcase helplessly and looked around the vast entrance hallway. My aching tiredness, the initial shrinking I always had to overcome in a new situation, and most of all, the mission which had brought me here, all seemed worse in the dismal, poorly lit emptiness.

In front of me was a wide curving staircase to an upper gallery, and on either side were steps leading down to rooms which flanked this center ballroom. In spite of the fact that it was large enough for a dance, the room held only one small mirror, a rickety little table and a chair. The one item originally meant for a house of these proportions was a wall tapestry, but it was tattered and faded.

I maneuvered around Daisy Barker, my shoes sounding loud on the bare boards, and headed for the gloomy staircase.

"—that tired, we can wait for tomorrow evening. They'll all be *so* disappointed they didn't stay. Incidentally, I believe I did write you when you answered the ad that I didn't serve meals, but I'm not the least bit uptight about hot plates and coffee makers in the rooms. I know how expensive it is to eat out all the time." The prolonged barking laugh again. "That is, I don't actually *know,* but I've *heard* that it's expensive to eat out all the time. Anyway, we're all like one family and we keep our liquor downstairs and have a happy hour each evening before the rest of you jazzy creatures go out to your *fabulous* rendezvous."

The Invisible Boarder

On one side, the gallery overlooked the center hallway. I glanced down at a dusty cracked crystal chandelier that hadn't been lit in years. Opposite the railing were rows of closed doors. Up here, there wasn't even the amenity of mirror, chair and table. The lighting was poor and the temperature couldn't have been over sixty. I stopped at the oval window at the end of the hall and stared down into the woods. I could make out the branches of a maple tree, which some time in the distant past had been planted too close to the house, and as the years went by, had been stunted and crippled by lack of room to grow in. Glancing covertly at my landlady, I wondered if the same thing had happened to her.

"Isn't the view marvelous? We can't see another house anywhere. We're *madly* lucky. We own only five acres, but we're surrounded by spectacular estates, so we get all of the advantages without the taxes. We snapped up this white elephant for a song, but even so, we couldn't afford to keep it without taking in boarders. Fewer and fewer people can afford these old mansions any longer unless they convert them into something else. Poor old things. They remind me of Sleeping Beauty. It's too bad there aren't enough rich young princes to kiss them back to life."

I took another look at her, half expecting to see a teenager. But although the skin and figure were nearly good enough, the expression in her eyes was too opaque, too indecipherable. Besides, teenagers didn't talk that way either.

She opened the last door with a flourish, as though uncovering a masterpiece. I could tell that someone had expended a great deal of effort on the room. Although the basic ingredients of bed, table, chest and chair were cheap, they had been made palatable the way the French make poor meat palatable with good sauce. On the chest was a dried leaf arrangement, the lampshade was hand painted, a variety of interesting prints adorned the walls, the chenille spread was newly laundered, the curtains were bright. On the night table was a catholic assortment of books: *The Cassell Book of English Poetry*, edited by James Reeves; *Mainstreams of Modern Art* by John Canaday; *Bird Migrations* by Donald R. Griffin; Thoreau's *Walden* and

Civil Disobedience; Stendhal's *Le Rouge et le Noir*; and *Great Tales of Terror and the Supernatural.*

"It's a lovely room," I said.

"Oh, I'm *so* glad you like it. I've spent hours—days, actually—trying to make it just right. You wouldn't believe what I went through. I feel it's difficult enough coming to a new house in a new town without having to live in dreary surroundings. Oh, I just *know* we're going to get along beautifully. I like filling the house with bright young people. Of course, Mrs. Webster could hardly fall into that category"—bark, bark—"but she was our first boarder and she's been here forever."

I put the duffel bag and suitcase on the bed and began to unpack. She didn't stop talking, but watched with interest as I placed three dresses, two skirts, three pairs of slacks, two long outfits, one pair of slippers, robe, boots and evening sandals in the closet. Six tops, a second purse, underwear, pantyhose, two sets of pajamas, and toilet articles went into the chest of drawers. A book and a magazine, thrown on the bedside table, finished my unpacking.

"Do you like the books I provided for you? I selected them carefully for variety, and for what I knew to be your interests." In our limited exchange of business letters, I didn't recall mentioning art, poetry, birds or civil disobedience, much less terror. "I'm very psychic. Johnny laughs, but I *really* am. We must have a séance some time. Wouldn't that be fun? What an *adorable* outfit. But is that all you brought? You do travel lightly, don't you? Not that I own much myself. Anytime you want to, I would love to show you some of the *fabulous* shops in town. I get a vicarious thrill out of watching others shop. Oh, and before I forget, you'll simply *have* to buy a car out here. We have absolutely no public transportation. Of course all of us will be happy to help you out until you find one. Verity goes in about the same direction and she can drive you when you and Johnny have different shifts. She's a lovely girl except for the fact that she's *madly* in love with Johnny." Bark.

I finished unpacking, and not knowing what else to do, sat down on the edge of the bed to wait for her to leave. It was useless studying her face to see what went on behind the chatter because it was perfectly motionless except for the mouth.

12

"I really ought to leave you alone so you can get to bed. I can't wait to introduce you to the others. We'll have so much fun tomorrow evening. And when you're not so tired, I can give you the vital statistics about where to bank and get gas and go bowling, if that's what turns you on, and let us not forget the liquor store—"

"Daisy!" It was a pleasant male voice, calling from down the hall.

"Oh, dear. There goes Johnny roaring for me again. He can't bear being alone for a minute. Well, I mustn't stay another minute. I'll see you in the morning. Let me know if there is *anything* I can do for you. All right, Johnny. All right. I'm coming—" She continued speaking even after the door closed behind her, the unseen Johnny taking over for me.

I leaned back on the pillow and took a breath, and then, noticing that there was a key in the lock, I turned it. For a while I lay on the bed, waiting for all sounds to die down before I went to the bathroom. It seemed to me that talking too much might be a better cover-up for a person with something to hide than silence. Gradually the hum of my landlady's voice died down, and I listened to my watch ticking until I fell asleep.

I came to gradually, wondering where I was and what had awakened me. The dim bedside lamp was still on, and I sat up and glanced at my watch. I had thought it would be near dawn, but it was only eleven-forty.

Then, just outside my door, I heard a man say, "Make it snappy, Verity." A door slammed, footsteps sounded on the stairs, and I stiffened, but no one approached my room. There was the sound of a toilet flushing, sink water running, a murmur of low voices.

When it had been quiet for about five minutes, I gathered up my bag of toilet articles, slippers, robe and pajamas, and went into the hall. It was deserted. Slipping into the bathroom, I found it steamy and filled with a pleasant fragrance. I bathed quickly.

Back in my room, I was no longer sleepy. I went to the window and looked down at the moonlit lawn. The shadow of a tree was black against the silvery grayness, every branch clean-cut. Something stirred in the ivy where the woods started, and as I watched, a cat appeared, partially camouflaged by the dappled light. Muscles taut, it crawled forward silently. And then it pounced. There was a squeak, a quick shuffle and it was over.

Then I recoiled. Just under the tree was a bright yellow spot, the one shimmer in the gray murkiness. For a moment I couldn't figure out what it could be, and then I realized that it was the back of my landlady's head.

Encased in what looked like an ancient army jacket, she was bending over something on the ground.

Frozen, unable to breathe in case she could hear me through the glass, I continued watching. Crablike, she moved forward and to the left. Finally she rose and went around the house. I peered downward, trying to find a logical reason for a grown woman to be hunched over the ground in the middle of the night.

The only explanation that occurred to me was that she was a witch hunting for herbs for her spell.

I went back to bed.

Two

It began to snow my third day on the job, just as I was getting ready to leave the office on an assignment. Through one of the dirt-caked windows, I could see the pure fluffy flakes trailing earthward. Almost immediately they began to smooth out the ugly lines of the streets, the business offices and the cars.

"Do you go on like that forever?"

It was Chris Upham, the news editor, who had come up behind me.

"Like what?"

"Lady, all day you've been humming, 'It's over. It's over.' Enough is enough already." He was a large, shambling man in his early fifties who was always in shirt sleeves, tie askew, pants baggy. He had a pleasant, once-good-looking face, dissipated by too much liquor and too little of the outdoors.

"Actually, I didn't know I was doing it."

Sticking his pencil behind his ear, he peered at me over the top of his eyeglasses. "I'll forget it this time if you let me buy you a drink after work."

"Your wife wouldn't like it."

"Why should she start objecting now, after twenty years?"

I began gathering up folded yellow sheets, pencils and my jacket. Most of the other reporters were reading their own stories in the afternoon lull. Only one typewriter was going. Looking up from his newspaper, Johnny Barker, Daisy's husband, asked, "Is that dirty old man propositioning you?"

Johnny was a ten-year-younger version of Chris Upham,

except that he was slimmer and sounded as though he'd had a more expensive education. His hair was too grizzled for his age, and his handsome face was worn down, eroded. When he smiled, however, the effect was unexpectedly pleasing, like a crocus in the snow.

"Chris is harmless," I said. "If I accepted, he'd faint."

The teletype machine burst into spasmodic sputters, and Chris went into the room to tear off the tape. I put on my coat, weaved in and out of the cluttered desks, across the large, messy news room, and not waiting for the elevator, walked down the iron steps.

The air was mild as I stepped outside the office. Soft flakes powdered my hair and eyelashes, touched my tongue with seductive coolness. But it was all deceptively benign, I thought, as I hurried to the car. Like Daisy.

My secondhand Volkswagen was equipped with snow tires, but I wasn't sure how good they were. If I didn't finish up the assignment early, I would have a hard time getting back to the house.

The streets were already completely coated, even in the center of the business and shopping district, and there was an air of suppressed tension as snow-powdered pedestrians hurried along with bent heads. The cars, windshield wipers spinning, crawled slowly. Only two children, trying to scrape up enough snow for snowballs, were pleased with the weather.

I parked in the crowded high-school lot, wondering to whom all those vehicles belonged. *My* way of getting to school had been on a bus.

At the front office, they directed me to a small cafeteria off the main lunch room. The high school was new, and my shoes echoed on terrazzo floors. I caught glimpses of classrooms with electronic equipment. The students, jeaned, sweatered and sneakered, spoiled the décor.

The tiled cafeteria was already filled with the hosting group and the lecturers for vocational guidance. There was a television actor, confident, aloof and bored; an intense-looking author who chewed his nails; a talkative, outgoing psychologist; a business executive who, oddly, was the only one with longish hair and

16

mod clothing; one each representing the medical, legal and dental professions; and finally a female dress designer.

At sight of the last, a warning tingle shot up my spine. When I had first decided to come back to Freetown, I had been sure no one would recognize me. We'd lived in the town only a month, I'd spent all my time getting settled, and it had happened four years ago. Now, back less than a week, I was confronted by someone who looked familiar.

Trying to remember where I had seen her and what name went with the face, I started to speak to the others. I jotted names and background material, hoping I could avoid the dress designer completely and get the information from the hostess, but inexorably, the latter led me to each one.

Then I saw it would be all right. The dress designer's mind was elsewhere. She was shivering uncontrollably and seemed about to have a nervous breakdown.

"Are you cold?"

"No, it's not that. Oh, dear, why don't they start? If only they'd get it over with. I can't remember one thing I planned on saying and I can't read my notes."

"Did you forget your glasses at home?"

She looked at me, blinked and tried to focus. "I mean my hands are shaking so much. I hate public speaking."

"Oh." I tried to dredge up something comforting but couldn't. "Well. Would you mind answering a few questions?"

She paid no attention. "When I was twelve, I had to give a speech in assembly. I knew it backwards and forwards—"

"Did that help?" I asked before I could stop myself.

"What?" Without waiting for an answer, she went on. "And then, when I got up on the stage and saw that sea of faces, I forgot the entire speech."

I began to doodle a barn door, a square with crossed lines and a peaked roof—it was a puzzle; one wasn't supposed to pick the pencil off the paper. The actor was entertaining the others with an anecdote, the author had begun on the skin around his nails, and the doctor was saying that sterilization was the only answer.

To the dress designer, I said, "If I were you, I'd simply get up and leave."

"I wish I could. But my boss told me to go out and get the exposure."

"In the dress business?" I murmured.

Again she didn't hear. "You see, I'm divorced, and I have three children to support."

As usual the word "children" had a depressing effect. I went to the coffee urn, poured two cups and handed her one. Hardly knowing what she was doing, she drank in small, nervous sips and watched the hostess. I stared into my cup, trying to find the unfindable and thinking that tragedy had its compensations. Once the worst misfortune occurred, one never worried about the minor ones.

Finally the woman in charge began shepherding her experts into the auditorium. I sat down in the front row. The doctor, lawyer, dentist, psychologist, author and business executive gave competent five-minute speeches. The television actor brought the house down four times and received a prolonged ovation. And then it was the dress designer's turn.

I could almost see the goose pimples on her arm as she rose unsteadily. When she looked in the wings, I thought she was going to run, but instead she stared down at "the sea of faces." The sight of the lollers, chewers and whisperers made her look up quickly at the rear wall. She smiled vacantly and said she had wanted to be a dress designer all her life. She had started sketching at the age of six. A teacher to whom she had shown her early designs had suggested that she take up cooking. She waited for titters, but the audience was too sophisticated. Glancing at her notes, she evidently found that she'd been right. Her hands shook too much for her to read them. I mouthed words at her, telling her to discuss her first job, but she wasn't watching me.

"It's a very rewarding profession," she said in a spurt, "and anyone who wants to know more about it can see me later." And she sat down.

There was a stunned silence. Next to me, a boy said, "Gee, that's the best speech I ever heard in my life." He applauded her even more enthusiastically than he had the actor.

The moderator said a few words and then it was over. A

group of teenagers converged on the actor, ignoring the others. No one, apparently, wanted to be a business executive, psychologist, author, doctor, lawyer, dentist or dress designer.

Outside it was still snowing. Every harsh line in the landscape had been erased, every branch brush-stroked in white, every person softly powdered.

Tossing my notes and coat on the car seat, I was about to slide in when a bundle of white fur descended on me.

"My God. I was even worse than I was at twelve. At least then I had a prompter."

"They enjoyed the brevity."

"It was awful. I won't be able to face a soul in town. Listen, I have to unwind. You were so nice, I'd love to buy you a drink—"

The warning bell rang again. So far I'd been lucky, but relaxing over a drink, she might remember. "Sorry, I have to get back to the office to write up the story."

"This late in the afternoon? Do it tomorrow morning. The *Gazette* has only one edition a day, and you've already missed that."

"I'm also worried about the roads. If this keeps up, I can get stuck."

"This stuff won't be bad for at least another two hours. Come on. I have a sitter at the house and I don't want to get back too early."

The last statement made no sense to me, but in the end, I gave in and agreed to follow her to a bar called The Pink Elephant. While I drove, I automatically began composing a lead. "Three hundred students at George Washington High School heard eight experts in their respective fields discuss vocational opportunities at an assembly yesterday afternoon—"

The thick flakes continued their unhurried, dedicated job of covering the earth, but the Volkswagen purred along steadily. She was waiting outside The Pink Elephant to make sure that I didn't go by. I found a parking space and hurried back. Inside, it was dimly lit and decorated to resemble an English pub, even to the dart board. The drinks, however, were American and we both ordered whiskey sours. I lit a cigarette and we began to talk about the latest public scandal. I was reaching for the plate of nuts when her voice broke off and I turned to see what had happened.

My hand froze for a moment and then continued to the dish. I had been relaxed, glad that I had accepted her invitation, and now I saw that my first instinct had been correct. She was frowning at me in sudden concentration. Tension gone, and alcohol circulating through her system, she was taking her first real look at me.

"How many children did you say you have?" I asked quickly. "How old are they?"

"Haven't we met before?" She pushed her coat away from her shoulders and allowed it to dangle behind her.

"I doubt it. I only arrived in town a short time ago. Do any of your children attend George Washington?"

Offended, she said, "Oh, no. My children aren't old enough for high school. They're six, eight and eleven. Are you sure—"

"Listen to those horns honking in the street. There must be some kind of a snarl in the traffic. I wish the snow would stop."

Frowning, she continued to examine my lowered face. I took out my notes and made a useless notation. "Boys or girls?"

"What?"

"Your children."

"Oh. Boys at both ends and a girl in the middle. I don't even know your name."

The part of my face closest to her was beginning to feel hot. I wished the place would fill up. "Norma Boyd. What are your children's names?"

"Why? Are you going to mention them in the paper? They'll love it." Her face resembled a ferret's. "How long did you say you lived here, Norma?"

"I only just arrived." Finishing off my drink in a gulp, I snuffed out the cigarette and slipped off the stool. "I'd better be going."

"Only just arrived? Did you ever live here before? I'm sure we've met. Don't go yet. Have another drink."

A tight smile on my face, I said, "You've certainly gotten over your embarrassment."

I felt ashamed of myself, but she didn't hear me. Her eyes

suddenly widened. "I've got it!" I watched a spate of emotions cross her face, from the briefest of triumph to sudden doubt and finally something entirely different. She fumbled in her purse, took out some bills and placed them on the bar. "I'm so sorry. I didn't mean to—but you know how it is when someone seems familiar. No wonder you didn't want to talk about it. It was unforgivable of me."

My face had congealed. She took hold of my arm in her excitement, and I allowed it to drop so that her hand slid off. "It's like having a word on the tip of your tongue," she continued. "You can't rest until you remember it. It was about four or five years ago, wasn't it? Yes, four. I was about to enroll Gail in nursery school. It was a terrible tragedy. Awful of me to bring it up."

By now we were outdoors, our shoes soundless on the muffling snow. A woman, head ducking into the collar of her coat, hurried by, ghostlike in the late afternoon gloom. Finally I looked straight at her, my mouth hurting from keeping it rigid. "You've got me mixed up with someone else. Thank you for the drink." Leaving her standing in front of The Pink Elephant, I hurried to my car.

It was more like June than September—the sun bright, the temperature balmy and the air so fragrant I could feel joy bubbling in my throat. Behind the house, phlox and zinnias and mums, a little ragged from lack of care, formed a rainbow of lavenders, pinks, yellows and oranges. We finally had a house in the country, I was giving up work to stay home with Teddy, and perhaps, this time, the company wouldn't transfer us too soon.

"All you do is be busy," he complained. "I wanna play."

"I know, darling. But I have so much to do. It's so gorgeous, why don't you play outdoors on your tricycle while I put the books away."

"You can't ride on grass."

"Take your gardening tools out and prepare a bed for next year."

"You help me."

"You know what, Teddy? They have a museum and live animal farm nearby. As soon as we're settled, we'll go there."

"Now?"

"No, in a few days."

"I wanna go now."

"Or perhaps you can dig up some worms and Daddy'll take you fishing on the weekend."

Complaining and protesting, he finally went outdoors. I watched him through the window, a small yellow-haired figure in stained polo shirt and shorts and torn sneakers. Then I went back to the books. I became so absorbed, I forgot to keep checking.

An hour passed before I heard him calling. Guiltily, I ran to the door. He was running from the direction of the woods, shouting for me.

Putting down the books in my hands, I grabbed him in my arms and kissed him. "Where've you been? You've been gone for ages."

"Mommy, I saw Hansel and Gretel's house."

"How about that? Where?"

"Back there. Far away."

"Was it made of gingerbread and candy canes?"

"I saw somebody—they was dragging something on the floor and they got awful mad when they saw me."

Feeling only the slightest tinge of uneasiness, I said, "Really? Where was this house? What did you say you saw?"

"Back there." A wide, meaningless gesture.

"Who was dragging what?"

"Somebody. Dragging a bundle. They got awful mad when they saw me. I got scared and ran."

"You sure they were mad?"

"Mommy, will they find me?"

"I don't really know what you're talking about. How did you happen to see this?"

"Through the window."

"Come on, Ted. The window would be too high."

"No, honest. It was low. Will they find me?"

"I doubt it. Let's have a snack. How about milk and cookies? Or tea?"

I took out a doll tea set I'd had as a child and prepared small sandwiches and cookies. Then I had to straighten up and start dinner. The incident slipped from both our minds.

22

Three

I was crying when I reached the entrance to the driveway. Because I wasn't paying attention, the car skidded. I tried several times but couldn't make the slight incline. Finally I backed down and left the car on the road, on the side away from town.

With the motor off, an unearthly quiet descended on the world. I sat for a while, drying my eyes with a tissue and blowing my nose. When the tears stopped, I took out a mirror and examined my face. Then, after powdering the skin around my eyes, I got out of the car. The softly descending snow had obliterated all tire tracks, or else no one was home. I couldn't hear anything but my shoes crunching as I walked up the twisting, tunnel-like driveway. Even the sparrows and squirrels were quiet.

The house looked deserted. No cars and no lights. Either the others were still at work or stuck in the snow. The flakes kept floating earthward gently but relentlessly, covering everything. Even my footprints were nearly wiped out.

It occurred to me that it was the first time I had the house to myself.

Unconsciously reluctant, I took a long time unlocking the door. It was as though I were opening a Pandora's box and unleashing something unspeakable. Finally my numbed fingers got the key to turn.

The cavernous hallway yawned in front of me. Every door leading from it was open, even the one to the butler's pantry, and I could glimpse the dim, secretive expanses beyond. I checked to see if a car was in sight. There was nothing on the driveway but snow. Shivering in the damp cold, I took off my wet shoes and hung my jacket in the closet.

Abruptly, like an underground motor beneath the foundation of the house, machinery sprang into life. I had a picture of a creature about to emerge, slither from the depths below, start up the cellar stairs, and while I waited, petrified, press open the door an inch at a time. Finally the thing that had been gestating all those years would be loose among men.

But the machinery was the water pump and the refrigerator, and the only creature which emerged was a scurrying mouse. It darted across the hallway and disappeared into a crevice. I was about to turn away when I caught the glint of metal near the hole. In the faint light from the front window, I bent down to examine it, and caught a movement from the corner of my eye. Whirling around, I saw it was only my shadow darting before me.

The metal was a gold pin with a letter on it. I took it to the window and saw that the letter was an M. Not knowing what else to do with it, I dropped the pin in my pocket.

Time was passing and at any moment, one of them might return. Quickly I went to the first door on the left of the hallway, the study. It was squarish, except for a curved bay window filled with pillows. The books on the shelves weren't the traditional leather-bound volumes belonging to a house like this, but a large assortment of paperbacks, worn copies of the classics, reference books, magazines and a few new hardcovers. The furniture, too, was untraditional. Instead of a massive English desk, leather armchairs, hunting prints and mellow lamps, there was a rattan couch covered with a Thai cloth, a straight French chair, a rickety desk with an ink well and quill pen, a Chinese rug with a hole in the center, and some plants. The walls were covered with museum prints of Picassos, Braques, Riveras and Woods.

Moving quickly now, I opened the top drawer of the desk. It was stuffed with canceled checks, mortgage slips, bills, department-store catalogs, tax and insurance data. The bottom drawer—there were only two—had the raw material for a scrapbook: snapshots, restaurant menus, newspaper clippings.

It was the snapshots that held my attention. There was one of Johnny which showed a boyish face, young and unworried-looking. The version I had met was a blurred, saddened copy. Daisy, on the other hand, didn't seem any older than the youngest picture I could find, as though she were Dorian Gray and Johnny her painting. The only alterations were in the roles she had taken on over the years. In one group of snapshots, she had been undergoing a sophisticated period, with hair piled high and clothing slinky. In another, she was the wholesome house-wife, hair plain and dresses running to checks and gingham. Both were different from her present teenage period.

I was putting the pictures back when I heard a car.

For a moment I didn't move. Then I ran to the window, forgetting I couldn't see the front drive from this window. I was about to head for the back stairs when I heard the rattle of garbage pails. It was only the rubbish truck.

Taking a deep breath of relief, I began sifting through the canceled checks. There were the usual doctor and dentist payments, fuel, one or two department stores, drugstores, car payments, gas and electric, mortgage and insurance. What was missing, I noticed, were newspaper and magazine subscriptions, which struck me as strange, considering that the house was filled with that kind of reading matter. Then I remembered that Johnny could bring them home from the office. Also missing were donations to charities.

Something rubbed against my leg, and as I glanced down at the cat, I noticed that I had dropped one of the pictures. It was an infant lying on a bed, with no identifying notation on the back. It resembled any other infant lying on a bed. It could have been Teddy.

I heard a dog bark just as I was replacing the picture, but I paid no attention because a canceled check caught my attention. It was made out to the state mental hospital for a small amount and was five years old. I kept staring at it as though expecting invisible writing to appear and explain it.

"Here Tolstoy. Here, boy."

It was Daisy.

Even by herself, she couldn't stop talking. "Tolstoy, I told you never to do that. You're incorrigible. I'm taking you to obedience school, you naughty thing. And no more car rides until you learn." Her footsteps sounded on the bare hallway floor, and I realized with horror that she was on her way to the kitchen, not upstairs. She would pass the study and the slightest turn of her head would show her where I was.

My paralysis didn't snap. I had to pry it loose. I shut the drawer, and then, looking around wildly, saw two escape routes—the French door leading to the outdoors and the closet. Just then, Tolstoy, a large, mottled-looking mixture of several breeds, came bounding around the back of the house, and I realized that she had left him outdoors. So I chose the closet. As I slipped inside, the hinges creaked faintly and Daisy's voice stopped short.

The full force of my mistake hit me then. If Daisy chose to open the door of the closet, I was trapped with no explanation of what I was doing. If I had shown any presence of mind and simply appeared to be browsing at the bookshelves, she might have been suspicious, but she could never be sure.

There was a long silence. I moved back behind a musty-smelling taffeta dress and listened, but all I could hear was the blood rushing through my head. I had no indication of where Daisy was until, close by, came the creak of a floor board and the sound of breathing.

Like a fish gasping for oxygen, I opened and shut my mouth. I pushed back until I touched the wall, and remembered the hide-and-seek games I had played as a child. Hating every minute of it, I had always been filled with terror when the one who was "it" came closer and closer.

I was considering surrender when the door opened.

Shutting my eyes, I waited for the startled gasp, the accusations, the demand that I leave the house immediately.

But nothing happened. The silence lengthened and then the door closed gently, leaving me in total darkness.

I felt confused. I didn't know if she hadn't seen me, or if she had gone quietly for the police, or if she had seen me and, inexplicably, decided to do nothing. The last seemed the most terrifying of all, and yet in keeping with her character, but I wasn't sure why.

Then, on top of that, came the sudden awareness of the

blackness. I had left the door slightly ajar, but Daisy had shut it completely. I put my hand up to my eyes but saw nothing.

I had always been afraid of complete darkness. First my mother and then Lawford had learned never to completely draw the curtains at night. Even the fear that it was a trap, that Daisy might be poised on the other side ready to pounce, couldn't stop me. I brushed away the taffeta, flung aside a coat and felt for the knob. For a moment I couldn't find it. Caution deserted me and I groped frantically with both hands. Just before I lost control, I found the knob.

As soon as I saw the splinter of light, the panic died. I waited, listening for a clue as to where Daisy could be. My left leg had gone numb, and I wiggled it to bring back the blood. Stinging needles shot up my side and I shifted my weight back and forth. Still I waited until I heard the clatter of cutlery from the kitchen and Daisy saying, "Just a minute, Dostoevsky. Stop that, you stupid cat. I have to open the can, don't I?"

I should have been reassured, but there was something in the texture of her voice that made me uneasy. It was too clear, too pat. It sounded as though she were performing for an audience. And the only audience around was me.

Water ran, a chair was pushed back, the refrigerator door banged shut. Everything was louder than life. Daisy began to sing off-key. " 'And it's too late, baby now, it's too late—' "

Tiptoeing to the door, I peered out. The hall was empty. Now or never, I thought, and made a dash for the stairs. I was halfway up when I heard laughter outdoors and the stamping of feet. Just as the door opened, I made it to the top.

Like someone who has been swimming for shore from a wrecked ship and finally touches ground, I tumbled on my bed, exhausted. I didn't bother turning on the light, but lay there, keeping my thoughts at bay. Gradually my breathing returned to normal.

When the activity in the hallway died down, I went out to the bath. I soaked for fifteen minutes, letting the tension and cold seep out. Sounds wafted up from below. The tinkle of glasses, voices, laughter, footsteps. Finally I got out of the tub, dressed, and went back to my room.

Now I was no longer tired but hungry. I had forgotten to do

any marketing on the way home, and the thought of struggling to my car and taking a chance on the condition of the roads depressed me. Another childhood memory came to me. My first week in camp I'd been homesick and shy and had refused my counselor's efforts to get me out of the bunkhouse. I had huddled there alone, listening to the others shouting, playing ball, swimming.

The knock at the door came without warning and every nerve jumped. "Yes?"

"It's me. Daisy. May I come in?" She opened the door before I could answer and stood framed in the light, a small figure in faded jeans and shirt. More than ever she resembled a fifteen-year-old. "So there you are, you sly thing." It was the same tone she used for Tolstoy or Dostoevsky. "Johnny said he saw your car on the road. Were you hiding in here all this time?"

"I was asleep. Is it still snowing?"

"Yes. Isn't it *fabulous*? It's simply gorgeous outdoors. And here we all are stranded in an isolated mansion, cut off from all other human contact. I wish the telephone would go dead. Maybe we'll pretend we don't have electricity and use candles. What a setup for a murder!" She laughed, her familiar pro-longed strident yelp. "No one wants to brave the storm and go out to dinner, so we're all pooling our provisions and settling down for a long session of eating and drinking. And we insist that you join us."

Although I wanted to go down, almost automatically I started to say, "Well, the only thing is—"

"I won't take no for an answer. Besides, the others still haven't even caught a glimpse of you, and they're convinced you're a figment of my imagination. It's lucky Johnny sees you at work. In any case, you *have* to have dinner—"

"That's the problem. I haven't done any marketing yet, so I can't pool provisions—"

"Not to worry. Don't you love that phrase? We'll treat you tonight and you can treat us tomorrow night. You needn't be afraid that we'll let you get away with it. In any case, I'm not leaving this room without you."

Getting off the bed, I turned on the lamp and combed my

hair. While I put on lipstick, she chatted about how unhealthy it was to "curl up like an animal in its lair." I agreed with her, but I didn't tell her that I had been unhealthy for four years. Steeling myself to face in the flesh people who had been wraiths until now, heard from afar or glimpsed in the hall, I followed her out of my lair and went downstairs.

The living room was badly lit. Only two lamps were turned on and the occupants were lost in the vast shadows, coming into focus only gradually. As Daisy introduced them, I tried fitting each one into the role I had come to cast. The eldest, a woman close to seventy, had grizzled hair, a body of no particular shape, and a pleasant face. The youngest, Verity Carlhian, was several years my junior, in her early twenties, with long straight hair, somewhat lighter than mine, and a slim athletic-looking figure. I was bothered by her appearance, but I wasn't sure why, and before I could pin down the source of my uneasiness, Daisy was presenting one of the three men in the room. Strandy Bourne had a feature I hadn't noticed in the dimness of the room until I got closer. He was a Negro. Between thirty and thirty-five years old, he would have been good-looking if his skin hadn't been pitted from a childhood disease. Johnny Barker I knew, of course. Both he and Strandy had risen when I'd entered the room, but the third man, Wesley Olson, remained seated. He too was in his thirties, and in his case, the good looks were marred by a surly expression.

"Verity is a secretary to an *extremely* important man," Daisy was saying, "and is a perfect darling about doing any typing we might need. And Mrs. Webster sells gorgeous boutique items and gets us all *fantastic* bargains. And Strandy is our lawyer and comes to our defense when we get into trouble with the law. And Wesley—well!" Her voice fell dramatically as she introduced the surly one. "You'll never guess what *he* does. He's our black sheep. We hide him when company comes. What do you think he is?"

"President of the United States?"

"Worse than that! He's in the military-industrial complex!"

"If you need a flamethrower, come to me," the black sheep said. He studied me carefully and then turned to the window where the snow had framed each pane. I felt appraised, labeled and rejected. As I sat down next to Mrs. Webster, as the most innocuous person present, Strandy handed me a drink.

"Strandy, may we borrow a wee bit of your Scotch?" Daisy asked. "Johnny just finished our *umpteenth* bottle and we don't have a drop."

Rolling his eyes good-naturedly, Johnny said, "There she goes again. We finished our biweekly quart two days ago and I told her to buy some."

Hastily, as though warding off a familiar scene, Strandy poured Scotch for her, and Mrs. Webster asked, "Where are you from, Miss Boyd?" Her voice was sweet, but I decided that I'd made a mistake about her innocuousness. Evidently she was the kind who couldn't speak to a new acquaintance without finding out about his place of birth, grandparents, position on the social ladder, business, marital status, religion and political preference.

"Ohio."

"Were you born there? I mean everyone moves around so much these days."

"Yes."

"Which part of Ohio?"

"Cleveland."

"Oh." I'd made a mistake being born in Cleveland. I could tell. "Oh, a big-city girl. Are your people still there?"

"I don't have people."

Getting up, Verity Carlhian offered me a plate of crackers with bits of food on them. I thought she winked, but I wasn't sure because of the low-voltage lighting. Thanking her, I helped myself to several crackers.

"Oh, I was telling everyone about the Seymour party," Daisy said, but I wasn't sure if she was interrupting the inquisition because of kindness or the inability to keep quiet. "They must have spent a *fortune* on it. She had hundreds of rented chairs and tables, and at least a dozen in help—"

"Three tables and two in help," Johnny murmured as an aside from his own conversation with Strandy.

"—and it's all so absurd because she was trying to impress

people who have *scads* more than she has. She wore this exotic gown absolutely *smothered* in sequins. It was hideous but it shrieked money. And the food! Of course she couldn't have ham and turkey like ordinary people. She had to have lobster and Beef Wellington—" Brightly, Daisy continued, an indefinable current beneath the gay surface.

To Verity, Mrs. Webster was saying, "But the queen has so much in the way of expenses. She has to travel and dress properly and entertain constantly. And she does so much for the English, they *owe* her a larger allowance—"

To Strandy, Johnny was saying, "—only interested in the superficial. They couldn't care less about the real texture of society—"

I found it hard to concentrate and the voices began to blend, covering the span from Mrs. Webster's light soprano to Johnny's baritone. I only half heard Daisy say to Johnny, "Get more ice, sweetie."

"—without realizing that we need a whole new concept of the world—"

"We need more ice, Johnny."

"—if we are to accomplish any of the aims—shut up a minute, Daisy."

"Did you tell me to shut up?"

Everyone stopped speaking. Not because Daisy raised her voice or showed any overt anger. Her tone was modulated, her features composed. In the brief time I had known her, I had never seen any particular expression on her face, or heard anything in her voice except dramatic inflections. Yet her stillness was more disturbing than contorted fury. "You've been interrupting me all evening," she said quietly. Mrs. Webster examined her fingernails, and Verity and Strandy began to chat feverishly about how long the snow would keep up. Only Wesley Olson wasn't embarrassed. Showing his first interest of the evening, he watched Daisy and Johnny like someone waiting for the curtain to go up.

Johnny took one look at his wife and put down his glass. Every line and crease in his face became more deeply etched. Then he grinned, got down on his knees and held up his hands in a parody of supplication. "Oh forgive me, fair one. Allow me this one trespass. I will get the ice forthwith." He rose, brushed off his trousers and disappeared in the direction of the kitchen.

There was a moment's pause before Daisy continued smoothly, "Even the flowers must have cost hundreds of dollars. The poor thing. What good did it all do her? Everyone was terribly bored—"

I noticed, for the first time, that the record player had been on all along. A male voice was singing, " 'Freedom is nothing left to do—' " As though the words were directed at me, I turned to look at the invisible singer and caught sight of Verity's face instead. Lack of expression was not one of her problems. She was watching Daisy with unconcealed hatred.

The talk swirled on. I noticed that Johnny didn't seem to be in a hurry to return to the living room. I also noticed that Mrs. Webster never turned her eyes directly on Strandy, as though she were afraid his skin had the properties of Medusa and could turn her to stone. Then: "What have you decided to do with the guesthouse, Daisy?" Mrs. Webster asked.

I forgot everything else—my brush with the dress designer, real or imagined undercurrents whirling around me, Verity's dislike of her landlady. Carefully, I placed my glass on the table and pretended to brush crumbs off my lap. I concentrated on keeping my hands from trembling.

"Oh, the guesthouse!" Daisy said enthusiastically. Instantly all the latent hostility in her voice evaporated. She was entirely different, bubbling with enthusiasm. "We've just gotten another estimate. This new contractor really sounds divine. He may be the answer to our prayers—"

"What guesthouse?" I asked. I tried to sound casual, but the words came through strained.

"Oh! That's right! You don't know about our guesthouse. What an experience we have in store for you!" Daisy clasped her hands rapturously. "We have this perfectly *dreamy* little cottage tucked away in the woods. I sometimes think it's the main reason that we bought the big house. But until now we haven't had the money to fix it up. I hope this new man won't want a *mint*. It would make a gorgeous setting for a party, or a guesthouse, or simply a retreat for me to run to when I have to get away from Johnny—" She broke off, noticing that Johnny hadn't returned with the ice. "If anyone ever leaves me money, the first thing I'll do, after taking a trip around the world, is fix up the cottage. You must see it, Norma. We'll take a walk there on the first sunny day—no, better yet, on a moonlit night. It's like the Taj Mahal and should be seen in moonlight to be fully appreciated. I'm *convinced* that wood nymphs carouse there under—"

"Gosh, I haven't caroused with wood nymphs in ages," Wesley said. Pushing with both hands, he got to his feet and swayed for a moment. I wondered if he was drunk.

Verity rose simultaneously, although more gracefully. "I'll help Johnny with the ice cubes," she said as though she'd been waiting for someone to press the button which would release her.

As she disappeared into the gloom beyond the stairs, Daisy watched her and then laughed. "Poor Verity. Suffering from unrequited love. She'll probably turn into a dried-up spinster waiting for Johnny to leave me and—" Distracted, she saw that Wesley was heading for the stairs. "Wait, Wesley, where are you going? You haven't had any dinner and we're just beginning this perfectly *fascinating* conversation about wood nymphs—"

"I'm bushed, Daisy. Besides, I have to catch a plane to Detroit in the morning—"

"You'll never get out. The snow will be ten feet deep by then, and we'll all be snowbound—"

"I think it's stopped already. Good night." He continued his awkward gait up the stairs, ignoring Daisy's protests.

"If it hadn't been for those lovely neighbors, I wouldn't have lasted for even one summer," Mrs. Webster was saying, and I realized that she'd been talking to me. "In spite of the fact that they were Episcopalians and I was a Presbyterian, they couldn't have been more friendly."

I wasn't sure I had heard correctly. But her enunciation was perfect and there was nothing in her bland sweet face to show she was joking. I got up. "I guess it's my bedtime too."

"You can't leave," Daisy moaned like an eight-year-old who

can't bear to have the party end. "You haven't had dinner yet. Let's fix some sandwiches, or would you prefer spaghetti? And I have a *gorgeous* dessert. I made an angel food cake—"

I hesitated only a moment. "I *am* starved. Can I help you with the sandwiches?"

Mrs. Webster picked up her bag of crewelwork. "I stopped off for something to eat before I came home. I think I'll watch television." She sat down in front of the set and Daisy and I headed for the butler's pantry.

"Well, we'd better get back." It was Verity, speaking from the kitchen. On the surface, the words weren't incriminating. Yet there was an intimacy, a resignation in the voice which embarrassed me.

Not looking at Daisy, I cursed loudly. "Damn it. I turned my ankle." There was a sudden silence from the kitchen, followed by a low laugh from Daisy. I couldn't see her expression in the dimness of the butler's pantry.

The kitchen door swung open and Verity said, "We were just getting the ice cubes."

"We've come to fix some sandwiches for the five of us. Wesley and Mrs. Webster don't want anything." My voice was too bright.

"What took you two so long?" Daisy asked banteringly. "It's lucky Norma made all that noise or we might have discovered you in a compromising situation."

"Yes," said Johnny, "there was that intimate moment when I held the door for Verity and our elbows brushed."

He rummaged until he found a can of tuna fish. Verity and I began spreading slices of bread and Daisy started the coffee. "Tell me about the house in the woods," I said casually, my head lowered as I diced celery. "Is it far from here?"

"Oh—it's an acre or two from the house. It's got another marvelous quality we haven't told you about. It's haunted!"

"Oh, God, Daisy, not again."

"But I'd like to hear about it, Johnny."

Sucking a finger, Daisy said, "Wait, let's get settled and I'll tell you all about the *ghastly* tragedy that took place there—"

"First of all, it didn't take place in the cottage. The body was found some distance from—"

"Johnny! You spoiled it. Will you please keep quiet and let me tell Norma. You don't know the first thing about how to build up suspense—"

"The body?" I managed to ask. I sliced the sandwiches in half.

"Yes. Wait until I tell you. It happened years ago—"

"Stop enjoying it so much, Daisy. You're a ghoul. A small boy was found strangled in the woods, Norma."

The room was silent for a moment except for the perking coffee. Verity went to the refrigerator and found a package of cold meat. Johnny took a jar of pickles off a shelf. Then Daisy laughed. "For a reporter, Johnny, you have a remarkable faculty for taking the drama out of the most exciting events. Oh. Speaking about reporters—"

I glanced up. Her eyes, birdlike and shining, were on me as she dug into her pants pocket. "Here it is." She held some folded sheets of yellow paper in her hand.

"It's the oddest thing. I was getting an old dress out of the closet in the library—" She stopped, as though expecting a comment from me, but I was running lettuce leaves under the tap. "—and look what I found."

We all looked.

"It's office paper. The kind of thing Johnny always carries around with him, you know, to take notes, when he's on a story. But the handwriting isn't his. It must be yours, Norma."

I dried the lettuce on paper toweling. Numbly I remembered that I'd put the notes of the high-school meeting in the pocket of my slacks, and then, when I'd been in what Daisy referred to as "the library," I must have dropped them. I could feel my face getting hot as, after waiting too long, I asked stupidly, "What does it say?"

"What difference—let's see. I can't. The handwriting is *appalling*."

"Yes. Those are my notes." I put out my hand. "Thank you. I'm glad you found them. I was looking for a book when I came home from work and I must have dropped them then, but I can't imagine how they got into the closet—" I began placing sandwiches on a platter. "Unless—that must be it. The dog or cat found them and dragged them into the closet."

"Oh?" There was skepticism in Daisy's voice, but she didn't pursue it. I couldn't understand why she had waited so long before mentioning the notes. She had been carrying them around for at least an hour. By now I was sure she had seen me in the closet, but for some odd reason of her own, had decided to play cat and mouse with me.

As we settled ourselves in the living room again with our sandwiches and coffee, it occurred to me that, diverse as they were, all of the inhabitants of the house shared a common denominator. Each was flawed.

First, of course, there was me, memory-haunted, guilt-ridden, thinking I could do what an entire police department had been unable to do. Then there was Wesley Olson, surly, rude, carrying his own invisible demon. Third, Strandy, whose taint in the eyes of people like Mrs. Webster was that he had too many melanin cells. And Mrs. Webster herself. Widowed, probably rejected by her only daughter, lonely, out of place on Circle Drive, she too was scarred. Verity's defect was that she was in love with a married man whose wife wasn't going to give him up. And Johnny's blemish was weakness, a willingness to be bullied by a strong wife.

Which brought me to my landlady, the most interesting of them all. On the surface, no one could be more pleasant, more agreeable, more vivacious. She laughed, she chattered, she worked hard to keep the house habitable, and she had a variety of interests. But underneath she was something else. A mirror image of what she appeared to be.

The gay, lilting voice she had used to describe the party had hidden envy and bitterness. The eyes she had turned on Johnny when he'd told her to shut up had been blood-chilling. The game she was playing with me was odd, abnormal.

If anyone in the house was a murderer, Daisy was the likeliest candidate.

Four

It was like revisiting a planet temporarily put to use by man and then abandoned. The debris of civilization—newspapers, rubbish cans, machines, desks, empty coffee cups, cigarette stubs, candy wrappers—was strewn around as though it had been in use up to the moment of cataclysm. I kept turning swiftly, sure I had just missed a movement beyond the reach of my eyes.

The silence was nearly absolute. No clatter of typewriters, no ringing of telephones, no thundering of presses, no chattering voices. Even the purr of tires from the street was hushed because of the closed windows. My footsteps echoed dismally as I returned to the deserted building with my notes from a civic organization brunch, a controversial church service and a police report of an accident.

I hated working on Sunday. When I'd been on the night or Sunday shifts on my first job, other people had surrounded me. But the *Gazette* was a smaller operation, and I appeared to be the only person in the entire building. I kept wandering nervously. I examined the notes on Chris Upham's desk, yesterday's stories on the copy horseshoe, and the picture assignment board: "Day: Wed. Time: 10:30. Date: Feb. 4. Location: First Congregational Church. Contact: Mrs. Stoneridge. Expect to use two-column spread. Shot of Mrs. Henry giving lecture on community service to go with story."

I wanted to talk to someone, but there wasn't even anyone I could call. I had pruned them all off gradually in the last four years—relatives, friends, acquaintances, until there was nothing left but me, a branchless stump. Finally I telephoned the publicity director of the civic group and asked her questions to which I knew the answers.

Abnormally loud, the stuttering of my typewriter bounced off the ceiling and the walls. I forced myself to sit still, without turning around, until I finished two stories. Then I got up, stretched my muscles and walked down the hall.

Again the sound of my footsteps rebounded throughout the length of the news room. At the door to the lavatory, I stopped and readied myself like a policeman about to storm the hideout of a dangerous criminal. Then I pushed the door open and stepped back out of the line of fire. There was nothing but the tapping of a faulty faucet. Once I was sure that the room was empty, I went in. I lingered for an unnecessarily long time. It was warm, safe and cozy, and I washed my face, reapplied make-up, combed my hair. The ringing of the telephone brought me out on the run.

"Is Mr. Van Fleet there?" a woman's voice asked.

"Mr. Van Fleet?" I repeated. Unnecessarily, I looked into the far corners of the room. "Is he supposed to be in today?"

"I wouldn't be calling if he weren't," she snapped.

"Well, I've been here for two hours and there's nobody here," I said, and nearly added, except for us chickens.

Without thanking me, the woman hung up. I went back to my last story. I was organizing my notes when I heard footsteps from the direction of the hall.

I don't know what I expected, but the atmosphere had affected me to the point where I dreaded turning. I wasn't sure what I would see. When the suspense became overwhelming, I finally looked up. It was George Van Fleet, a copy man.

He was middle-aged, middle-sized and had a dour expression, and at the moment, the smell of bourbon on his breath. Eyes slightly glazed, he barely nodded in my direction. He picked up the stack of stories and sat down at the copy desk.

"Mr. Van Fleet, your wife called. At least, I think it was your wife. A woman called, anyway."

His eyes shot up over the rim of his glasses. Tensely, he asked, "What did you tell her?"

"What did I tell her? That you weren't here, of course."

He had started to reach for the telephone, but then he stopped and stared at me. "You did *what?*"

"I told her you weren't here. I mean, I assumed—"

"You *assumed?*" His voice was deadly. "What right did *you* have to assume?"

I stared at him dumbly.

"You could have said you weren't sure. You could have said I went to the can. If you don't know the right answer, don't give the wrong one." The back legs of his chair slammed and he got up. Instead of using the telephone nearest to him, he went to the furthest end of the room and began to dial.

I kept my back rigid and pretended to be typing, but my fingers trembled on the keys. I could hear his voice, although not the words, and the tone was soft and conciliatory. It was nothing like the voice he'd used for me. I wondered what he'd been doing aside from drinking. He didn't look like the type to have a girl friend.

When I saw I was typing nonsense, I pulled the sheet out and threw it away. I lit a cigarette and tried again. Coffee would have helped, but in order to reach the machine, I had to pass Van Fleet, so I remained where I was. He went back to his desk and I heard the angry scratching of his pencil. She must have given him a hard time.

Nevertheless, I was pleased with his presence. Outside, it was getting darker and the lights in the room did nothing to dispel the infinite dinginess. Without people to distract the eye from the peeling walls, mutilated desks, mildewed muck, and black, encrusted windows, the room resembled a terminal to which no train ever came.

Again the telephone broke into life. I picked it up. *"Gazette."*

"Is this the *Gazette?*"

Since she sounded elderly and feeble, I said patiently, "Yes, ma'am."

"I told the police, but they won't listen. It's so dreadful. They are monsters, simply monsters, and they're going to kill it. They've got it trapped on top of the garage and they're looking for a ladder so that they can go up and capture it. Please send somebody to report it. If they see a reporter, perhaps they'll stop. They wouldn't want their pictures in the paper while they're torturing some poor creature to death. Please hurry—"

"Are you talking about a kitten, ma'am?"

"Yes. Didn't I tell you? It's that terrible Sharp boy and some of his friends. I can see them from the corner of my yard. They're looking for a ladder right this minute. If you—"

"I'm awfully sorry, but we don't have anyone to send."

"Nobody to send! That's the trouble with this world. No one cares if a fellow creature is tortured to death. They've just found a ladder. They're carrying it to the garage right this minute—"

"Perhaps you can call Mrs. Sharp."

"She won't care. She's as bad as her son. What will I do?"

"I'm sorry, but if the police won't help—"

"You're sorry, but you won't do anything. It's the same everywhere."

She hung up and I sat for a while with the receiver in my hand. The words "Nobody to send" kept echoing unpleasantly in my mind.

From behind me, I heard Van Fleet push his chair back. He was finished for the day, evidently. When the creak of his shoes died away, I turned. His hat and coat weren't there.

I missed him now that he was gone. I also missed the woman who cared. I wished I had her telephone number so that I could find out what had happened to the cat.

Out there in the world, I thought as I typed, were normal people with normal jobs and normal lives. Right now some of them were sitting around fires in cheery rooms, adults reading the Sunday newspapers, children playing games on the floor. Or they were at family gatherings. Or they were planning on going out to a movie.

Or they were torturing cats to death.

Abruptly, from somewhere in the building, came the sound of a loud crash.

I was so startled, I didn't have the breath to gasp. For a while I remained where I was, listening. There was no further sound. The normal thing to have done would have been to check the various rooms and find out what had happened. It was probably a cat which had knocked over a book. Or the watch-man had come in from his outside post and had accidentally turned something over. Finally the prickling sensation on the back of my neck was too much. I looked around. Nothing.

I went to the coffee machine, put in twenty cents and got a cup. Back at my desk, I kept making mistakes. My notes were sloppy and hard to decipher. I searched for a pencil and could only find broken stubs. "Story of my life," I muttered aloud.

Every time I surveyed the shadows, the room seemed subtly changed. I had seen a movie once about a department store at night, with the mannequins coming alive as soon as the last human being was gone. I had a sensation of constant movement which stopped when I looked; of constant murmurs which were silent when I listened. Beyond the range of my senses was a whole world I couldn't quite perceive.

Finally I was finished. I didn't like the stories, but I was too jumpy to do better. I still had to run the gauntlet of hallways, stairs and reception room before I reached humanity. It occurred to me that half of my life I avoided people, and the other half I kept trying to surround myself with them.

Dropping the stories into the basket, I picked up my purse and jacket and went to the ladies' room again. The faucet had stopped dripping and I couldn't remember if I was the one who had turned it off. Hesitating, I began to imagine that someone might be in one of the stalls, crouched on a bowl so that I couldn't see his feet.

I walked quickly to the stairs. Passing an open window which overlooked an alley between the building and a warehouse, I could see time-faded bricks, a rickety fire escape and a cluster of garbage pails. A dog prowled in the refuse. One of the windows of the warehouse was lit up and I caught a glimpse of a man passing back and forth. Fleetingly, I wondered if he were a burglar, but I didn't plan on doing anything about it.

I was at the head of the stairs when the telephone at the downstairs reception desk burst into life.

I had never understood how the telephones were hooked up when the switchboard was closed, but I was surprised that it was the reception desk telephone. It should have been the news desk on Sunday. However, I was happy not to have to go back, and I ran for the stairs.

My legs shot out from under me, my purse flew into the air,

and although I tried to grab the railing to save myself, I went crashing down the stairs.

I ended up at the bottom, one leg twisted under me, the other straight out, and my head resting against one of the steps. For a while I did nothing. I stared at the wall and waited for my breath to come back. Gradually the inner churning and thudding subsided.

When I tried to get up, however, I realized that my troubles were just beginning. Something had happened to one ankle. I clamped my teeth on a gasp and craned to look over my shoulder to the top of the stairs. It was dark and still, but someone could have been there, lurking in one of the glassed-in offices, waiting for me to be helpless.

I couldn't understand how it had happened. I'd been in perfect control, I was wearing flat heels, and then, for no reason, I'd careened down the stairs. Of course the sound of the telephone had made me run.

By now it had stopped ringing. Glancing at it, I wondered whether to telephone for help. Or wait for the next shift. Or try to make it to the car on my own.

Fortunately, since the parking lot was empty on Sunday, the car was next to the entrance. I held onto the railing at the bottom of the staircase and tried to put my weight on the injured foot. It was agonizing. Hopping to the chair at the desk, I sat down.

If I tried to get a doctor, he would take ages to arrive, and then I would have to go through the red tape of my life's history. Besides, he wouldn't arrive at all. He would tell me to get to his office under my own steam, or since it was Sunday, go to the emergency room at the hospital. Or get a friend to drive me.

A friend. My mouth twisted. Daisy?

In the end I did what I knew all along I would do. I got up, and holding onto the wall, hopped to the door. I got down the steps by sitting down, and then I hopped to the car.

Worn out, I threw my shoulder bag on the front seat and leaned back to rest. Oddly, I was less fearful now than I'd been all day. Whatever I'd feared was going to happen, had happened, and now I was safe. For the time being.

When a few minutes had passed, I pressed gently on the

clutch. The pain shot up the leg. Less predictably, however, the shoe slid off the pedal.

Swearing at myself for not having an automatic shift, I reached down, and gently as I could, removed the shoe. The bottom was partially coated with a dark greasy substance, like automobile oil.

I shut my eyes and tried to think where I had acquired it. Instead a picture began to take shape in my mind: A girl working alone in a large gloomy building. From somewhere, a partially closed office, another room, behind a door, eyes had been watching, ears listening, a mind planning. Then, grease at the top of a flight of stairs, a telephone jangling below at the crucial moment. And the girl tumbling, turning over and over in midair before coming to rest at the bottom.

What had been the purpose? Death? Not likely. Just a warning. Get out, get lost. Stop trying to find a murderer.

Five

The ankle was twice its normal size by the time I reached the house. I got out of the car, held on and tried a tentative step, but it was too much. Sitting down, I honked the horn.

I had hoped for Verity, but it was Wesley who appeared in the doorway. He stared questioningly a moment, and then recognizing the car, walked toward me slowly.

"You'll catch a cold like that," I said idiotically. He was wearing only slacks and a sport shirt. "I sprained my ankle and I need help."

I was examining my leg, trying to assess the damage, but when he didn't answer, I glanced up and felt a sense of shock. Instead of what I had expected—easy assent and a helping shoulder—he was looking at me almost with aversion. He turned away and said over his shoulder, "I'll get Strandy to carry you in."

I started to shout that I didn't need carrying, but the door had shut. Swearing, I got out and leaned against the car, measuring the distance to the entrance.

Before I could get started, however, Strandy came hurrying out, also in shirt sleeves. "What did you do to yourself?"

"I fell down the stairs at the office. I hate to be a nuisance—"

Before I could finish, he had lifted me in his arms and we went in, with Wesley holding the door for us. "Where to? Upstairs? Downstairs?"

"Or in my lady's chamber," I finished. "Upstairs, please, Strandy."

He carried me up, bending so that I could open the door, and then he deposited me on the bed. "Are you all right? Uh—how about the facilities?"

"I can manage if I sit on the floor and push myself."

Verity stood in the doorway, watching. Evidently fresh from the bath, she looked pretty in a long house robe, her face flushed and her hair damp around the edges. "How do you know it isn't broken?"

"Oh—it would hurt more, I'm sure."

"Thus spake Dr. Boyd," said Strandy. "I walked around for half a day once with a cracked ankle and didn't know it."

"I'll wait until tomorrow morning. Actually, I'm not terribly fond of doctors."

Verity insisted upon helping me to the bathroom, getting my pajamas and generally behaving like a frustrated nurse. When she finally left the room, I fell back exhausted.

The instant I shut my eyes, disagreeable images floated into my mind: The massive, depressing news room, the heavy sensation of being watched, the helplessness at the top of the stairs when I'd lost my balance, the sickening inability to stop myself, the agonizing crash at the bottom. And the grease on my shoe.

I opened my eyes, searching for the shoe, but I couldn't see it. Evidently, Verity had tucked it away, along with my other things. Just then I noticed something strange. The closet door was slightly open, the books on the chest were out of line, one of the drawers was gaping. Always neat, I had left everything trim before going to work. And Verity had touched only the closet door.

I lifted my bad ankle over the side of the bed, and holding onto the chest, hobbled in front of it. Sitting on the floor, I opened the bottom drawer. I was sure of it. The changes were minor, but someone had been going through my belongings.

Slowly, I pulled myself erect, and hopped to the window, as though the darkening sky could help me think. In the fading light, the lawn below was intermittently green and beige. Red berries popped from the maple tree like sores. A short distance off I could see a rusted outdoor grill, neglected for years, with a yellowed matchbook resting on the wooden shelf.

I turned as I heard the clatter of cutlery and voices. It reminded me of when I'd been a child, sick in bed, listening to the cheerful sound of my mother approaching with a tray.

Three of them came in, Verity and Strandy balancing dishes, and Wesley holding the door. They were in the midst of a conversation, Verity asking Wesley, "Don't you ever do anything spontaneously?" and Wesley answering, "I'm as spontaneous as the next guy, but I never do anything without thinking it over carefully."

Wesley had to steady the tray as, laughing, Verity began arranging a makeshift picnic on the floor. "We decided that you probably didn't have a chance to eat before the accident," she explained as she spread a tablecloth over the rug. Strandy helped me down, and I saw that they had Scotch, glasses, ice, cheese, bread, sausage and a bowl of celery. "I didn't bother with coffee," Verity said, "because I thought I saw a jar of coffee in your room and an electric pot."

Without thinking, I glanced at her sharply and asked, "How did you know?"

"I saw them when I helped you to bed," she said in surprise.

"Oh, yes. I managed to stop at a store the other day when I was coming from an assignment."

But she wasn't listening. To Wesley she was saying, "You don't have to ski. Just come along with us and watch."

"Thanks. Maybe I can take my knitting."

I glanced at his leg, stuck out stiffly in front of him, but Strandy distracted me by handing me a drink.

I leaned back against the bed, sipped my drink and relaxed. Watching the three of them, I was conscious of something I hadn't planned on. I was beginning to like them. And liking them could only interfere with what I had come for.

Strandy and Verity began arguing about a piece of sausage, and Verity cut it in half and told him to pick. He shut his eyes and got the smaller half. "You lose," she said.

"*You* gain," he retorted and for the first time in years I

found myself laughing. Laughing out loud. The aimless chatter blended with the Scotch and the warmth of the room and the taste of the cheddar and boursault and the fragrance of Verity's perfume.

When there was a pause, I asked idly, not as part of my investigation but out of friendly curiosity, "I wonder what brought you all to this house?"

"I fell in love with Daisy," said Wesley promptly.

"I fell in love with Mrs. Webster." That was Strandy.

"I fell in love with Johnny," Verity said and there was a brief silence.

"And what about *you*, Norma?" Wesley asked. "What brought *you* here?"

I wondered what they would say if I told them I'd come to find a murderer. "Oh, I got this job on the *Gazette* and I needed a place to live and I saw Daisy's ad. It isn't easy for a single person to find an apartment in Freetown." I hesitated and then added, "Especially in a happy little home like this."

"What I mean is, what made you pick Freetown?"

"Oh, I don't know. It's a lively town with some big companies and a good newspaper. And I wanted a change. You may say it was the spirit of adventure that brought me to Freetown." I wondered what was making me so talkative.

Wesley nodded. "Right on. If there's one thing Freetown caters to, it's the spirit of adventure. There are those switch-blade-toting boy scouts, the jealous undercurrents at the garden club meeting, the fury at the bridge table when someone trumps his—"

"*My* life is exciting," said Strandy. "I'm preparing to sue a roofer who did a lousy job for a client."

"And now to get back to your 'happy little home' crack. I couldn't agree more. Mrs. Webster supplies us with intellectual stimulation, Daisy and Johnny are a shining example of marital bliss, I am the picture of the well-adjusted young executive happily climbing the ladder of success on the bodies of—"

There was a quick knock followed by the opening of the door, and our landlady was with us. "So there you all are! We just got back and we were wondering where in the world you all were hiding. We could see the cars, but no people. I caught you in the act. Imagine having a party and not inviting us. Here you are gorging yourselves on all these fabulous goodies—"

While she went on and on, Strandy handed her a drink and Verity a wedge of bread. She settled herself on the floor, cross-legged, her cheeks rosy from the cold. Instead of her usual jeans, she wore a print blouse and a dark skirt, stockings and heels. Her hair, softly curled, hung loosely on her shoulders.

I wasn't sure if it was only in my own mind or if the others felt it too, but subtly, it seemed to me, the atmosphere began to change. It was like a slow insidious leak, seeping in through the cracks in the wall, along with the wind. As the voice trilled on, Verity's face seemed to harden into a brittle mask of politeness, her relaxation to evaporate. Strandy and Wesley stopped talking entirely and their eyes began to glaze. In my own case, I began weaving a cocoon around myself through which I could hear only occasional phrases. I was back to where I had been when I first arrived. They were nothing but pawns on a chessboard.

I heard snatches of Verity's explanation of my accident, Daisy's story about what a boring time they'd had at the art show they'd attended. Then, casually, Verity asked where Johnny was and Daisy told her he was reading the Sunday papers. No one, I noticed, bothered to inquire about Mrs. Webster. After a while Wesley began pushing himself up from the floor awkwardly. Strandy put out a hand to help him and then changed the gesture to brushing his pants leg. Rising, Verity began cleaning up the remains of the picnic.

"Hey, where's everybody going?" Daisy yelped. "Don't break up the party. I just got here. You'll give me a complex." Muttering various excuses about being tired or wanting to watch television or read the newspapers, the others drifted out, leaving Daisy and me alone. I struggled back to the bed to lie down and Daisy sat on the chair. I was trying to think of ways to get the conversation around to the house in the woods when I heard the phrase, "accident prone." Daisy was saying, "—couldn't drive a car without denting a fender, or walk outside without cracking an ankle."

Defensively, I said, "I haven't had any other accidents that I can remember."

"I wasn't talking about *you,* you silly thing. Heavens, don't be so paranoid. Can you spare a cigarette? I ran out at that horrid art show. You know, you look so comfortable, I'm thinking of breaking something too so we can both spend a week in bed and be waited on like queens."

"What happened to Wesley's leg?" I asked abruptly. I had interrupted, but it was impossible to be with Daisy and not interrupt unless one were a mute.

This time she didn't mind. Lighting a cigarette, she said enthusiastically, "Don't you *know?* Hasn't anyone *told* you?" She lowered her voice dramatically. As my energy ebbed, hers flowed in, as though, vampirelike, she was sucking it out of me. "It's all so *tragic,* but on the other hand, I've known many people who have had misfortunes and risen above them. Wesley has simply allowed *his* misfortune to ruin his life. He sinks more into himself every day."

She looked around for an ashtray, found a dish and settled down again. "Of course he's terribly reserved and it's impossible to get the details, but I'm sure he was a hero. I knew something was wrong when he first came to the house in answer to my ad. I could see it in his face before I noticed the limp. Come to think of it, I've never known him to be this social before. Do I sense the beginning of a romance? Wouldn't that be thrilling? We could have the wedding right here and you can be eternally grateful to Johnny and me for bringing you two together. I've always wanted to see a bride come down those gorgeous steps."

She stopped and held up her hand as footsteps sounded in the hallway, but they went past.

Watching Daisy's face, I wondered if witches ever came pretty and delicately made instead of like the illustrations in Grimm's. I couldn't get over the sensation of something stirring beneath the surface. She made me think of a placid-looking loch with a fissure below where a bizarre prehistoric creature lurked. She both fascinated and repelled me.

"Daisy, I wonder if you would mind getting me coffee? The smallest effort seems enormous just now."

"Of course." She jumped up with alacrity. "We'll both have some." Going to the window sill where I kept the jar of instant coffee and the electric pot, she looked around, couldn't find what she wanted and went down the hall to the bathroom. She returned with two plastic cups. "I hope I'm not tiring you. If I am, I'll continue tomorrow. You know, like a serialization. Although when I'm sick—which isn't very often—I love to have company. I think it's selfish of the others to leave you alone when it's still so early."

Her back to me, she began measuring out the coffee. Verity had plugged in the pot and the water was hot.

"You were telling me about Wesley," I reminded her.

"Oh, yes. I hope you don't take sugar or cream because there isn't any. On second thought, I don't think I'll have coffee. It keeps me up at night. Anyway, do you know that although Wesley has lived here for years I've never met a girl of his? I suppose he has some, but he's never brought them here. He's almost always alone. Sometimes I've almost imagined that I've caught him looking at me wistfully as though he were trying to get up the courage to make a pass." Hoot. "But he never did. And now that he's met you, you gorgeous creature, he doesn't know that I'm alive. But anyway, as soon as he'd come home at night, he'd go straight up to his room and never say a word to anyone. Especially at the beginning. He's been loosening up lately. Here's your coffee. I could tell that he had this mysterious weight on his shoulders—"

"Thank you." Without meaning to, I began to tune out. I stared at the black rectangular windows, trying to concentrate on keeping awake, but the warmth, the food and the relaxation after the tension of the day all combined to hypnotize me. I was nearly asleep when I became conscious of a pause.

"*Don't* you think it's awful?" Daisy repeated.

Sitting up straighter, I realized that I'd missed the story and didn't know the correct response. "Well—"

"You're as bad as Johnny! Utterly calloused. He's so philosophical about other people's problems. Wesley isn't the first man to lose a leg in a war, he'll tell me when—"

"Oh," I said.

"—when I try to get him to show some sympathy for

Wesley. Of course, part of it he's annoyed at Wesley for paying so much attention to me—"

"Daisy!" Johnny called from the hallway.

"Oh, that man. Come in, Johnny. I'm in Norma's room."

The door opened and Johnny stood on the threshold, smiling at me. "How's our invalid?"

"I'll live."

"Come on, Daisy. Let Norma get some sleep."

"Get some sleep! It's early. She doesn't want to be left alone."

"And besides, I'm hungry. What's for dinner?"

"Let's skip dinner tonight. You had an enormous lunch and besides, it's good for you to skip a meal occasionally."

"Daisy, it's Sunday. Haven't you planned—"

"I was just hearing about Wesley's leg," I said hurriedly. The latent volcano in Daisy was beginning to bubble and I didn't want it erupting near me.

"Wesley again. One of Daisy's favorite ways of whiling away a winter evening. It's her frustrated mother complex. For five years she's been talking about having a party for him to introduce him to a girl who's going to accept him, peg leg and all, but the best-laid plans of Daisy and Bobby Burns oft gang a gley."

"'The best laid schemes o' mice and men gang aft agley,' " Daisy corrected. "And isn't it rather ugly of you to talk about frustrated mothers?"

I looked at her sharply, but the remark had nothing to do with me. There was an undercurrent between them that I couldn't understand.

Smiling lazily at me, Johnny said, "It's just as well that we don't have children. No human child could live up to Daisy's expectations. By the way, did you ever see her collection of dolls?"

Mercurially, Daisy jumped to her feet and exclaimed, "No, she hasn't. Wait'll you see. I have one doll that was my mother's when she was three, and I have the most *fabulous* outfits for them. I must—"

"For God's sake, Daisy, Norma is tired. Show her the dolls tomorrow."

"She is not tired. I'm sure she's dying for company. You *are* dying for company, aren't you, Norma?"

I didn't answer immediately. Her eyes, flat and opaque, turned on me, and absurdly, I felt afraid, as though she would find some way to punish me if I answered incorrectly. I unglued myself and looked at Johnny. We were like two children clinging together in the presence of a not quite balanced schoolmaster. I wanted to back him up, but then, cowardice, not politeness, took over and I said feebly, "Well—uh, yes, I love company."

"See, Johnny? She *does* want me to stay."

"For Christ sake, Daisy, she's being polite."

Her face remained pleasant, but underneath, the change was taking place. "Why should she say she wants company if—"

"I tell you what," I said desperately, afraid I might start to laugh or cry, "I'll probably have to remain home tomorrow. I'll look at your dolls then, Daisy." The last sounded as though I, too, were becoming unhinged.

There was a pause. I'd lost the brownie points I'd earned a moment before. "Of course," she said finally. "I hope I wasn't being inconsiderate. I certainly didn't mean to tire you out." She gathered up the last remains of the picnic and they both left. I felt sorry for Johnny.

Chilled, I burrowed under the blankets. I felt that I'd been running uphill for days. I couldn't even summon the energy to reach out and turn off the light. And yet I was afraid that I'd spend another restless night, unable to sleep. I was still worrying about that when my mind went blank.

"When can I go on the school bus?" he asked plaintively.

"When you get to be in first grade."

"I wanna go now."

Lifting him, I whirled him above my head and kissed his nose. He struggled, not interested in levity. "I wanna go on the bus."

"Tell you what. Maybe we'll take a bus this afternoon if we can find one going anywhere. We'll park at the bus stop and take off. I have to do some errands."

"Now."

"Let me finish painting this one wall."

"We won't go. I know."

"Just wait a little longer, Teddy. Honest."

"You always say wait. We never do anything."

"I know how you feel, honey, but I simply have to finish this one wall—"

"You don't even read. At night Daddy calls you and tells me to go to bed. You never have time."

"Moving to a new house is a lot of work. But you'll be starting nursery school soon and meeting lots of friends. And Mummy isn't going to work any more so we'll have time to go places like museums and zoos—"

I didn't hear the knock, but suddenly a head peered around the front door and a voice said, "Hello—I've been banging and trying to get your attention—"

We were too far from town for casual saleswomen and I was surprised. Putting down the paint brush and stripping off my work gloves, I went to the door and opened it wide.

She was a nice-looking woman, only a few years older than I, with softly curled brown hair and a neat figure. But she was overdone. If she'd spent a month at Maine Chance, a week at I. Magnin and a day at the hairdresser's, she couldn't have been more slimmed, made-up, coiffed, manicured and dressed. Ready for a series of photographs in Town and Country, she was wearing the "country" look—hand-finished pink silk shirt, pink and green plaid silk slacks, and green flats, all, I was sure, with impressive labels.

"I'm Beth Threlkeld, your closest neighbor. I came to welcome you to Freetown. I think I've picked the wrong time."

Conscious of my paint-stained jeans, Lawford's discarded shirt, and torn sneakers, I laughed nervously. "In terms of being organized, every time is the wrong time for me." The words sounded rude. Hoping she wouldn't misinterpret them, I added, "I'm happy to meet you. Please come in, if you don't mind the mess. This is Teddy. I'm Norma Garretson."

"Hi, Teddy."

Teddy, clinging to my pants, disappeared completely behind me.

"Poised, isn't he?" I twitched a tarpaulin off a chair and motioned her to it.

Looking around with frank curiosity, she said, "I'd better not stay. You're busy. But anyway, I have a little girl about the same age as your little boy. We'll have to get them together."

"Oh, wow. You don't know how happy I am to hear that. Teddy's dying of loneliness. Please sit down. Would you care for a cup of tea?"

In the end she stayed and I put on the kettle to boil. I quieted Teddy with hot chocolate and cookies, and carried the cups and tea pot to the living room. She told me about the local nursery school, the shops and the availability of sitters. I was so happy to have an adult to talk to and a possible budding friendship that I forgot my promise to Teddy to take him to town. I also forgot the painting. Disconsolately, Teddy wandered outdoors.

While she chatted, my new acquaintance kept examining the furniture, the few paintings hanging on the papered wall, even my outfit. "Are you going to do the house traditionally or are you one of these modern buffs?"

"I'm an eclectic buff. A little of this, a little of that. Actually I don't have that much choice. A lot of it is inherited."

"Oh, dear. It's a little depressing to have to start with someone else's castoffs, isn't it?"

Well, perhaps it wasn't a budding friendship, I conceded, but it was someone to talk to. "If everyone agreed with you, what would happen to the antique business? Are you an interior decorator?"

"No, a dress designer, but I love all kinds of beautiful things. I can't bear being surrounded by the second-rate. What do you do? I mean, aside from being a wife and mother?"

"I've been a reporter, up to the time we moved. We got married quite young and I had to finish college at night after Teddy was born. Then I got a housekeeper and went to work. We needed the money. But with Lawford in this new job, we're better off and I can stay home with Teddy."

I'd never known myself to talk to a stranger so much, but I'd been lonely. We learned an incredible amount about each other in a short time. She, too, had stopped working for the sake of her children, but now she had to go back to work because her husband had left her. The last fact depressed me. I had envisioned a foursome.

Finally she got up, brushed the seat of her pants and said she had to go. We parted with promises of getting together soon and having the children meet one another. At the mention of children, I jumped up guiltily and looked out. Teddy was at the edge of the clearing, digging.

I watched her walk across the lawn and then I turned back to the room. I would have to give up the errands and work fast to paint the wall, clear the mess and fix dinner before Lawford came home.

Six

I woke up, knowing something was wrong. Usually it was the familiar agony which overcame me, but tonight it was different.

The light was still on, and I stared at it numbly, waiting for full consciousness to return. I had been half dreaming, half remembering, reality knitting in and out of sleep.

Beth Threlkeld. The last person to whom I'd spoken before my world fell apart. A woman whom I had even blamed, as I'd thrashed around trying to escape the full burden of guilt, for taking up so much of my time that afternoon.

I wasn't sure if my denial of identity had deceived her. If it hadn't, it would only whet her curiosity, perhaps even to the point of getting in touch with Daisy. In which case it wouldn't take Daisy long to realize why I had returned to Freetown.

I stared at the windows, black because of the lamp inside. Being damned, I decided, was having to wake up in the middle of the night.

And then, gradually, it crept up on me, what had really jarred me out of sleep. It wasn't the four-year-old torment, and it wasn't the realization of the dress designer's identity. It was a stomach ache. I felt queasy, nauseated, without any localized pain.

Lethargically, I remained where I was, hoping it would go away. As the minutes passed, it got worse, the ache growing until I couldn't lie still. My lower abdomen was gripped by a spasm and I had to get out of bed. Attention divided between the pain in my swollen ankle and the one in my midsection, I limped and hopped to the bathroom.

I couldn't make myself throw up. I drank a little water and tried to retch but nothing happened. I sat down on the edge of the bathtub and rocked back and forth, trying not to make a sound. My watch, which I had forgotten to take off when I'd fallen asleep, said it was two o'clock.

The window of the bathroom shone eerily as a car approached from the direction of the town. The beam hit the glass and then disappeared around a bend. From the direction of the woods, a cat howled with unearthly sadness. I wasn't the only one awake in the world.

A lurch in my stomach brought me upright, and holding onto the wall, I lifted the toilet seat and began to throw up. Four painful spasms wracked me before I began to feel some relief. Finally I washed up and went back.

Sweating and shivering, I crawled into bed and lay in a stupor, my skin sensitive but the torture gone.

And then, as the aching receded, something else flowed in to fill the vacuum. I had eaten nothing all day between the civic organization's early brunch and this evening's supper. The brunch had been over at eleven, and my afternoon coffee had come from a machine which had never affected me before. It had to be the supper. Except that we had all eaten the same things, drinks from the one bottle, sausage, cheese, bread. I wasn't sure, of course, that they weren't sick also, except that I'd been awake all this time and hadn't heard a sound.

Something could have been dropped into my drink. Or my coffee. Paranoid, Daisy had called me. It was probably only a twenty-four-hour virus.

I had thought that nothing could make me get out of bed again during this endless night, but something did. I crawled out, held onto the wall and went to the window sill for the coffee jar. I peered inside, expecting I don't know what, and then, spreading a tissue on the night table, I sprinkled coffee on it. I separated the grains with my fingers, thinking that I could detect miniature whitish particles mixed in with the dark ones. Finally I funneled it back and put the jar in the closet.

I lay in the dark wondering if I'd have the courage to take the coffee to a drugstore or a laboratory to be analyzed. Or would I do what was easier, forget about it. Then I speculated, since calamities came in threes, what else would happen. Finally I fell asleep.

Seven

Holding onto the sill, I looked out. The sky was overcast, and a sifting of snow was blowing sideways more than down. The lawn had the insubstantial appearance of the English moors, and appropriately, a dog resembling the hound of the Baskervilles slunk by. Everything normally visible was lost in swirling murkiness. As I watched, Verity's car started up as though by remote control, the headlight beams flickering on and off as they went past the driveway trees. She was the last one, leaving me alone with Daisy.

Even though the blue and swollen ankle ached, I remained standing at the window because I didn't want to face the nothingness of the day. From the direction of the road came the shouts of young voices, and I caught patchy glimpses of the yellow school bus, enveloped in scarves of snow. For a while the air was filled with indistinguishable cries, and then they were lost in the distance, leaving an echo in my mind. In the early morning stillness, I could hear the hum of traffic from the new highway. Shivering, I shut the window.

Finally I hobbled to the bathroom. The stomach ache was gone, leaving me weak but hungry. I washed and went back to put on slacks and a turtleneck. In a sitting position, I slid down the steps, one at a time.

From the kitchen came the clink of silver. I managed to navigate past the high-ceilinged butler's pantry, filled with a miscellany of trays, candles, unmatched salt and pepper shakers and broken-handled sugar bowls and creamers, and reached the kitchen.

It was a large, depressing room, originally intended only for servants, and so the architect hadn't provided for airiness or a view. The windows were too small and high to let in much light, and the walls were papered with a peeling brown-and-mustard print. The original wood floors, which Daisy said she would restore some day, were covered with faded linoleum. Cobwebs festooned the ceiling.

Daisy was nearly lost in one corner. She was drinking coffee and had the newspaper propped up in front of her. "Oh, there you are, Norma! Good morning. How's the ankle?"

"Better, thank you."

"Good. There's coffee on the stove if you'd like some."

Before leaving for work, Verity had offered to get my breakfast, but I'd assured her that Daisy would do it. Now, strangely obtuse, Daisy was back to reading the newspaper. I couldn't decide whether it was deliberate, or whether some vital part had been omitted when she'd been put together. Holding onto the counter for support, I said, "Thank you. Uh—would you mind if I helped myself to toast? And may I call the office?"

"Sure. Help yourself. By the way, I have a pad next to the telephone so that anyone who makes a toll call can mark it down and we settle up at the end of the month. Honor system." She laughed.

There was no chair next to the telephone and I leaned against the wall while the call went through. I asked the switchboard operator for the news desk. "Chris? This is—"

"Don't tell me. I'd know that voice anywhere. In the Himalayas, in the middle of the Sahara, on an island in the Pacific—"

"And I'd know that line anywhere. Did Johnny tell you? I sprained my ankle at the office yesterday."

"Are you planning on suing us?"

"Only if the damage is permanent. I'm sorry I can't make it today."

"I'll be glad to go over there and stroke your ankle for you."

"The excitement would be too much. If the swelling goes

60

down, I'm hoping to be in tomorrow. Maybe I can work on rewrite for a day or two."

"I can always find *something* for you to do." His voice had the automatic, undangerous leer to it. "We'll miss you."

After hanging up, I limped to the stove and poured myself a cup of coffee. Then I waited for two slices of bread to toast, and spread them with margarine. I joined Daisy at the table.

Pushing aside the newspaper, she asked, "Did that wicked Chris Upham make a pass at you yet? I couldn't help hearing that 'I'd know that line anywhere.' He's the most lecherous man I ever met."

"He's all bark."

"He goes after every girl when he first meets her. As soon as Johnny went to work for the *Gazette*, we were invited to the Uphams' for a cocktail party. I made the mistake of going to the bedroom to comb my hair, and he followed me and pushed me down on the bed—"

"Was everyone all right this morning?"

I hadn't meant to interrupt, but my mind always wandered when Daisy began an extended story. Her bright gaiety faded. "What?"

"I had a terrible stomach ache last night. I wondered if anyone else did."

She got up, went to the stove and poured herself more coffee. Over her shoulder, she said, "Not that I heard of. It was probably a virus. Are you ready to see my dolls now? I'm beginning to be glad you hurt your ankle. As soon as you've finished your coffee, we can go up to the attic—"

"The attic? I don't know if I can climb attic stairs today." It was more than the climb. For some reason being in an attic alone with Daisy, far from any telephones, made me afraid. Irrationally, I felt helpless, like a patient locked in a private sanitarium with a mad doctor.

"No, of course not. I wasn't thinking. Oh, I have this *fabulous* idea. Since I have to do errands this morning anyway, *scads* of them, we'll wait until I get back, and then I'll fix us a proper English tea and we'll bring the dolls down here."

While she swept on, I looked at the table or the gray cutout of the sky or the spider on the ceiling, anywhere except at Daisy, as though, like Mrs. Webster, I might turn to stone, but at the sight of a different object.

"—and pick up things for you while I'm out. You'll need food, won't you? And I don't mind shopping as long as it's with someone else's money."

I hoped the relief wouldn't show. With Daisy away part of the day, it might not be so bad. "Oh, yes. Thank you. If I could have a pencil and paper, I could make out a list. You're sure you don't mind?"

"No, I *adore* shopping. I ought to be a professional shopper." She rummaged in the drawer near the telephone and returned with a sheet of paper and a pencil. She continued talking while I made out the list: milk, juice, eggs, bacon, butter, bread, sausage, cheese, tinned vegetables, fish and soups, a chicken, fruit, a carton of cigarettes and three quarts of bourbon.

"—heard of these people who buy gifts for you and do your marketing— Wow! Are you stocking up for a siege?"

"Everyone's been so nice to me, and I keep forgetting to shop. Or else the stores are closed by the time I finish work. You're sure you don't mind?" Just then I remembered the coffee. If someone *had* doctored the jar, I was taking a chance with all these groceries. Unless I left them with all the other provisions in the pantry. No one would try to poison an entire household.

"Great. We can have a party tonight. I'd better get dressed. Do you mind giving me the money? I'm always short of funds."

"Of course." I rose slowly and started for the door.

"Don't be ridiculous! You mustn't go up the stairs again. Just tell me where your purse is and I'll get it for you."

Too late, I realized what I had done. I hadn't given it enough consideration. If she went for my purse, there was a chance she might look inside and see the name on the license. "I want to go up and lie down anyway."

"Why don't you lie down in the library?" Her eyes flickered.

"You might not be able to find the purse. Besides, I would prefer bed." I began to hobble a little faster, and the pain shot up my side. She took my arm and helped me solicitously. When we got to the bedroom, the purse was in plain view on the chest.

The Invisible Boarder

"And you didn't think I would be able to find it!"

"I forgot where I'd left it." I fished out two twenties and a ten and handed them to her while she exclaimed she hadn't seen that much money in years. Finally she left the room.

I lay down and listened to the sounds she made. Her footsteps receded down the hall, a door slammed, a drawer creaked, water rattled down the drain. Finally I heard her go down the stairs, the front door slammed, a car motor started up.

I remained where I was. I was waiting for the throbbing in my ankle to die down, and also to make sure that Daisy hadn't forgotten anything and returned. Outside my door, Tolstoy pattered by, his nails clicking on the bare floors.

When ten minutes had passed, I got up, limped to the window and made sure that there were no cars in the driveway except for my own. Aside from the few flurries of snow, nothing moved.

I limped down the hallway to the Barkers' bedroom. There were all the usual articles of clothing, both feminine and masculine, but fewer of them, of poorer quality and longer usage than what I had come to expect as normal. In the bathroom, however, I was surprised by the extensive supply of cosmetics. Daisy had splurged on creams, lotions, lipsticks, eye make-up, hair conditioners, hair lighteners and shampoos. Johnny's equipment, however, was as minimal as his meager supply of clothing—toothbrush, comb, shaving cream and razor. In the medicine cabinet, among the usual array of aspirin, iodine and bandages, I found rat poison.

The latter, of course, attracted my attention. It was a perfectly plausible item in an old house, but nevertheless, I took the box down and saw that it had been opened. Inside was a beige, cerealish looking mixture. I wondered if a small amount could be ground invisibly into coffee grains.

Putting everything back more carefully than had the person who had searched my room, I tried to picture what was missing. For one thing, letters and personal papers. Since they hadn't been in the desk either, they were probably in a safe-deposit box. Also missing was birth-control equipment. Whatever that meant.

I was about to leave when I noticed the telephone on the

bedside table and remembered something else I had to do. I sat down on the bed, got the telephone book from the shelf beneath, and found the number for the state mental hospital. It wasn't local, and I hesitated a moment, wondering what Daisy would do if she noticed the item on the bill and checked it. Then, recklessly, I got the operator and asked for the number. She would never be able to check which one of us had made the call, and the discovery of it might catapult her into an impulsive mistake. Or into arranging another accident for me.

"State hospital," a voice on the other end said.

"I'd like some information about a patient, please."

"One moment, please." The next voice said, "Dr. Umberger's office."

"I'd like some information about a patient, please."

"What kind of information?"

"I'd like to know if a Daisy Barker was at the hospital five years ago, and if so—"

The voice, several degrees colder, said, "We don't give out information of that nature."

"All I want to know is—"

"Who's calling, please?"

"My name is Mary Stone and all—"

"If you come here with a court order or written permission from the patient, Dr. Umberger might speak to you."

The conversation was over. "Right on," I muttered.

I stood in the doorway a moment, looking along the hallway to the other rooms. Then, instead of following through and searching them all systematically, I turned back. In theory, I knew, any one of them could be the person I wanted, but because one was elderly and the others likable, I couldn't make myself invade their privacy.

Cursing myself for being such a lousy detective, I went back to my room and lay down. Odd sounds filled the house. Some were accountable, others had no traceable source. Then, down the hall, I heard a creak.

I stopped breathing. Absolutely still, I waited for something else. There was nothing. It was my imagination, or the wind shifting the ancient shingles, or the dog. Knowing as I did what had taken place in the woods nearby four years before, I was conjuring nonexistent evils.

Further down the hall, another creak. My eyes rolled to the wall as though I could see through it.

Perhaps Daisy had left the car on the road and doubled back to see what I would do. Or perhaps it was someone completely unknown. Searching a monstrous house like this one would never reveal an intruder. He could always keep one room ahead and start at the beginning again. He was almost taking shape, a faceless stranger, living in the house for years and never discovered. Flitting from room to room, coming out at night to steal food from the kitchen. An invisible boarder.

I was afraid to move, to leave the safety of the bed. But finally I made myself get up, hobble to the door, and as soundlessly as I could, turn the key in the lock. How long would a locked door keep out someone determined to come in?

For a moment I considered going down the hall to Daisy's room and calling the police. Hesitating, I reminded myself that I'd be leaving the safety of my room. Besides, what would I tell them? That I'd heard a creak? I would sound as senile as the woman who had telephoned me about the cat.

I kept wavering indecisively. Any line of action seemed to lead to a dead end, so I didn't do anything. Turning back to the bed, I noticed my purse on the chest. I would have to carry my wallet at all times, I reminded myself. And then a movement caught my eye.

Sucking in my breath, I whirled to the window. I was just in time to see a figure, nothing more than a darker shadow against the gray of the trees, disappearing in the direction of the woods.

For a moment I was so dizzy I had to lean against the wall to steady myself. Then it hadn't been my imagination. Someone had been in the house all along, creeping stealthily through the halls, perhaps prowling in my room while I'd been in Daisy's. Someone watching me, listening to me make the telephone call.

The quiet and the cold numbed me. After a while I pried myself away from the wall and went back to bed. I lay stiffly, weighing alternatives. It was no better telling the police that I'd seen someone running into the woods than it was to tell them I'd heard a creak. They would tell me it was a neighborhood kid taking a short cut.

The best plan would be to get the coffee analyzed. If it was mixed with poison, I would have something concrete to show them.

The minutes ticked by. It was as though the house had been abandoned years before, and not knowing of my existence, no one had told me.

Finally I tried to read the book I had taken from the library, Kozol's *Death at an Early Age*. I read for more than an hour and then dozed off.

When I woke up, the light was unchanged, colorless and dismal. Outdoors there wasn't even the sound of a bird or a squirrel. Glancing at my watch, I was surprised to see that it was nearly three in the afternoon. Then I remembered the figure running through the woods.

The key, I saw, was still in the lock. I was famished, but I didn't want to go downstairs unless I was sure Daisy was back. The contradiction struck me. Daisy prowling around stealthily was a source of fear, but Daisy returning openly through the front door was a source of safety. Perhaps she had returned, knocked, and since I'd been asleep, gone downstairs again.

Stiffly, I forced myself out of bed again. Not only the ankle but every part of me ached. I went to the door and listened. From below came the sound of a radio.

Relieved, I turned the key and opened the door cautiously. Daisy was speaking to Tolstoy. I washed up and began my slow journey down.

"Both sides rested their case," the radio announcer was saying. "The jury isn't expected to stay out more than a few hours. And on the local scene, this morning the police found the remains of a cat that had been burned to death. According to Mrs. Alvin Lindsay of Pine Drive, a group of boys had been chasing the cat yesterday afternoon—"

Dizzy, I sat down on a step and shut my eyes. I could hear the elderly voice again: "Nobody to send! That's the trouble with this world. No one cares if a fellow creature is tortured to death—"

It's only a cat, I whispered to myself. The world is full of cats. And an echo from the past whispered back, It's only a kid. The world is full of kids.

Daisy was leaning over the counter, her back to me. She was completely engrossed. Either the radio masked my footsteps, or I was making very little noise in my soft-soled slippers. I was about to speak up when I noticed something which made me feel sick.

The round kitchen table was meticulously set with a printed cloth, a small vase holding one artificial flower, and delicate, old-fashioned china. What was horrifying was the group of guests. Six chairs had been pulled up to the table, and four were occupied by staring, shallow-eyed dolls. All of them appeared to be watching me. One, the most decrepit, was a large, china-headed apparition with the wispy remains of blond hair and a yellowed christening dress. Next was a baby, bald, scarred and wrapped in a shabby old blanket. The other two were more recent acquisitions, modern suburban types with long silky hair, one dressed in a snappy-looking pants suit and high heels, the other in a long flowered gown and silver slippers.

I must have made a sound finally because Daisy whirled with a gasp. For a moment, her face reminded me of the dolls'—flat, frozen and moronic—and then it was lubricated by a more human expression. "Good heavens! What do you mean by sneaking up on me like that?"

"I'm sorry. I didn't realize how quiet I was being."

"Now you've spoiled my surprise! I was just fixing this *marvelous* tea. What a shame you didn't wait until I called you. Your goodies are in sacks over there, and the change is there too. Oh, well, since you're here, come meet my family. That's Seraphina, my most precious darling. She belonged to my grandmother and needs a little medical attention. I'm planning on taking her to the doll hospital one of these days. The christening dress belonged to my mother and it's all handmade. She has the best character of all—"

For a moment I thought she was referring to her mother, but then I saw she meant Seraphina, and she continued to describe the names, lineage, birthplaces, birthdates and idiosyncrasies of her guests. I expected that any moment she'd mention their social-security numbers and educational credits. While she spoke, she poured tea from a china pot into the six cups, and placed two serving plates on the table, one containing sandwiches, the other iced cakes.

"—Verity's discarded dresses and I cut them up for clothing. Aren't their outfits darling? I have to do something about Matilda. She can't keep wearing that blanket, even if she *does* need it for security. Do you think I'm a complete nut? I can tell by the expression on your face that you consider me *absolutely* mad. But since I don't have any children, why not?"

I gave her another few minutes on the subject of dolls—she had an encyclopedic amount of information on them—and when I couldn't bear it any longer, I interrupted in my usual manner.

"How long ago was that picture taken?" I pointed to a framed photograph, in color, of Daisy and Johnny in bathing suits on the beach. Both looked young and tanned, Daisy in an orange one-piece, and Johnny in flowered trunks.

"—my next birthday, Johnny promised to get me—what? Oh. Do you like it? It was taken in Florida." She didn't seem to mind my rudeness. She was as enthusiastic about vacations as she was about dolls. "Johnny had to do a big series about vacation spots for the paper, and we got this *fantastic* free week on the beach. I wish we could get more assignments like that. Didn't I look great with that tan? We were out from dawn to dusk, swimming and sailing. There was this darling boy from Coral Gables who owned his own boat and he followed me everywhere. He was *madly* in love with me, and it made Johnny furious—"

I was staring at the picture, fascinated. It was the same reaction I had had when I'd been searching Daisy's desk. Without thinking, I said, "It's funny about all your pictures. No matter when they were taken, you never look a day older, but Johnny ages normally."

Her voice broke off, but this time she didn't launch into the new subject. Suddenly noticing the silence, I snapped my attention from the image to the reality, and I felt as though I'd been knocked over. I had thought she'd be flattered, but instead her mouth was twisted by a faintly unpleasant smile. "Where did you see other pictures of us?"

My throat felt dry. "I—uh—I don't really know. Don't you

have others around? Maybe Verity showed me one. I can't—"
More quickly I babbled, "Anyway, I can't get over how marvelous you look. You never change. You must have drunk from the fountain of youth—"

Our roles had reversed. While she answered perfunctorily, I couldn't stop talking, and since the other four guests contributed nothing to the conversation, the mad tea party went into a slump.

Finally she rose and said, "I'd better get my little darlings back to bed. They've had their tea and now they need a nap." Limping, I cleared the table, washed up and unpacked my groceries. Then, taking the cigarettes, I began my painful ascent.

Back in my bedroom, I thought of the coffee jar again. I wanted to place it next to my purse so that I would remember to have the contents analyzed the next day. Dragging the chair to the closet, I managed to get up. Then, unbelievingly, I stared at the shelf. The coffee jar was gone.

Eight

By the end of the week the ankle no longer bothered me, and when the police reporter left for a southern vacation, I was assigned to cover the station house. Although I should have been pleased at the respite from town-board meetings, fund-raising drives, school activities and local politics, I still felt twinges in unhealed nerves whenever I had dealings with the police. Four years wasn't enough to mend the scar.

All the branches of local government were contained in a new-looking brick building in the main part of town. I went down the hall to the section marked "Police" and nodded at the man at the raised desk. The immense switchboard in front of him was alive with blinking lights and rattling voices erupting from unknown sources. Talking to a patrolman, the sergeant ignored me. "Damn it. Tell her it's always the fault of the moving vehicle."

"She says this station wagon was stuck in the middle of the road around a bend. She couldn't stop."

"She went into the other car, so it's her fault."

"How about the old lady in the first car, sitting there in the middle of the road?"

"Listen, I don't have time—yes, miss?"

"I'm Norma Boyd from the *Gazette*. I'm taking the place of Sherwood Craubart this week."

"Oh, yeah. He said he was going on vacation. Here's the blotter, miss. Call me if you need help."

I accepted the red and black record book and went down the

hall to an unused room where I sat at a table and examined the notations. Each entry was preceded by a date and a number, and I checked them slowly to see if there was anything worth pursuing. As I went down the list, I could hear the board in front of the sergeant crackling and sputtering with various bits of information from around the town. Someone came in and began complaining about hunters dropping beer cans and paper bags on his property. "What I can't understand is why they drink so much beer. There must be something about hunters that makes them drink more beer than anybody."

There was nothing in the book or the court calendar to interest the news desk, and I left.

For the first time since I had arrived in Freetown, the street was flooded with brilliant sunshine. Every surface was clear-cut as a diamond in the icy cold. I passed a group of children chanting to the tune of "Frère Jacques":

> "Marijuana, marijuana
> LSD, LSD
> College kids are making it
> High school kids are taking it
> Why can't we? Why can't we?"

One of the children was a five-year-old boy with an angel face and filthy clothing. When he saw my eyes glued to him, he stuck out his tongue and laughed delightedly at his witticism. I would have to stop staring at small boys, I reminded myself. Instead of being a dirty old man, I was a dirty old mother.

The office was humming with the usual pre-presstime activity: typewriters clattered, a boy tore copy off the teletype machine, telephones rang constantly, Chris shouted for a re-plate because of a burglary at Lelenko's in the downtown shopping area, rewrite men with headsets were taking notes and calling for copy boys, and three men on the rim of the horseshoe were checking copy and writing heads. I noticed that George Van Fleet was in the slot. He no longer nodded to me since the day I'd given his wife the wrong message.

Dropping my day's stories in the wire basket on the copy desk, I wandered into the composing room and watched Chris checking the front-page layout with the make-up man. He was asking about a jump on "accident victim" and paid no attention to the picture editor standing beside him with a glossy. The smell of paste was pungent as they put the front page together like a scrapbook.

Even though it was a process repeated at the same time daily, there was always the same frenetic activity. Johnny went by and winked at me. Sotto voce, he whispered, "Stop the presses. Stop the presses."

I considered lunch, and then remembering the snugness of my slacks, decided to skip it. Momentarily I wondered why, after four years of never experiencing hunger, I was beginning to take an interest in food. If it was a sign of returning mental health, the fact didn't please me. Losing my obsession would be the worst betrayal of all, and I had already betrayed him, fatally, long ago.

Suddenly I remembered something I had to do. Going downstairs to the *Gazette* library, I refused the offer of help from the girl at the desk and asked if she would mind if I checked the file on my own. Since she knew me, she motioned me to help myself. I found the correct drawer and took out the manila envelope marked "Garretson." Inside were seven stories, all dated four years before.

In chronological order, the first reported the disappearance of Theodore Garretson, four years old. The second described the town-wide search for the missing boy. The third read:

"Theodore Garretson, four years old, was found, strangled to death, in the woods behind his house on Old Dam Road yesterday evening by a group of boy scouts on an all-night outing. The son of Mr. and Mrs. Lawford Garretson, the boy was reported missing Tuesday. According to Mrs. Garretson, he had gone out to play early in the afternoon. She hadn't noticed that he was missing until close to six P.M. when she began to search the woods for him. The police were called shortly before nine P.M.

"The object of an intensive search for three days, 'Teddy,' as he was called, had told his mother a confused story of seeing someone dragging 'a heavy object' across the floor of a cottage he had explored the day before he disappeared. The only cottage in the area is a small guesthouse on the property of Mr. and Mrs. John Barker of Circle Drive, a road running parallel to Old Dam Road. The Barkers knew nothing of the matter and a search of the cottage didn't reveal anything.

"The body was found by Robert Oppenheim, nine years old, of Oak Drive, one of the boy scouts. He told the police that he had been gathering twigs for a fire when he had caught sight of a shoe under a pile of leaves. Poking aside the leaves, he had uncovered his grisly find and run to inform the boy-scout leader. Medical reports indicated that the boy had been dead for three days."

The story went on about the Garretsons' recent arrival in Freetown, the company with which Mr. Garretson was affiliated, and the fact that Mrs. Garretson had been a reporter in the Midwest. The subsequent stories were usual follow-ups about false leads. Then they stopped. Seven brief clippings in the life and death of one Theodore Garretson.

"Did you find what you were looking for?"

I whirled around and found the girl behind me. She hadn't been particularly quiet, but I'd been too absorbed to hear her. Putting the clippings back carefully in the envelope, I went back to the files and slipped the envelope in the right drawer. "Yes, thank you."

The naked, flat words—strangled, grisly—burned through my brain as I went back. If my resolution ever flagged, if I ever decided it was over and done with, all I had to do was read the story again and it would be back in its full horror: the first onslaught of creeping fear, the three days which I would never forget, the final inexorable reality.

Back upstairs, the process of getting out a newspaper was still under way. Girls were typing at machines from which yellow tapes snaked to the floor. Robotlike boxes projected images of the stories onto galleys, which, wrapped with the original stories, were sent back for correction. After the galley proofs came the page proofs. An elderly man was melting cakes of wax for the glue. All around was the frenzied activity.

Half-mesmerized, I followed the raw stories along their processing route as though I were committed to the full gamut. In the press room a plaque warned, "Do not run with guards open," but the blue sliding door was gaping, and inside, I could see the machinery whirring as the presses began to rotate. The noise was picking up, and below, in the reel room, the mammoth rolls of paper were feeding in faster and faster until they reached the rate of 3,000 revolutions a minute. The leviathan cylinders thundered along with such velocity they turned into a blur. Newspapers began spewing out from a chute and someone snatched one off the line and checked the front-page layout. He shouted a direction about a margin adjustment, and then, on the next level, men began cording papers for the delivery trucks.

When I'd finished my assignments for the day, I put on my jacket and ran through the dark icy streets to my car. I drove slowly through the downtown section and noticed that the department store was still lit up. Parking in the municipal lot, I went inside. The store was bustling with late shoppers, men doing errands for their wives, women with small children, girls from nearby offices. Everyone seemed to be in a hurry except me. I wandered up and down the aisles and bought some cosmetics and a knitted top. Then, passing a telephone booth, I hesitated. Finally I went over, put down my shopping bag and leafed through the local book. I found three Oppenheims, but only one lived on Oak Drive. When I'd dropped the dime into the slot and dialed, I had to wait for five rings before someone was sucked out of the vacuum at the other end to answer. "Yes?" she asked breathlessly.

"Mrs. Oppenheim?"

"Yes."

"I'm Norma Boyd, a reporter from the *Gazette.* I'm doing a series of stories about unsolved murders and I was wondering if I could interview your son—"

"What!"

"We're doing a series of stories—"

"I heard you. What do you want to dig all that up again for? It happened years ago. Bobby told the police everything he knew and he isn't going to remember any more now."

I swallowed and wet my lips. Resisting the impulse to hang up and run, I said, "Could I just speak to him for a few minutes? I won't upset—"

"He's not here now."

"I didn't mean on the telephone. Will he be home soon?"

"Not until seven."

"That would be fine. If I could just pop over for a short—"

"I'm sorry, Miss—Miss—I'm expecting some ladies for bridge after supper and I'm getting ready—"

"Maybe I could take Bobby off your hands for supper—"

"No." The woman's voice sharpened with suspicion. "He'll be busy doing his homework when he gets home. I've got to hurry—"

Outdoors, streams of cars inched by as offices and stores began emptying. The revolving door spun to let in a never-ending flow of shoppers. "Could I stop by on Saturday morning, Mrs. Oppenheim? I'll speak to him right in the house, and I promise it won't take long."

Her voice was nearly a wail. Evidently it was as difficult for her to refuse as it was for me to insist. "But I don't want to bring it all up again. It's something I want him to forget."

"Yes." I wished I could forget it. My hand tightened on the telephone as though, by breaking it, I could break the sequence of time, erase what had happened and do it all differently. "Mrs. Oppenheim, the *Gazette* will pay your son twenty-five dollars for a few minutes of his time. Whether we print the story or not."

There was a brief silence. When she spoke again, her voice held a mixture of self-contempt and anger. I couldn't tell if the anger was directed at me or at herself. "Oh, darn it all. Bobby's desperate for a record player and he's almost saved enough. Will there be any pictures of him in the paper?"

"No. And we might not even use the story if nothing new surfaces. I mean, we need a new angle, but if we don't get it, Bobby gets the money anyway."

"Do you have to mention his name?"

I hesitated, wondering how much she'd swallow. "I tell you what. I'll call him a young eyewitness."

"Oh. Well, in that case—I guess it's all right. Come around on Saturday. Not too early. My husband goes to work at nine. Make it ten."

I thanked her and hung up before she could change her mind. Watching a girl picking slacks off the racks, I remained where I was. A man was examining women's sweaters. A saleswoman was folding a blouse into a gift box. Two children were running up and down the stairs. Then someone rapped on the glass and I woke up like a sleepwalker who finds herself in an unknown landscape. Outside was an irritated middle-aged man who wanted to use the telephone and saw me standing there doing nothing.

I walked past him briskly, as though I had an appointment, and got into the car. The traffic was bad, bumper to bumper, with the going-home crowd. I drove listlessly, watching the passers-by on the streets. Then, stopping for gas, I asked the attendant to recommend a restaurant. He suggested a place uninspiredly called the Freetown Inn and gave me directions.

It was in the heart of town, but inside it was pleasant enough. Ordering a drink and a chicken dinner, I continued my principal activity of recent years—watching other people live. There was a group of businessmen discussing a contract, a few couples whose conversation was more intimate, and at the table nearest to me, a woman and man with three children. It was the last, as usual, which occupied my attention. Ranging in age from about three to eleven, the children were fair-haired, good-looking, and all of them wore eyeglasses. They were excitedly discussing a forthcoming trip. After a while they became aware of my attention and glanced up, uncomfortably. I turned away, took out the *Gazette* and pretended to read.

Less than an hour later, I was out on the street again, wondering what to do. I felt that I had been running all my life toward a nonexistent rendezvous. The two movie houses I passed didn't tempt me, and when I went by the bowling alley and saw the cars turning in, I wished I knew how to bowl and had someone to bowl with.

Just as I entered the house, Wesley appeared at the head of the stairs, and I had a fleeting impression that he'd been standing at the window, waiting for me. The hallway was dimly lit as usual and his shadowed face seemed oddly sinister. Then he came into full view and I saw the weariness on it. He looked as though he'd had a hard day. Without speaking, we stared at each other like acquaintances meeting after years of separation and not knowing what to say. Finally the absurdity of it made him smile. "And what have you been up to all day?" he asked.

"Oh, the usual. Listening to a debate about whether the new garbage dump ought to be on the north side of town or the south side of town. The proponents of the—"

"Make it the middle, and then people can say they were born on the wrong side of the garbage track."

"I'll propose it. And what have *you* been up to all day?"

"Oh, the usual. Making napalm for little children." He hesitated. Then, "I was just going out to dinner. Join me?"

I was surprised at the strength of my disappointment. Just a short time ago I had been convinced that I'd been hurrying toward a nonexistent rendezvous, and now I'd found out that it existed after all. But I couldn't keep it. Slowly, I said, "I feel like that little boy in the play who was invited to stay for dinner and called his mother for permission, and then turned back sadly and said, 'I've already had it.' Me too. I've already had it."

He continued staring a moment longer and I knew he didn't believe me. All friendliness evaporating from his face, he said coldly, "Too bad," and limped to the door, slamming it behind him. I heard him start the car with a grinding of gears and race down the driveway. At the bottom, he evidently didn't stop and I heard a car honking angrily.

Johnny appeared from the direction of the kitchen. Swallowing hastily, he asked, "What's going on around here? Who just came in?"

"I just came in and Wesley just went out."

"What was the racket about?"

"He was mad, I guess, because I refused to go out to dinner with him."

"Oh," he said neutrally.

"Don't look at me like that. The only reason that I refused was that I ate before coming home." I wondered at what point I had started to think of the house on Circle Drive as home.

"I'm not looking at you like that. It's all in your own mind. And as for Wesley, he's always been prickly. Don't worry about him."

"Where's everybody?" I asked. The question surprised even me. It had never interested me before.

"Daisy went to an adult education course, Mrs. Webster is at her daughter's, I think, and Strandy has a date. Verity—"

We heard another car coming up the driveway and I was struck by the expression on his face. Unaware of it himself, he opened the door and looked out, letting in a draft of cold air. "It's Verity," he said. He didn't notice when I went past him up the stairs.

I didn't turn on the lights, but remained in the dark, looking out. I saw the lights of Verity's car go out and then I heard the click of her heels below. The conversation was muffled. Outside, the moon hadn't risen yet, but it was a clear night, with each tree etched in charcoal. I opened the window, enjoying the discomfort, and wondering what I was going to do with myself for the next few hours. Or weeks. Or even the rest of my life, after I had finished the one thing left to do.

And then, a sensation began creeping up on me. At first it wasn't a clear-cut idea, only a gossamer layer of feeling, a miasma, invisible and without odor, rising stealthily to enclose me in its vaporous fumes. I was weakening, losing my grip on the one obsession which had sustained me for four years. Something else was trying to take its place, usurp its territory. And then it crystallized. The something else was Wesley. If I wasn't careful, I might lose my lust for revenge.

Nine

It was still dark outdoors when I woke up, but my inner clock told me it was close to dawn. I turned on the light to see my watch. It was shortly after five A.M. For a while I tried to get back to sleep, but when I saw it was hopeless, I got out of bed, threw on my robe and pattered down the hallway to the bathroom. This was as good a time as any to take another step in my mission.

The house was freezing. Back in my bedroom, I dressed warmly in slacks, sweater, heavy socks and shoes, and then, carrying my jacket and gloves, I went quietly down the stairs. The house was still, but filled with the breathing rhythm of sleeping occupants.

Outside, it was much lighter than within, and it was easy to see where I was going. Walking briskly, I headed for the woods, in the direction of Old Dam Road. I had no intention of visiting the house in which I had spent the most unspeakable month of my life. What I wanted to find was halfway between there and the Barker place. Now and then I glanced back to see if anyone was watching, but the windows were opaque.

Twigs crackled underfoot on the hard, rutty ground. Ahead of me, dead leaves rustled as an animal scurried out of my way, and from nearby came the sad, rhythmic creaking of a broken branch, still clinging to the mother tree, but doomed to break off with the first strong wind. As I got further from the house, I began to see the black round pellets of deer. To make sure I wasn't losing my bearings, I looked back and saw that the roof of the tall, graceless house was still visible.

Then, without warning, I came to the clearing.

The cottage was made of native stone, and it blended so well into the grays and beiges of the morning light, I nearly missed it. Perhaps it was the suddenness of its appearance, or the woods encroaching on it, smothering it, or the hushed stillness of the morning, or the one piece of information I had about it, but immediately I felt afraid. I kept glancing over my shoulder as though I were playing giant step and each time I turned away, the trees moved a little closer. If they reached me, I'd be finished.

I had to force myself to take the last few steps. The windows were sightless eyes watching me approach, the stones were huddled together like a gang bristling at the appearance of a stranger.

As Teddy had said, the windows were low enough for a child to peer inside. But the grime of years and the poor light made it hard to see. Walking to the door, I turned, for no reason, to look at my tracks, and was relieved that the ground was too hard to show any. The door was unlocked.

The interior was filled with sound. As though it had been waiting for a signal to break the spell, the house erupted into a maelstrom of flurries, whisperings, scurryings. The air was saturated with the polyphony of tiny creatures emerging from subterranean passages into the light of day.

But that wasn't all. I who had always laughed at those who believed in the occult, was overpowered with the sensation that something or someone had been waiting in this cottage for four years. Waiting to tell me an important fact.

For a long time I stood there, afraid that once I made the fateful step, I would be trapped for eternity. The magic spell would engulf me, prevent me from returning to the land of the living. Finally I went back to the woods, found a large rock and propped open the door. Glancing in the direction from which I had come, I saw that the big house had blended into the shadings of trees and sky.

The three small rooms on the ground floor had the moist, rotting smell of disuse—the moldy odors of ancient human activities were imprisoned within. And whatever remnant of quaintness the cottage had on the outside had been obliterated within. Almost as though it were deliberate, a former owner had conscientiously covered the austereness of an earlier period with the sleaziness of a later one, so that the wooden floors were covered with linoleum, the walls with plaster, the cabinets with paint. All of it had been cheapened and coarsened; somehow I was certain that it hadn't been Daisy who had done it.

The only furniture in the living room consisted of a blue-velvet armchair with its intestines hanging out. The kitchen had a porcelain-topped table, and chromium and plastic chairs, chipped, ripped and rusted. Although the bathroom had once held a tub, someone had ripped it out, and now there was only the sink and toilet, and a scar to show where the tub had been.

I stood at the intersection of the three rooms, turning constantly to make sure nothing could creep up behind me, and studied them as though I were going to be tested afterwards. I couldn't see any closets or hiding places. Then I checked the kitchen cabinets. Here, in the wet filth, were encased layers of refuse in which various meals could be traced the way geologists can trace the history of the earth in rock strata.

A tiny staircase wound upward, the top lost to sight. It was almost doll-like in its proportions, built for people who had lived when men were smaller. Evidently there were no windows immediately above; it was dark.

I peered overhead, hesitated, and without thinking, pressed the light switch at the bottom. Immediately the stairwell was illuminated. It was startling, like finding life in a corpse.

The presence of electricity in an unused house made me more uneasy than the dimness, the scurryings and the filth. Quickly I pressed the switch off. Then, testing the stairs carefully, I started up. They creaked, but held. I wound around the tight spiral, and on the seventh step, a board cracked. Clutching the wall, I went hastily to the next, treading lightly until I reached the top. My experience at the *Gazette* had made me wary of stairs.

Upstairs there was one room with a sloping roof. The only place I could stand erect was in the center, but at least it had been left in its original state with rough wooden planks on floors and walls. The bed which took up most of the space was worn and gutted. Again there was no sign of a hiding place. Instead of a closet, there were hooks on the wall. Spider webs wreathed every corner.

As insubstantial as a shadow, something flicked past my face, and I stumbled backward in fright. I clutched the bed post to keep from falling. The thing dipped and rose and slashed back and forth in pendulous arcs. A bat.

I ducked my head superstitiously and dashed for the stairs. Just in time, I remembered the broken step and avoided it.

The house had affected me to the point where I was almost surprised that everything downstairs was the way I had left it: the door propped open and the crisp air freshening the musty atmosphere. Whatever it was that was waiting for me in this house hadn't revealed itself. Perhaps it was waiting for a better time when I would be more receptive. Or perhaps I had to come at midnight when the moon was high. Or perhaps there was nothing and it was all a delusion.

But Teddy's death hadn't been a delusion.

I checked my watch to see if it was time to get dressed for the office. Then, glancing at the awakening day outdoors, I was startled to see lights through the trees, until I realized that they came from the big house. Everyone was up. Quickly, I went to remove the rock from in front of the door and I noticed something behind it. I touched it with my shoe to make sure it wasn't alive, and when it didn't move, I bent down to pick it up. It was a baby rattle. I was still frowning at it when Daisy's voice said, "What in the world are you doing *now?*"

I jerked so hard I hit my shoulder against the door. Fright and pain fought for a moment and the pain won out. "All I ever do since I came to Freetown is hurt myself."

She was standing on the frozen ground in the clearing, an old coat thrown over her nightgown, boots on her feet. With the light behind her, I couldn't see her features. She was only an outline.

I wanted to see her face, and I walked close to her to get her to back out so that we'd both be in the clearing, but she continued to block the doorway. A tiny flicker of fear ate at my bowels.

82

"What are you doing here, Norma?"

Trying to sound surprised at the question and even a little aggrieved, I said, "Nothing. I couldn't sleep, and so I came out for some fresh air and exercise. Then I saw the cottage and decided to explore. I remembered you discussing it and I was curious."

"Did you find the three bears?" There was nothing light in her voice.

"Not even their porridge." I hesitated. "How in the world did you know I was out here?"

"I was putting on the coffee and happened to glance out and saw the light in the cottage."

"And you came out to investigate? How brave you are."

"Not as brave as you. Walking in the woods alone at dawn." She still hadn't moved.

A little breathlessly, I asked, "How come there's electricity in the house?"

"It was there when we bought this place, and we never got around to having it shut off. What's that in your hand?"

"What? Oh, this." I looked down at the baby rattle. It was, like everything else in the cottage, soiled and old. "I happened to find this behind—"

The hackles on the back of my neck tingled and I broke off. Daisy had moved back slightly so that the light touched her, and the expression on her face nearly paralyzed me. There was so much concentrated hatred in it, it was worse than a blow. Without thinking, I dropped the rattle. She bent and dropped it into her coat pocket and I went past her, hurrying. Although I didn't like to have her behind me, I was anxious to get away from both her and the claustrophobic woods. I didn't stop until I reached the back lawn of the house. From upstairs came the muffled sound of whistling and a shower going full force. Safe again, I was able to turn around and look at Daisy.

Her face was exactly as usual, polite and expressionless. Gradually the tension seeped out of my shoulders, and the hairs on my neck settled down. It had all been a trick of the lighting in the woods. Or my overheated imagination. There was nothing in an ancient baby rattle to upset Daisy.

Ten

It was in a neighborhood of lower-middle-class two-story detached houses separated by narrow driveways, and each with its own tiny lawn in front. In the case of the Oppenheims, the lawn featured one large hydrangea bush and a row of sticklike rose bushes. The house needed paint and repairs, but was otherwise neat.

When I rang the bell, the woman answered immediately as though she'd been watching from the window. She was unexpectedly young and pretty, and wore brilliant yellow wool slacks and pullover. I was sure that she had polished both the house and herself for my benefit, and the fact that she had a head full of curlers only meant that she didn't see anything wrong with curlers.

"Mrs. Oppenheim? I'm Norma Boyd. I have my identification—"

"You don't have to show it to me. I telephoned your office and they gave me a description of you. But they didn't know a thing about the story."

I wished I could get over the habit of flooding my face with blood at every moment of stress. It hadn't occurred to me that she would contact Chris Upham. I floundered. "Well—you see, I didn't want to tell the office about the story until I was sure it would pan out. We frequently dream up our own features."

"Well, it's all right. Come in. The only thing is, Bobby slept at a friend's house last night, but he promised to be back at ten.

You're a little early. He'll be here any minute." She spoke over-carefully as though afraid of making an error.

"Thank you. Don't let me interfere with anything you're doing. Perhaps I could wait in Bobby's room and be out of your way."

A baby wailed from the direction of the kitchen, and she turned, undecided.

"Or," I said carefully, feeling a tightening in my chest, "I could help. Perhaps I could look after the baby if you're doing something else."

"No. Thank you. I guess you can go up. It's the first door on the left."

Turning away so that she couldn't see my eyes, I went upstairs. I felt tattooed: "Danger: Keep away from children."

The room she had indicated, one of three off a tiny landing, was unnaturally neat for a boy's. It contained two cots covered with red-white-and-blue cotton prints, and the walls were dotted with posters of football players, baseball players, basketball players and skiers.

I caught a movement at the outer corner of my eye and turned. A small girl was in the hall staring at me.

"Hi," I said. She fled.

I wandered to the window and stared down at the crowded, seedy houses occupied by lower-income accountants, dentists or engineers, for whom this represented the first step; or assembly-line workers, garage attendants and salespeople for whom it might be the ultimate step. The street was filling with older people heading for the shopping areas, young housewives pushing baby buggies, children squalling and playing hopscotch.

Finally I turned back to the room. I opened the door of the closet and peered inside. It occurred to me that I was becoming a professional snoop—before, nothing could have induced me to examine people's desks and closets. This particular closet, I noticed, wasn't nearly as neat as the parts of the room which showed. Evidently Mrs. Oppenheim didn't penetrate this far. Surveying the objects on the shelf—cleated shoes, parts of uniforms, shin guards, torn nets, broken badminton racquets, torn pads and crayons, old stuffed animals, shell and rock collections, candles, dismembered games, models of frogs and skeletons—I saw a card hidden behind an old wine bottle. It showed a naked man and woman making love. I put it back exactly where I had found it.

None too soon. I heard footsteps bounding up the stairs, and Bobby shot in just as I moved innocently to the window. Throwing jacket, wool hat and a pair of ice skates on the floor, he turned the room into a shambles almost before entering it.

"Bobby," his mother called from below, "don't mess up your room."

"I won't, Mom." He sat down on the bed, and taking off his shoes, began to scratch the bottoms of his feet unself-consciously. He was nice-looking, healthy, and rosy-cheeked from the cold. "My mother said you were writing a story about that kid that was murdered. Did you find out who did it?"

"I'm hoping to. That's why I'm here."

"Gee, it happened a long time ago, and I told them everything I knew."

"I want to hear it straight from you."

"Will I be in the papers again?"

"Well—your mother doesn't want your name mentioned. Anyway, it all depends upon whether or not I get a new angle."

"Okay. I don't care. Like I told them, we were on this overnight hike. That's really a laugh. We were near these houses but we pretended like we were miles from nowhere. Anyway, our scoutmaster sent us out for firewood. I found a dead tree with a lot of branches we could use and I began breaking them off, and then I saw an eye."

He stopped, not for effect, but because he was trying to see the bottom of his foot. He wouldn't have noticed anything wrong, but nevertheless I turned and pretended to be studying the book titles. I kept telling myself it was all four years old, but the sickness started up in my chest.

"Just one eye. A human eye and it was wide open. I remember it was kind of a greenish color. Light-green. Man, was I scared. I was only a little kid myself, and I screamed so loud you could've heard me in China. At first the guys thought I was playing a trick on them—" He was quiet so long I thought he was overcome with emotion, but all he was doing was examining the bottom of his foot. "I have a funny hard spot there."

"Go on." I rummaged in my purse, brought out a sack of mixed candy and handed it to him.

"Thanks," he said, digging into the bag with the hand which wasn't scratching. "Anyway, the scoutmaster came running." His voice was indistinct as he bit into a nut. "He pushed away the branches and I thought I would die for sure. Honest, it was awful. The eyes being open and all, and the face was kind of dark-looking and the mouth open. God, he must have been scared out of his head. I could see marks—"

"Bobby," I said, and my voice must have sounded odd because he glanced up. "Bobby, I'm not really interested in that part." Why was I doing it? Was this another way to punish myself? I cleared my throat. "What I am interested in is clues. You know, like footprints. Or perhaps the murderer dropped something. Did you notice anything at all? After all, you were the first one there, presumably, after the murderer."

"You look funny. Do you want a candy?"

"No—well, yes, maybe. One of the hard ones. The murderer might have torn his clothing or, well, lost an object from his pocket. I suppose it sounds far-fetched, but it's possible."

"I wasn't thinking about clues when it happened, like you know, I was so scared. But it's funny you asked. The next day, after the police took the body away, a bunch of us got brave and went back to poke around. You know, like detectives. How come you're not writing down what I'm saying?"

"I have a good memory."

"A lot of reporters came to interview me after it happened. They wrote everything down and I got my picture in some of the papers and I was a real hero. This is good candy."

"Let me see," said a voice from the hall. It was the little girl, back again.

"Go away, greedy eyeballs," he said. But he reached into the bag and handed her a tootsie roll. She grabbed it and ran. "My mother told us never to take candy from strangers," he said, grinning.

"You said that the next day you went back to poke around.

Did you see anything else?" I lit a cigarette and put the match in a shell on one of the shelves.

"No. Nothing like torn clothes or foreign coins. You know. Wait a minute. I just thought of something. Your cigarette reminded me." He got up and went to the closet. Evidently he noticed the pornographic card and he glanced back at me furtively. Shoving it further behind something, he said ramblingly to distract me, "I always wanted to be a detective. Before I wanted to be a baseball star. We have this code. It's kind of stupid, but our mothers never bother to decode it, so we can have some privacy—"

"You said my cigarette reminded you of something."

"Oh yeah. It could have been there for years, except it was kind of fresh-looking. No rain or mud on it. It's probably nothing, but I picked it up anyway because I have this collection—"

"What is it?"

"A matchbook. I collect them. My dad's a traveling salesman, kind of, and he brings me matchbooks from all over the country. One of the guy's fathers goes to places like Tokyo and I have a good one from a place called Tempur Ten-chi—"

Still talking, he pulled down a scrapbook, sat down on the bed, and opened the book carefully. It was partially filled with neatly folded and pressed flat boxes and books pasted on the pages. "I keep it hidden so my pesky sister won't get at it. Here's one from a fancy restaurant in San Francisco—"

"Which is the one you found in the woods?"

"Let's see. Wait. It goes back a long time—here." He stopped flipping and pointed with a chocolate-covered finger to a white match folder with heavy black lettering saying FREDDY'S. On the back was a picture of a scantily dressed go-go dancer. "May I have it?" I asked.

His jaw dropped. "Gee, I hate to tear it out. And besides, if it helped to solve a crime, it could be valuable, couldn't it?"

"Yes, of course. I don't really need it. I'm sure there wouldn't be any fingerprints on it after all this time. I just want to see the back. Could we take it off and then paste it back again?"

He hesitated and then nodded. Carefully he pried it off and I

88

examined it. There was nothing else. No address, no telephone number. "Well, thank you, Bobby." I began buttoning my jacket. "I'll leave my name and telephone number so that if you think of anything else you can call me. Here's your twenty-five dollars." I drew two tens and a five from my wallet.

He looked embarrassed. "Gee, I didn't do anything. I didn't even give you the matches."

"A deal's a deal." I held out the money, but although he looked at it longingly, he didn't reach for it. "Gee, you gave me candy and all."

Putting the money on the desk, I said, "Use it for your record player." I reached out, nearly touched his hair, and changed the gesture to a handshake. "And thanks. If this helps solve the crime, you'll get the credit."

He was looking straight at me for the first time, and I saw his eyes widen with surprise. Still holding my hand, he said, "Jesus."

I blinked. "What's the matter, Bobby?"

"Nothing, I guess. I mean—remember how I told you the dead kid had these light-green eyes?"

I turned away and started for the door.

"Your eyes are the same color!" he blurted.

"It's just a coincidence." Quickly, brushing past the little girl who was in the hall again, I went downstairs, and not saying goodbye to Mrs. Oppenheim, rushed out.

The wall was painted, the meat and potatoes in the oven, the table set, and all I had to do was shower and change. Glancing out of the window, I was startled to see that it was getting dark and realized that Teddy was still outdoors. With a sense of irritation, I ran to the door. "Teddy! Teddy!"

Outdoors, there was enough light for me to see that he wasn't close by. Muttering under my breath, I shut the door and went to look for him. It was a warm evening, with the glory of the day lingering in the fragrance of roses climbing the fence, a mourning dove cooing invisibly behind me, the sweetness of apples lying under the tree. Teddy had gathered a pile of fallen apples the day before so that I could bake a pie, but I hadn't gotten around to it yet. The pile was still there, pockmarked with brown spots. Flies buzzed around them. I walked past a neglected rock garden, only a few yellow and pink portulaca, orange marigolds and stooped white petunias peering from the crevices, and thought to myself that I would have to get to work on it in the spring.

I still wasn't alarmed. Orbiting in ever-widening circles, I kept shouting for Teddy. Two cardinals fluttered out of an azalea bush and winged away. Perhaps there actually was a cottage in the woods and he'd gone back to explore it. Or he'd wandered to a neighboring house and was getting acquainted. Or, always fascinated by insects, he was absorbed by an ant hill. I stopped at a gray clapboard house and knocked. The elderly woman who cautiously unlocked the door told me, no, she hadn't seen any small boys, but she would call me if she did.

And then, slowly, very slowly, the fear began to creep up on me. Suppose there were ponds in the vicinity, hidden bodies of water where a small boy could slip in and never be found. Suppose there were tramps around, perverted, unbalanced men who might react in unpredictable ways at the sight of a lost child. Suppose there were wild dogs loose, abandoned animals left to hunt in packs.

As it grew darker, the tension mounted.

Finally I decided that I needed help. Wheeling, I ran back to the house. I wasn't sure if it was relief or added apprehension I felt when I saw Lawford's car parked in front. He was in the kitchen, taking cheese from the refrigerator. At the sound of the door, he turned. "Hey, what's going on around here? Where were you?"

"Lawford, I can't find Teddy. He was playing outdoors—"

"What do you mean you can't find Teddy?"

"I was painting the living room wall and fixing dinner and he was outdoors. Then, when I was finished, I remembered—"

"You remembered!"

"Well, I got involved."

"I can't understand how one wall could take you so long. You started this morning—"

"A neighbor dropped in." I was oddly reluctant to tell him how much time I'd wasted chatting.

"And so you forgot about Teddy."

"*Look, what do you think we ought to do?*"

"*How about look for him?*"

Again I was out in the dusk, this time with Lawford, circling and calling. And all the time, the chill within me grew. Lawford did nothing to help. He pointed out that I'd left Teddy with sitters for years so that I could work, that when I'd finally stopped working, the first thing I did was let him get lost, that if I'd been satisfied with less money, I would have been a mother instead of a career girl. Each word was a knife, and I agreed with them all.

In the end we went back to the house, and I stood and watched as Lawford called the police. Even at that point, some part of my brain kept assuring myself that it would be all right, that Teddy would be safe.

When the police arrived, I'd been almost embarrassed. It seemed to me that they were regarding me with hostility. What a way to start in a new town, I thought.

Fear kept alternating with confidence. First the sharp teeth of anxiety would tear at my viscera, and then anger would take over at Teddy's stupidity. The minutes ticked by. I watched the flashlights blinking in the woods, waited for the telephone to ring, and listened to Lawford's bitter comments. And then, gradually, the horror took over completely. Both irritation and hope seeped out of my bones. Ten o'clock passed, eleven, midnight. At best he was lost, cold, hungry, terrified and crying for me.

It became a never-ending nightmare. Dark hours without food or sleep. I kept wishing I could lose consciousness, but when a doctor arrived, summoned by the police and not Lawford, I wouldn't let him near me. I couldn't accept relief while Teddy was alone in the woods.

Incredibly, it was morning. Another bright sunny fall day, filled with promise. I tried to remember what had been in my mind only yesterday morning, what unimportant problems had troubled me. In the first of a million times, I prayed to be allowed to relive the past twenty-four hours. Do it over. Take Teddy on the promised outing. Bake him a pie. Read to him. I stared at the freshly painted wall and wondered what had made me think it was more important than my son.

By now the police were no longer passing judgment. Instead they were telling me stories about children who'd been lost for as long as a week and been found alive and healthy. I scarcely heard them. I was in a clear bowl through which I could hear and see the world through distorting glass. Odd-looking people made senseless gestures and disconsonant sounds. I couldn't communicate. And instead of drawing us together for comfort, the fear separated Lawford and me. Strangers came to the door to ask if they could help, but I couldn't bear talking to them. I remained isolated, alone in my own private hell, neither dead nor alive.

I don't know how many hours or days or weeks passed when I heard the knock that changed my life. Numbly, I listened to the footsteps, the hushed voices and the piercing cry from Lawford. Unmoving, I remained where I was. When the policeman stood at the door of my bedroom, I remembered thinking that the stairs must have been too much for him because his face was so red. "Mrs. Garretson, I'm sorry I have to tell you—"

I never heard the words. I covered my ears with my hands. I wanted to faint or die, but nothing happened. Until finally the doctor arrived. This time he didn't wait for permission. I felt the stab of the needle, and finally came oblivion. Kind, merciful oblivion.

Eleven

"Why did you go see the Oppenheim kid?"

I didn't have the control to keep from whirling around. Chris Upham, head bent over a story, had tossed the question out without even looking up. And several people, Johnny among them, had heard it.

"Oh, Mrs. Oppenheim," I rambled. "Oh, yes. She called in to verify my identity, didn't she?"

This time Chris did look up. Placing his pencil between his teeth, he tilted back with his feet on the desk and peered at me over his eyeglasses. "Oh, Mrs. Oppenheim," he mimicked. "Yes, she did call in to verify your identity." The front legs of the chair came down with a crash. "How about canning the act and telling me what you were up to?"

"Nothing. I happened to be reading about the case and I thought I could do a follow-up—"

"You *happened* to be reading about the case? Where?"

Deeper and deeper every minute. "I can't remember. I think it was a magazine article about unsolved murders. After all, a little boy was killed—"

"Little boys are killed every day. Big boys too."

Johnny lifted his hands, holding out an imaginary newspaper. "I can see it now. Eight-column head. 'Beautiful girl reporter solves four-year-old crime.' "

" 'Attractive girl reporter,' " I amended modestly. The same seeping poison. Not only was I losing my taste for revenge, but I was beginning to joke about it. Joke about Teddy's murder. My head lowered, I began to leaf through the stories on Chris' desk. I was looking for a change of subject and I found it. "Say, you guys. Look at this. The story is about a children's doctor and the head says, 'Podiatrist seeks legal aid.' "

It worked. Slamming his pencil on the desk, Chris roared, "What ass wrote this head?"

"You know something," Johnny said, ambling over and sitting on the edge of my desk. "That's not so far out. I mean about your solving an old crime. Did you ever hear about the case in which an entire city police force was searching for a wanted man, and a cub reporter consulted the telephone book, dialed and found him at home?"

"Exactly," I agreed. "What we need is the innocent approach. I'll probably get a prize for innocence."

He looked at me a moment and then shook his head. "I doubt it." In spite of his smile, his face was melancholy, the lines etched in, the skin worn and eroded over the years. "For niceness, yes. For innocence, no." Not even niceness, I thought. I glanced at him, and against my will, our eyes locked for an instant. I was irrationally convinced that he could read my mind and knew that I was measuring his wife for a noose or the electric chair or whatever was currently in fashion. I yanked myself loose and went back to my story, while Johnny got his coat and left on an assignment.

As was usual when I was finished for the day, I found myself hurrying until I remembered that I had no place to hurry to. I parked on the main street and went into different stores, stocking up on food supplies and a paperback. I couldn't bear the thought of eating alone in a restaurant that evening.

Lights were flickering on along the countryside as I drove, making the area look more populated than it did during the day. Hugging the right side of the road so that people with destinations could pass, I examined the closest houses, trying to imbibe vicariously other people's lives. A woman was getting out of a station wagon at a split level, a child tucked under one arm like a package and three others spilling out.

"Lousy hoarder," I said aloud and a car honked at me, as, without warning, I shot back to the center of the road and speeded up. I had just remembered that possibly there *was* something and someone to hurry to.

The long driveway, shadowed by evergreens, was more suffocatingly claustrophobic than usual, and the few dim lights did nothing to dispel the gloom. Then I caught sight of his car parked in the shadows near the pines.

I hurried upstairs, deposited my purchases on the bed, showered, and put on a long culotte outfit. Then, carrying purse and jacket, I went down again.

I could hear the low rumble of his voice from the living room and various functions of my body—pulse rate, heart beat, adrenalin production—all accelerated. I hadn't felt this way since before I had married Lawford. I waited a moment and went in.

"A warm room is a happy room," Mrs. Webster was saying as she shivered in the icy air. We greeted each other politely and I saw that Wesley had the newspaper spread out on his lap as though he'd been reading before being interrupted. When I entered, he folded the paper quickly, but not before I had glimpsed my by-line on a conservation story.

"Are you a fan of mine?" I asked lightly to show how relaxed I was.

"Actually I was reading a story about the adventurers' club. They had to cancel their Thursday night meeting because of rain."

I laughed nervously and sat down, wishing Mrs. Webster were someplace else. Wesley, noticing my manner, watched me with interest. "That's a very pretty outfit. Are you going out?"

"Well, you know, it's Friday. T.G.I.F. I always feel festive."

"What's T.G.I.F.?" asked Mrs. Webster.

"The Thank-God-It's-Friday club. I'm a charter member."

"Waiting for your date?" Wesley continued.

I felt my face getting red, but Wesley was watching his own legs, holding them out aggressively.

I plunged. "Did you ever hear of a place called Freddy's?"

"No."

"It's a kind of bar or discotheque."

"Oh, wait a minute. I think I know the place you mean. I pass it on the way to the airport. A kind of tacky shack?"

"What's it like?"

"A kind of tacky shack. Why?"

"I mean, is it jammed with people smoking pot or is it just what it's supposed to be?"

"What is it supposed to be?"

"A place for dancing. Do you know where it is?"

"We could look it up in the phone book."

The "we" encouraged me. "I'm going to do a feature on local hangouts. You know the sort of thing. Do-you-know-where-your-children-are routine. I thought I'd start with Freddy's, and well, I'd love company. Will you go there with me? Dutch, of course. You too, Mrs. Webster," I added lamely.

"You're asking *me* to go to a discotheque, Norma?" Mrs. Webster smiled and her smile was sad.

"You're asking *me* to go to a discotheque, Norma?" Wesley echoed. In his case, the smile was sardonic.

"You don't have to dance. I just want to sit and watch and take notes."

Tactfully, Mrs. Webster stood. I glanced at her fleetingly and then with more attention. Immersed in my own problems, I hadn't given much thought to what it was like to be close to seventy, widowed, living in a house with much younger strangers, never actually accepted as a person, but only as a type—older woman to whom one must be polite and indifferent. If she didn't make a pest of herself.

Instead of saying goodbye, however, she hesitated. "Norma, a funny thing happened—"

I frowned, half trying to be courteous, half wishing she'd leave. "What, Mrs. Webster?"

"I'm not sure I ought—it's so hard to know what's right when you've given your promise—"

If I hadn't been thinking about Freddy's, if I hadn't been overly conscious of Wesley's proximity, I might have given her my full attention. But as it was, I must have shown, either in the expression on my face or the timbre of my voice that I was afraid she had decided to accompany us after all. "Is something wrong, Mrs. Webster?"

She glanced at me sharply, considering. Then she made up

her mind. Over her shoulder, she said, "Have a nice time, children," and left.

I wiped her out of my mind. The words, "Norma, a funny thing happened—" and "I'm not sure I ought—it's so hard to know what's right when you've given your promise—" would come back to haunt me, but at the time they meant nothing.

When she was out of earshot, Wesley asked, "Couldn't you find anyone else to go with?"

"I don't know anyone else." I waited for him to look at me instead of his legs, and added, "When are you going to stop licking your wounds?"

He was silent a moment and then he said conversationally, "Do you know what I've noticed ever since I got my leg shot off? Other people are very brave about my troubles."

Sorry I'd started it, I snapped, "Do you think you're the only one in the world who ever lost anything?"

I was sure I'd blown any chance I'd had of his accompanying me when I noticed a common phenomenon. As my aggression grew, his diminished. He was even faintly amused. "Is that supposed to make me pull myself together and say, 'I'll show you. I'll go to your adolescent discotheque'?"

That was exactly what it had been supposed to do. Slumping, I wondered if I had the courage or the energy to go to Freddy's alone.

"And what did *you* ever lose, Norma?"

The words took a little time to filter through my self-absorption, but when they did, I got to my feet. My throat had tightened to the point where it was hard to speak. "Forget it. I didn't think it would be such a chore to go out with me."

"Stop fishing." He began the operation of heaving himself out of the couch. It was so deep he had to put one hand on the refectory table behind it and the other on the chest beside it before he could make it. "I'd love to take you out. But why can't we have a good dinner instead of going to that ridiculous teenage hangout?"

I was so relieved that I didn't have to go to Freddy's alone that, without thinking, I put out a hand to help him. He ignored it. "I told you. I want to do a story about it." A thought occurred to me. Watching his face, I asked, "Why are you so reluctant to go to Freddy's?"

"Do you know something? You make everything so complicated. Let's go if we're going."

"Thank you. But I didn't actually mean this second. It's early. Let's have a drink first."

Nearly at the archway to the hall, he stopped. He leaned back on the wall and studied me. "Since this is our evening for being frank—I'm referring to your crack about my licking my wounds—you won't mind if I tell you that you've been twitching ever since you entered the room. Your hand has been groping for a drink that isn't there."

I was taken aback. Without looking at my hand, I clenched it. "Is that supposed to make me pull myself together and say, 'I'll show you. I won't have a drink all evening'?"

"Jesus." Suddenly he began to laugh. It was a real laugh, not a sarcastic one. Then, shaking his head wonderingly, he said, "Norma, love, let's go to gay, jazzy Freddy's, and you can drink yourself under the table for all I care."

Freddy's fitted Wesley's original description. Like a blemish on an already unattractive face, it stood on the edge of the road on a deserted section of scrubby, flat country. There was no particular reason for it to be there instead of someplace else—no graceful topography, no crossroad, no nearby recreational area, no shopping mall. It had simply erupted, apparently because of an internal disorder. A small, once-white building with a porch, it seemed to have been built for a purpose other than its present one, but I couldn't tell what. The biggest thing about it was a neon sign with a go-go girl jerking on it. Around the building, the witch hazel and other small growths had been cleared for a parking lot, but nothing had been planted in their stead.

Four figures, all in jeans, scruffy jackets and boots, and with hair streaming down their backs, preceded us at the entrance. From the front, they turned into two girls and two boys, and all four had just gotten under the wire of eighteen.

The din was incredible. A bald man stood at the entrance to the red-lit interior as though he were collecting tickets at an amusement park, and asked for a two-dollar cover charge. In addition, the teenagers had to show their ID cards, but Wesley and I were not challenged.

I was digging into my shoulder bag for the two dollars when Wesley, muttering, "I think I can scrape it together," pushed me ahead and paid.

The room was no larger than a fair-sized living room, and not a quarter the size of the one at the Barkers', but there were at least a hundred people jammed into it. We managed to squeeze into one of the benches along the wall, as far from the band as possible, but it didn't help. Beside us, three girls, their freshly scrubbed faces a mixture of expectation, embarrassment at being without escorts, and sang-froid, were passing around a marijuana cigarette. I was filled with gratitude to Wesley for not letting me come alone.

As though sensing the thought, he put his mouth next to my ear and said, "Next time do a story on a French restaurant." The proximity to my ear evidently had some chemical effect on him, and I thought I felt his teeth. Then, abruptly, his mouth was withdrawn. Disappointed, I wet my lips and pretended not to notice. He grinned. "Tell me, Norma, love, are you the type who allows a chaste kiss on the first date?"

"At least," I said, without thinking, and then turned away to hide the ubiquitous flush.

I was beginning to wonder what I was doing here. I wanted to get away from the blasting noise and the wild-eyed teenagers and go someplace quiet with Wesley.

"Ready to order?" a girl asked, dropping a food-stained menu in front of us. She was young, nice-looking, and dressed exactly like the customers.

We had a choice of eight sandwiches and twelve drinks. I ordered bourbon, and ham and cheese on rye. Gloomily, Wesley echoed me, and we sat like two octogenarians at a nursery-school party. Under lurid lights, a girl on a raised platform near the bar was grinding and bumping to the music. She wore a white tassel-fringed bikini. A few older men lounging at the bar were ogling her, but the kids were immersed in their own twitching and jerking.

At the other end of the room, the band, consisting of three long-haired boys who were bare-chested and wearing Indian headbands and loincloths, were determined to break everyone's eardrums. One played on bongo drums, another shook a tambourine, and the third yanked on an electric guitar, and all of it was magnified by loudspeakers. If that wasn't mind-blowing enough, strobe lights began to revolve, transforming the dancers into old-time cartoons, moving erratically on a slow reel. A girl who looked to be in her eighth month gyrated like a loose balloon.

Dazed by the din and the dizzying effect of the unstable lights, I was slipping into a trance when a voice roused me. "Wanna dance?"

A shaggy-haired boy with the stubby beginning of a beard and skin that hadn't settled down yet was leaning over the table.

I crushed out my cigarette and jumped up. "I was hoping somebody would ask me."

Wesley made a halfway attempt to rise, as though he'd misplaced fifteen years and a war, and was back at dancing school. Then reality returned, and he bowed mockingly. "She kisses on first dates," he told the boy.

On the floor, I fell right into it. "It's like swimming," I said to my sometime partner. "One never forgets." But at the moment he happened to be out of earshot.

When he returned, he asked, "What did he mean by that crack?"

I touched my head. "Pay no attention. He isn't all there."

"Hey, cutie." One of the older and scruffier-looking of the barflies touched my shoulder. "You shouldn't rob the cradle." He was a little unsteady on his feet and his eyes were bloodshot. I smiled, took the boy's hand, swept around another couple and went on with it. All the while I bobbed and swayed, I kept looking around, searching for I knew not what answer to what question. If I spoke to the man at the door, what would I ask? Please describe anyone who was here four years ago who looked like a murderer.

"How about it, cutie? Come and dance with a grown man." The barfly had followed us, and on the boy's face was a mixture of truculence and apprehension. Not wanting to maneuver him into a Galahad position, I said okay to the older man. The latter grinned in triumph, and unable to leave it alone, said, "Go find a teenybopper, kid."

I wiggled between them and babbled, "I never was here before. You know? Isn't it neat? It really turns me on." I wished I had gum to chew.

Instead of keeping his distance and swaying like everyone else, he grabbed me in both arms and pressed me close. The air around him was saturated with a mixture of alcohol, cigarette smoke and garlic. Instinctively, I put up my hands and tried to push him away. His grip tightened. Although we were surrounded by people, I felt frightened. "Listen—cut it out—"

Behind me a voice said, "The lady is with me." Galahad had shown up after all, in the form of Wesley. He appeared big and solid, with no indication of the fact that he had left a leg and part of his ego on another continent. He took my hand, and relieved, I leaned against him with exaggerated kittenishness. The minute my shoulder touched his chest, the joke turned into something else, but I had no time to analyze it. "Come on, cutie," Wesley said. "Your sandwich is getting cold."

The barfly hesitated. "You with him?"

"Oh, yes." My voice sounded breathless and I took a gulp of tainted air and slowed down. "I am. He's my guardian. He never lets me out of his sight. Thank you for the dance. I enjoyed meeting you."

Still holding my hand in his large warm one, Wesley led me back to the bench. Then he shoved me firmly behind the table and dropped my hand. "Enjoy having three men fighting over you, cutie?"

"Oh, you bet. I haven't had this much fun in ages. I really dig this scene—" The last words boomed out loud and clear because, just then, the music stopped for an intermission. There was a tinkle of laughter, followed by heavenly silence. Or comparative silence. I took a sip of my drink and started on the sandwich.

"Then it hasn't been a waste," Wesley muttered. Suddenly his eyes focused with surprise on the doorway and I turned. What I saw made me forget everything else. Coming in were the majority of the Barker household: Daisy, Johnny, Verity and Strandy. Only Mrs. Webster was missing.

101

They were in the midst of an argument, Daisy wanting to sit near the band, the others opting for the wall. Then Daisy saw us. "Norma! Wesley!" she shrieked. Titillated by being out, by the atmosphere, by the joy of seeing a familiar face, she began angling toward us, excusing herself left and right in her pleasant but uninhibited voice.

"What are *you* two doing here? How'd you discover Freddy's? Isn't it *wild*? I had the most *agonizing* time getting all these deadheads rounded up. They'd never do anything without me. Guess what happened at the door? That lovely man asked me for my ID card. Isn't that *fabulous*? He thought I was under eighteen!" Her laughter bubbled around the room.

"Daisy," Johnny said. "You're stopping traffic."

The teenagers obligingly squeezed even closer so that Daisy and Verity could join Wesley and me against the wall, while Strandy got chairs for himself and Johnny.

"All *they* wanted to do was sit around in the house all night and drink. It's lucky they have me to stir them up occasionally or they'd grow roots. I told Johnny we simply have to take up something new together—"

"And I suggested divorce," Johnny said, motioning to the waitress.

"—but he—" She broke off to shriek with laughter. When she was able to function, she said, "Actually I had something more active in mind—"

"Don't you two do anything active together?" asked Verity. She looked very pretty in her long outfit, and watching her, it occurred to me that I hadn't given any thought to my own appearance in years.

Again Daisy was convulsed with laughter. "In *addition* to that. I'm getting fat from all our drinking and I've decided to take up dancing and give up breakfast—"

"How long will *that* stage last?" asked Strandy.

"Until breakfast," Johnny said.

"Now tell the truth, sweetie. Aren't you glad you came? Isn't this place *marvelous*?"

"I'm ecstatic," Johnny said.

"Me too," Strandy agreed. "They need a token black around here. Have a joint."

Everything was making Daisy laugh. With the music off, her laughter reverberated around the room and heads kept turning in our direction. The attention increased her intoxication.

When the waitress arrived for their orders, Daisy asked for two beers before Johnny could open his mouth.

"What will you have to eat?" he asked her.

"We've eaten. Look, Norma's hardly touched her sandwich. We can share it." I pushed my plate toward her, while the others ordered. Then the musicians returned, and Daisy pulled Johnny to his feet. She was bizarrely dressed in a purple shirt, fringed vest and green slacks. Two purple ribbons were tied around her pigtails, and her face was as flushed and smooth as a child's.

On the floor, Daisy gyrated with loose-jointed abandon while Johnny moved woodenly. I couldn't tell what was wrong with her dancing except that it didn't come naturally and for some reason it embarrassed me. Johnny glanced back at the table, caught Verity's eye and turned away again. Compared to Daisy's, his face was ancient.

"Daisy's a horse's ass," Verity said conversationally.

"I don't know," Strandy said. "She's right. If it weren't for Daisy we'd do nothing but sit around most evenings."

Mimicking Mrs. Webster's voice, Wesley said, "And besides, you mustn't look for the worst in people, dear."

"The worst! That's the best."

Strandy changed the subject. "Wesley, I've thought of a good investment for you and me."

The din started up again, and unable to follow the conversation easily, I got up and went to the man guarding the entrance. "Excuse me. Do you have any matches?"

Collecting money from new arrivals, he said hurriedly without looking at me, "Ask one of the waitresses."

Back at the table, Wesley was saying, "We could get it for a song."

"Sure. They're probably the only undeveloped beaches left in the whole world. All they need is a little fixing up."

"We would have to get rid of the unexploded bombs though," Wesley said, "and the parts of bodies—"

"Get rid of, hell. We'll sell them as souvenirs. I can see the posters now. 'Step right up and get your relics of the Vietnam

War before they're all gone. Almost perfect legs and arms'—"

I was surprised at Wesley's laughter. Either the healing process had started with him too, or he had a special relationship with Strandy. Then I was caught by my use of the word "too." *I* wasn't healing. I wouldn't allow myself to heal.

Snapping her fingers and gyrating her hips, Daisy returned to the table. Johnny trailed her. "You all look as though you're at a prison party. Why don't you dance? I'm surprised the men aren't swarming all over you two *gorgeous* creatures. Someone tried to take me away from Johnny. Was he furious!"

I waited for her to be seated before getting down to what I had come for. "Do you and Johnny come here often?"

"I wish we could. It's not all that expensive. But it's so hard to get Johnny to do *anything*. I love this place. It's so alive and so young. The most I can manage is to get Johnny here three or four times a year. And he complains so bitterly, it's almost not worth it."

I offered her a cigarette, lit it for her and kept my eyes lowered. "For how many years have you been coming here? I mean, when did you start?"

"Oh, we've known this place *forever*. Ages and ages. Once I even organized an office party and we got *scads* of people, from Chris Upham down to the copy boy. Even Mrs. Webster came once. The only one who has resisted so far was Wesley. You must have special influence with him. I must get started on dreaming up another bash for this group before they all sink into their graves. Oh, look at that *darling* boy. He's been staring at me ever since I arrived."

Putting down the cigarette and beer, she jumped to her feet and wiggled her way across the dance floor to a boy sitting by himself. He glanced up, startled, then grinned and got to his feet.

Shaking his head ruefully, Johnny caught the waitress's eye. He ordered a Scotch, and before she could leave, I asked her for matches. From her pocket she produced a folder and dropped it on the table. It had a large black "Freddy's" on it and a go-go girl. It was the same Freddy's.

"I feel like a damned fool in this place," Johnny said.

"Then why did you come?" Verity asked. I could see she was getting drunk.

Johnny lifted his eyes to hers and the two of them stared at one another with a mixture of antagonism and something else, a mixture I knew well. They'd forgotten the existence of the rest of us. Then Johnny shrugged and turned away. "Because it gives Daisy pleasure."

"Then quit complaining."

On the dance floor, Daisy's movements became wilder and more abandoned. She was self-conscious, as though performing for a large audience. Beside me, Wesley had switched subjects. "—were born at a time when the baby books insisted upon strictness and schedules. You know, four-hour feedings and not a minute sooner. But the current crop of teenagers were brought up on the demand-feeding routine. So, if the cops break up demonstrations, they have to know if it's the disciplined lot or the undisciplined lot, and treat them accordingly—"

"He asked for my telephone number!" Daisy was back at the table, even happier and younger-looking, her laughter loud as the music. "He's going to call me and ask for a date. Isn't that *crazy?* I'll wait for some night when Johnny is working late—" She stopped as her eyes lit on the Scotch, and the animation drained away as though a suction cup had been applied to her skin. "Did you order Scotch, Johnny?"

I got up. "We ought to be leaving, don't you think, Wesley?"

Wesley continued sitting. "Why?"

"Well—I mean, you weren't very anxious—"

"But now that I'm here, I'm used to it. I'm getting to dig this place. Sit down and have another drink."

"I don't really want another drink."

"But *I* do. Actually, Norma, I can't stand bossy women." He was grinning, watching Daisy. I sat down.

"I told you not to order hard liquor," Daisy was saying, "and you went and—"

"—and disobeyed you," Johnny finished. "Daisy, I'm a big boy now."

"You know we agreed to have only beer—"

"*You* agreed, Daisy."

Grabbing Johnny's hand, Verity said, "Let's dance. Come on. I haven't danced yet." She pulled him toward the dance floor.

Standing, Wesley said, "I hate to tear myself away, but since you would like to leave, Norma—"

"Wait a minute," Daisy said, distracted. "Where are you two going? We all just arrived."

"I'm dead tired," I said untruthfully. Actually I was feeling stimulated, excited, but I wasn't sure why. "Besides, I had to twist Wesley's arm to get him to bring me here at all, and I promised not to stay late—"

"He said he digs this place." I could hear the quotation marks dropping around the word "dig." Then her eyes narrowed. "If you're so anxious to leave, why did you come here so early? I mean, what made you come in the first place?"

"I'm thinking of doing a story about teenage hangouts—"

"Just what I thought! *Another* story. First the Oppenheim boy, and now this." Forgetting about Johnny's transgressions, she fixed all her attention on me and I felt like a butterfly pinned to a board.

I took out my cigarettes and dropped them in front of her, on the subconscious principle of the Russians who dropped babies in front of wolves to distract them from the main course. "Keep the cigarettes, Daisy. I don't need them any more this evening."

It didn't work. "Sit down a minute, Norma. I *insist*. I shall feel terribly hurt if you leave so soon after we arrive. Besides, now that I have you all together, I have to ask you something."

Weakly, I sat, and after glancing at me, Wesley did the same. Daisy leaned forward. "One of you naughty boarders made a long-distance telephone call and didn't put it on the board." She was smiling pleasantly, and looking only at me.

I felt feverish and headachy, as though coming down with an infection. I couldn't pull my eyes away from hers. "It was me, Daisy. Sorry, I forgot to make a note of it."

"Ah ha! And the rest of you will never guess to whom the call was made. I checked with the telephone company." She waited, but no one guessed. "The state mental hospital!"

I reached for a drink, realized that I no longer had one and brushed my hair back instead.

"Is it in connection with another story you're doing, Norma?"

"Yes."

"Wow. Johnny had better watch himself or he'll be out of a job. I think you're going to take over the entire news department."

She continued in the same joking vein, but there was no humor in her eyes. My chest felt squeezed.

As she went on, I composed a scoreboard. In my column was the fact that I'd found a canceled check made out to the state mental hospital, and I'd located a matchbook leading to Freddy's and discovered that all of the boarders, except Wesley, had been here at one time or another. On the other side was the fact that Daisy probably knew I'd searched her desk, I'd fallen down a flight of stairs, I'd been suspiciously sick one night, and I'd been recognized by the dress designer, Beth Threlkeld.

There was no doubt that "they" were ahead.

Twelve

Although I had tried to resist Daisy's pressure for days before I gave in, the first dive into the warm chlorinated water pumped my blood into a warm glow. I came up spitting and blinking, and then went into my own version of the crawl along the length of the Boys' Club indoor pool. As usual, Daisy had been right. It was exhilarating.

Familiar heads, wet and oddly changed by the unfamiliar medium, glittered through a watery haze. I had trouble recognizing some of the people I had heretofore only seen in ordinary daytime clothing.

Sidestroking beside me so that we could chat, Daisy said, "Now, admit it. Aren't you glad that I made you come? Isn't this *fabulous?*"

"Right on, Daisy. Right on."

"Do you know what I'm planning for next summer? We're all going to get out on the tennis courts—the public ones in town—every morning before work and play a couple of sets. And next winter, if we can afford it, we'll all go skiing. I may up your rents so that I can scrape the money together." Her laughter bounced back from the beamed ceiling.

Next summer. Next winter. What a lot of chickens Daisy was counting. Hopefully, by next summer my mission would be accomplished. And then what? Aloud I said, "You ought to be a social director, Daisy."

"That's a *marvelous* idea. I can start a whole new career.

I'm getting tired of cleaning up after all of you. I bet I'd be *fantastic* at it." She kicked off vigorously.

It was actually a dreary room with its no-color walls and no-color tiles, and the stacks of kickboards, lifesavers and ladders in the corners. But the brilliantly colored caps and swimsuits and half-naked children livened it up. The faces glided by, Verity, Strandy, Johnny, people from the office—Chris Upham and his wife, two or three reporters, a man from the business office, another from the composing room. They had all been organized by Daisy and invited back to the house for a spaghetti dinner afterward. It was the club's free swim for men, women and children, a regular Sunday afternoon event, and the pool was crowded.

Someone tickled my stomach, and I splashed water out of my eyes in time to see Chris surface beyond me. "You ought to come to work in that bikini. It would do wonders for morale."

"Isn't this fun? I haven't gone swimming for years."

"Even in the summer? Why not?"

A slip a day. Could keep the job away. The reason I haven't gone swimming for years, Chris, is that every time I was near water and heard the little children laughing and splashing, I wanted to kill myself. Aloud, I said, "Because I didn't have Daisy around to force me to."

I swam on, lazily breaststroking. I enjoyed watching people's varied methods of attacking the water. Verity's strokes were indifferent, like mine. Strandy's were the best, powerful and graceful. The Van Fleets, who had arrived when my attention had been elsewhere, were surprisingly strong swimmers. Johnny and the two Uphams were mediocre.

Daisy was the most interesting of all. Her swimming was an encapsulation of her personality. It didn't come naturally or spontaneously as it did with Strandy; it wasn't uncaring as with Verity and me; it wasn't mediocre as in the case of Johnny. Born without natural athletic ability, she had attacked swimming the way a mathematician attacks a problem. Instead of a casual leap, her dive involved standing stiffly on the board, pointing her arms like arrows and then cutting the water precisely. Her strokes were neither fast nor slow, but studied, hands correctly coiled, legs accurately positioned, face concentrated. The only thing she lacked was grace.

Since I hadn't done anything more active than walk in a long time, I tired quickly, and climbed out to rest for a moment. Just as I lifted myself over the edge, I caught sight of a face which twisted my viscera with the familiar stab of fear.

At first it was unfocused fear. I didn't recognize her immediately because of the cap and swimsuit, but my glands told me she was associated with something unpleasant. Slightly plump, with an unexercised figure, she came into the pool area accompanied by three children. It wasn't easy to tell if the two younger ones were male or female because of the shoulder-length hair and half-suits. The eldest, about eleven or twelve, was a boy.

Then I knew who it was. Beth Threlkeld. The woman with whom I'd spent my last peaceful afternoon on earth.

I looked around quickly to locate Daisy and saw that she was at the other end of the pool. I didn't want Beth Threlkeld to speak to me within earshot of my landlady.

Hoping to avoid her entirely, I started to get up and she saw me immediately. Probably because of the movement. "The guilty flee when no man pursueth." Or was it the wicked?

She headed straight for me. "Why, hello there. It's a small world. What are *you* doing here?"

"Swimming. That is, until a minute ago."

She laughed politely. "You may go in, children. Stay at the shallow end, Keith. Is your family with you?"

"I told you. I'm not married. Unless by family you mean my mother and father."

"Oh, yes. I forgot. I can't get over your resemblance to that woman, Mrs. Garretson, whose son was murdered. I can't seem to remember her first name. None of the newspapers mentioned it—"

"You checked the newspapers?" I felt the muscles of my face stiffen and I tried to smile.

A little embarrassed, she said, "Well, I was so sure. I mean, you know, curiosity—"

"—killed the cat." There was something about the woman

110

which brought out the hostility in me. Momentarily, I considered telling her the truth and asking for her silence. Then I decided against it. Explaining that I was looking for a murderer would sound insane. And as for her maintaining silence, my newspaper experience had taught me that no one could resist talking. It had been a mistake coming here anyway. Too many children.

"Well, since I'm here, I might as well go in." She dived in and disappeared in the welter of heads.

Her youngest child, Keith, elected to remain with me. "Lady, why don't you swim? You know how?"

I glanced at his shining hair and skinny body and then turned my attention to the cinder-block walls. A bulletin board in one corner listed the boys' red team, the boys' blue team, instructions on diving, and a typewritten sheet from the aquatic director. It listed the date, and the subject was safety. "Drowning and pool accidents," it said, "are apt to happen when we relax our vigilance or neglect to fulfill our responsibility—"

"Can't you swim?" Keith persisted.

"I'm resting."

"If you can't, I'll teach you."

"No, thank you."

"Then I'll push you in." He came up behind me, eyes glinting with admiration for his own daring, and reached out. I grabbed him playfully, but then, without meaning to, I tightened my grip. His eyes widened with fear. At the touch of his cool, smooth skin, something happened. I dropped his arm, and blindly, I turned away. I started down the hallway to the dressing rooms. My vision was blurred. But not so badly I couldn't recognize the new arrival.

His face was strained and he stared straight ahead. He was wearing brightly flowered trunks, and he was well made, with muscular shoulders, narrow hips, one long leg and one artificial contraption.

He passed me without a word and my eyes dried as I watched him stop at the edge of the pool, neatly detach the limb which didn't belong to him, set it down and do a beautiful dive into the water. His crawl resembled Strandy's.

Slowly, I went back. As though Wesley and I were engaged

in a childish game, I told myself that if he could do it, so could I. Ignoring Keith, who by now had switched his fascinated attention to Wesley, I dived in.

When I came up, I heard Daisy's uninhibited voice. "Good for you, Wes. I was considering returning to the house and dragging you here by your good leg." I saw two women, chatting at the edge of the pool, exchange shocked glances. Wesley was treading water. Gradually he lost his hard, vague look, and grabbing Daisy by the shoulders, he ducked her beneath the surface. The two of them began splashing at one another until the lifeguard approached and told them that they would have to get out if they didn't stop. Shaking his head, he told a man nearby about a drowning the week before.

I continued my mild breaststrokes, listening to snatches of conversation. I searched for Wesley, but couldn't find him. It didn't matter. Knowing he was in the vicinity had changed the texture of the afternoon. Forgetting Beth Threlkeld and the danger of her speaking to Daisy, I floated on my back and noticed the rainbow hues around the lights. They were probably due to the chlorine in my eyes, but I attributed them to Wesley's proximity. The entire atmosphere was heightened, not entirely pleasantly. For one thing I began to worry about how my figure compared to those of girls who hadn't given up swimming for years. On the other hand, I felt sorry for all the married men and women around me, facing a dull evening, feeding children, washing dishes, staring at the television set all evening. I had come a long way since I had envied everyone and felt sorry only for myself.

I bumped into someone and went back to breaststroking. And then I noticed Verity. One moment she was idling along on her back the way I had been, and the next she was gone. She had been frog-kicking peacefully, almost sleepily, and then she had flung up her arms and disappeared.

My first thought was that it was a joke. I watched stupidly, waiting for her to reappear. But she didn't. It took me a moment to become galvanized. Pushing people out of the way, I began splashing toward her. I had lost sight of the lifeguard or anyone I knew, so I doubled up and surface-dived myself.

Vague, shadowy arms and legs weaved around me. The

chlorine stung my eyes. Then, below, I caught sight of a vertical figure, kicking and struggling frantically, while another, a horizontal one, clung to its ankle. I felt myself trying to scream silently, and I gulped in a mouthful of water. A suffocating ache in my chest made me kick upward, but there were bodies in the way. I lost my head and began to tear and scratch as panic overcame me. Incredulous, unbelieving, I thought, I'm going to drown, I'm going to die. Whoever had said that drowning was peaceful was insane. It was agony.

And then I hit the surface.

My lungs bursting, I dragged in sobbing gulps of air. Nearby, someone said, "Hey, what do you think you're doing?" The pool was too crowded and the din too great for him to notice my condition. I shook the blur out of my eyes and started to call for help, and then I caught sight of Verity.

She was in the same state I was in. Clinging to the wall at the side of the pool, she was gagging and sputtering. I paddled around a father telling his son not to be a sissy, and reached Verity. "What happened to you?"

Still choking, she was unable to answer. She shook her head and dragged herself out. I followed her to the dressing room, where one woman was under the shower, another drying her hair, and a third trying to find her clothing in the welter of hangers. The room was a shambles, filled with scrambled shoes, small steel lockers for underwear and purses, scattered combs and lipsticks. Two of the curtains over the showers were half ripped, and one of the doors to the toilet stalls wouldn't lock. From below we could hear the jukebox in the recreation room wailing Carole King's "It's Too Late."

For a while Verity leaned against the mirror, her breathing gradually slowing to normal. When she could speak, she said, "Some idiot grabbed my ankle and dragged me down."

"And then?"

"And then he let me go."

"Who was it?"

"If I knew who it was, I'd strangle him."

"Are you sure it was a man?"

"What? No. I always use the masculine—I'm not woman's lib, I guess." She went to one of the stalls, got bathroom tissue and blew her nose. Then she began rubbing her face with a towel. "What a sense of humor."

Slowly, I said, "Are you sure it was a joke?"

She removed the towel from her eyes so that she could see me. "What else could it have been?"

"Well, you might have been drowned."

"So could he. Or she. I mean, there wasn't any scuba-diving equipment around, so I couldn't have been kept down too long."

"Yes, but he could have prepared himself with a lungful of air, while you went down unprepared."

She turned on one of the dryers and stood under it. "Norma, do you know what you're talking about?"

I didn't answer. I was staring at the reflection in the mirror opposite us. We were both wearing flowered bikinis, both had long straight hair, and we had similar figures, although mine was taller and heavier. Slowly I said, "Maybe whoever it was thought you were me."

She too was caught by the reflection. For a moment she examined us critically, and then she shook her head with impatience. "Are you really saying what I think you're saying? That someone tried to drown me because he thought I was you?"

More to myself than to her, I went on, "And then he saw he had the wrong one and he let go."

"Listen, Norma, all ankles are the same under water—no, wait, I take that back. Not Mrs. Van Fleet's. What am I talking about? Who would want to drown you anyway?"

I almost told her. I needed someone to talk to, and she was close to my age, I liked her, and the attack seemed to prove she wasn't the one I was looking for. But the habit of repression had become a part of me. "I don't know."

"Then what are we talking about? Honestly, Norma, I can't figure you out. You've had something on your mind ever since you arrived at the Barkers', and I sure wish I knew what it was."

"Everybody has something on his mind," I said lightly and got under the dryer beside her.

As I listened to the whir of blowing air, the full implication of what was happening began to overwhelm me. A fall down the stairs, a bad stomach ache, a near-fatal attack under water.

None of them was meant to kill, but each was a little worse than the last. Get out or else. And yet I had nothing concrete to tell the police. Even Verity, the mistaken victim, didn't believe the attack had been serious.

Gradually, from being the hunter, I had turned into the hunted. If I didn't get out, next time it might be too late. But I'd been obsessed by revenge for four years—breathed it, pampered it, hugged it close day and night—and I wasn't going to abandon it now.

And it wasn't only revenge. Underneath the surface of my mind was a knowledge I didn't want to face. It was Wesley who was keeping me here. Erratic as he was, blowing hot and cold, he might make no effort to see me again if I moved out. And where would I go? Back to nothing in Ohio? Another apartment in town?

The possibilities, the alternatives kept blowing around in my head, keeping pace with the heated air fanning my hair.

Thirteen

The state hospital was a huge, rambling complex of red-brick buildings set in the middle of flat, decimated fields stretching to the hazy rim of the horizon. From the public point of view, it was in a perfect location for a mental institution: the land was dreary enough not to be wanted by anyone else; it was miles from centers of recreation; it was situated next to the railroad station for the convenience of visitors. From the point of view of the patients, however, it couldn't have done much to improve their condition.

In the changing, wintry light, men wandered around aimlessly, a nurse with a black coat over her uniform walked to the station, a woman sat on a bench in the cold, reading.

Inside, it was better. It had terrazzo floors, and it was clean and freshly painted. Empty except for a reception desk, the large entrance hall echoed to my footsteps. There was no one behind the desk. I was still considering what to do when a man emerged from one of the offices and glanced at me inquiringly.

"I'd like to speak to someone in charge of public relations."

"We don't have a public relations man. Is there something that I can do for you?"

"I'm from the Gazette and I want to speak to somebody about an attack on an attendant by one of the patients—"

"Why would you be interested in that?"

"Well, the incident was important enough to make the town police blotter," I said, and added a lie. "And my editor asked me to do a story about it."

"I don't know anything about it."

"Could I speak to the attendant? I have his name right—"

"No, I'm afraid not. They rotate and he's probably not even here today."

"Could you check and see if he is?"

"It wouldn't make a good story. Some poor soul got upset and attacked the nearest person—"

"You mean you know who it was?"

He blinked. Then, his voice neutral, not antagonistic and not friendly, he said, "No. I mean that sort of thing happens occasionally in a place like this."

"Is that a fact?" My own words echoed unpleasantly in my mind. Nature hadn't intended me to be a reporter with the persistence and aggression necessary to get certain stories, and I had to push myself, with the result that occasionally I pushed too hard. More politely, I said, "If there's no public relations man, could I speak to the director of the hospital?"

"He's away."

I took a deep breath. "Does he have an assistant? I mean, someone must be minding the store." Again it sounded impertinent.

"Yes," he said reluctantly. "Dr. Umberger is here. Will you sit down? I'll check and see if he's in the office."

I stared at a wall because I couldn't see any paintings or magazines, and finally he returned with a girl. She led me up a broad, winding staircase to the second floor, which was different from the first floor in that it had even more empty space. I wondered if the dormitory part of the hospital was as spacious as the administrative. We went past a series of closed offices, each with a neat white sign indicating the name of the person within.

Dr. Umberger was past middle age, bald, and looked as though he'd never done anything active in his life. I sat opposite him in the large, pleasant office, and went through the same routine with him as I had with the first man, but in this case it was more difficult because he was German and we had a communications problem.

"This is not important. It would not make a good story."

117

"Well, actually, I don't mean to talk about the knifing alone. I want to do a feature about the state hospital."

"What is this feature?"

"A story. A human-interest article. It will be good publicity."

"Publicity? Why do we need publicity?"

"Every public institution needs a good press. You know," I added lamely, "when the budget hearings come up next time, you might need larger appropriations."

"You write down your questions and send me a letter."

"A letter!" I said in dismay. "It took me nearly an hour to get here. I know you're busy, Dr. Umberger, but couldn't you assign someone to show me around?"

"I am sorry. It is not a good story. We are ordinary people with ordinary jobs."

"Me too. And my job is to get a story."

"Then you send me a letter with these questions. I think about it."

To hell with it, I decided and plunged. "Did you ever have a patient here by the name of Daisy Barker?"

Lines etched themselves into his forehead and he stared at me as though considering me a candidate for permanent residence. "What did you say?"

My instinct was to run, but quaveringly, I repeated, "Daisy Barker. Was she ever a patient here?"

He stood up. "Miss, what is this? What do you want? You say you work for this newspaper and you come here with a story about an attack, and now you ask me confidential information about the patients. Miss, if you come here and you are a patient, how do you like it if somebody, anybody, comes here and asks us questions about you?"

I was still sitting. "But—I'm not asking about her psychological problems. Only if she was here at all. Surely it wouldn't be—uh—betraying a confidence if you told me if—"

"I am sorry. No more questions, miss. I have no more time."

Still standing, he waited for me to leave, but did not accompany me to the door. I found my own way out, and stood on the chilly pavement, wondering what to do. The light was no longer changing, but had turned uniformly gray. A pigeon waddled up to my shoe. I wanted to go home, but my conscience wouldn't allow it without one more try.

Finally I walked to the next building. This time I didn't bother with the reception desk, but went past briskly as though I belonged. Unlike the administrative building, this one was older, shabbier and not freshly painted. The walls were hung with notices of Valentine parties, bingo games and movies, and the halls were crowded, but no one challenged me as I passed rows of small offices. So far I hadn't encountered a single patient, or anyone whom I recognized as a patient.

Glancing into each open room, I finally saw one filled with stacks of filing cabinets. There was a woman at the desk, and I didn't break my stride. Turning a corner, I came upon a closet and had an inspiration. The closet held buckets, mops, brooms and uniforms. Hanging my purse and jacket on a hook, I picked a uniform at random and put it on over my sweater and skirt. It was small, but I left it unbuttoned. Then I went back to the file room.

The woman at the desk glanced up. "Yes?"

Sounding hurried, I said, "I have to get a patient's record."

She stopped me as I started to brush past. "Which patient?"

"Daisy Barker."

"On whose authorization?"

"Dr. Westwood's."

"Westwood? I never heard of him. You'd better get written authorization."

Back in the hall, I went past the broom closet where I'd hung my coat and purse and considered how to forge a note from a doctor. First, of course, I would have to steal his stationery. To think, I found a bench within sight of the file room. Passers-by glanced at me occasionally, but without undue curiosity. Sooner or later, I reasoned, the woman in the file room would have to go to the bathroom or take a coffee break. Nearly half an hour passed before I saw another woman enter the file room, and a moment afterward, the first woman emerged. It was not left unguarded.

I got up and continued glancing into offices to see if any one of them was empty. All the open ones were occupied. I noticed a sign pointing to the cafeteria and I had an idea. A friend at my first newspaper office had told me that if I ever wanted information not readily available, never to ask for it in a forthright manner. People who would balk at an open breach of confidence would gossip readily if approached in a roundabout way.

Following the signs to the cafeteria, I stopped to retrieve my purse but not my jacket. The cafeteria was below street level, cement-floored and tile-walled and utterly dreary. I passed a series of laboratories before I found myself in a large, cheerless room filled with tables and chairs, one wall lined with counters. The room buzzed with conversation and the clink of china. I got on line, bought coffee and Danish pastry, and looked around for a likely prospect.

An elderly woman with grizzled hair was sitting alone at one of the tables. Approaching, I asked permission to join her.

"Of course. Help yourself." She waited until I was seated and then opened the conversation. "Are you new? I don't remember seeing you here before."

"I'm an assistant in one of the labs," I said. "I just started. Have you worked here long?"

"I've been a nurse here for nearly forty years. My husband and one daughter work here also."

"Oh, my. Forty years. Do you like it?"

She burst out laughing. "What do *you* think? I wouldn't be here if I didn't like it. Nurses are in great demand. I watch the patients come in—dazed or violent or depressed—and I see them leave—healthy and able to cope. It's very satisfying."

"They're lucky to have a nurse like you. I hear that a lot of the people who work here hate it and mistreat the patients."

"Where did you hear a thing like that?" She pushed away an empty plate. "It's not true. Most of the nurses and attendants are kind people who really want the patients to get better."

I offered her a cigarette, but she shook her head. "I quit eight years ago."

"Not according to a friend of mine who was a patient here once," I continued. "She told me she was treated abominably."

"She must have been sick in the head." The woman, whom I was beginning to grow fond of, laughed at her own joke. "What was wrong with her? Who was she?"

"Her name is Daisy Barker. Since you've been here so long, perhaps you knew her."

"Daisy Barker. Let me think a minute. I have an excellent memory. Barker, Barker. It sounds familiar all right, but it isn't an unusual name. I *did* know one Barker once, but her name was Margaret."

I swallowed some coffee the wrong way and began to choke. Putting down the cup, I wiped my mouth. "How long ago was that?"

She thought a moment, cocking her head to one side. Near us, a group of interns were laughing noisily. I caught the word "euthanasia" and then the loudest of them said, "Who has a better right to kill them than those who *bore* them?" and they all roared at an obscure joke.

"It was the year my mother was dying. She was ninety-one when she died. We're very long-lived in my family. Anyway, that was the year my mother was dying, so it must have been about five years ago."

"Five years ago," I repeated, trying to suppress any sign of interest. Crushing out my cigarette, I said, "That was about when my friend was here. What did your Margaret Barker look like?"

"Margaret? Let me see. I don't remember anything about her except that she was fat—I remember thinking that my mother, who weighed seventy pounds when she died, could have used some of Margaret's fat. And she was dark-haired—"

I stopped listening. I remained at the table a little longer and then rose. Telling her that it was nice meeting her and I hoped to see her around, I went back upstairs. A wasted day.

Fourteen

I finished my last assignment early on Monday, and it was still light when I arrived home. There were no other cars out front. For a moment I hesitated, debating, and then, reluctantly, I told myself that I wouldn't have many opportunities like this to go back to the house in the woods. Part of me wanted to relax, forget it, begin to live; the other part knew that I would never get over the guilt if I didn't follow every lead. Sighing, I went upstairs and changed. Just as I was going past his room, Wesley's door opened and he stared at me, surprised as I was. Consciously, I didn't want to run into him at that moment, but unconsciously my body reacted independently of my mind.

"What are you doing home?" I asked. "I didn't see your car out front."

"I left it at the garage and they drove me back. Something's wrong with the starter. Aren't you early?"

"I finished all my assignments."

"Judging by your clothing, I'd say you were going for a walk in the woods."

"Right on. I need some fresh air."

"Like some company?"

He must have noticed something in my face or in the way I let out my breath. It was enough for his prickly personality. "Never mind."

The hell with the cottage. It could wait for another time. Grabbing his arm, I said, "Don't be an ass. Let's go."

"I no longer have the urge."

"Your urges don't last very long, do they? If you don't come with me, I just may throw you down the stairs. I'm big enough to do it."

For a moment we glared at each other, and I wasn't sure if it mightn't be the other way around. Then I could feel the muscles in his arm relax, and he grinned. "Wait. I'll get my coat."

Since I no longer had an object in mind, I let him choose the direction and the pace. He avoided the woods and went down the driveway, turning away from town. I had never gone that way before. The road curved and swooped around the bends, beckoning us onward with each turn. We passed an impressive stone entranceway, each side topped by a lantern, and I peered down the driveway, trying futilely to see what was at the end. A little further on was a modern house, unpainted cedar, starkly part of the woods, with a bridge over a pond leading to the front door. Dreaming, I thought I would have a hard time choosing between an old-fashioned mansion and an unusual modern, but I suspected that I would settle for a split-level if Wesley were the other occupant. For some reason, I remembered the woman I'd seen unloading groceries and babies from her station wagon, and thinking how I'd like to trade lives with her, when a dog emerged from a driveway and began barking at us half-heartedly. Tail wagging, he began to follow us. We moved to the shoulder when we heard a car behind us, and the driver turned to stare as though walking were an archaic activity.

"If we were jogging," I said, "we'd look normal. Or bicycling—"

Too late I remembered that jogging and bicycling were activities no longer available to him.

"If every remark is going to lead to a dead end," he said, "we're never going to be able to carry on a conversation."

"*You're* the touchy one. If I so much as stop to take a breath when you suggest anything, you think I'm rejecting you because of your lousy leg. Or lack of it."

"You're not too normal yourself."

I scuffed along, watching my feet in the fading light. For once there was no hum of traffic, only the clucking of chickens and the chirping of a bird I couldn't recognize.

"You can't have been this way all of your life," he went on.

Knowing I was making a mistake, I gave him the opening anyway. "What way?"

"I was hoping you'd ask. Preoccupied, withdrawn. I sometimes get the impression that when you're with me you're between crying bouts and can't wait to get back to your room to carry on where you left off."

Roughly, I pulled him to the shoulder as a car came around the bend at about sixty miles an hour. The car swerved abruptly, and I realized that the driver hadn't seen us in the dusk. It was a dangerous time of day for a walk. Then we rounded the curve and came upon a scene which stopped us.

For a moment I wasn't sure it was real. It was as though the inhabitants of another world had returned to earth for a once-a-century rite celebrating an ancient festival.

Long ago I had owned a child's storybook, which, when opened, revealed cardboard landscapes rising from the pages in three-dimensional woodland visions. The picture in front of us reminded me of that book.

It was an ice-covered pond lit by lanterns and a huge bonfire. Colorfully jacketed and sweatered children and adults darted around like water bugs, skimming across the smooth surface, bumping into one another occasionally and shrieking excitedly. Parked along one side of the pond was a line of cars, and gathered around the bonfire were clusters of people laughing and chatting.

The two of us were transfixed, outsiders with noses pressed against the window watching the party within. Shadowy figures cut off forever from the happiness before us. I was afraid that if we moved closer, the entire scene would disappear, leaving nothing but dead embers. Here on the outskirts we were invisible, unseen and unheard.

I caught sight of a small boy with a blue, pinched face, circling awkwardly, trying to imitate the more adept children. One shouted a derogatory remark at him as he sped by. It threw him off balance and he fell flat. Crying quietly, he picked himself up, and then, half walking, half skating, he approached one of the cars and opened the door. From within came a woman's voice: "Can't you do *anything* without whining?"

The words echoed familiarly. I knew them well. I had an

irrational impulse to run to the woman and tell her to take them back, to hold her son and soothe his bruise, kiss him and tell him that skating wasn't all that important. I wanted to warn her that she might have to spend the rest of her life regretting this moment.

But of course I didn't. Instead I remained where I was, a being from another world. From one of the cars, a man called out that it was time to be going home. A child protested. Near the bonfire, a group began unpacking a picnic basket.

I turned away. "I'm getting cold. Let's go back."

Gradually the laughter and voices died out behind us. I didn't realize how fast I was walking until he said breathlessly, "I can't keep up."

I slowed down and waited until he was alongside of me, panting. "What are you running away from?" he asked.

"You have the oddest way of expressing yourself. Let's cut through the woods. It's shorter."

He hesitated only a moment before following. The air was hushed now except for the dry crackling of twigs underfoot. Spongy with the tramped-down leaves of a hundred autumns, the ground was treacherous, but the stars gave us enough light to see where we were going. A squirrel skittered home from a foraging trip, scolding us for disturbing his territory. The land sloped down and we came to a rocky bed which probably housed a stream in the spring, but which was dry now. Spindly birches grew along both banks, tufts of moss clinging to them. As I crossed a path with deer droppings on it, I checked to see how he was getting along. Keeping his head down, he used the saplings occasionally for balance. And then we came to a pasture enclosed by chicken wire, and I stopped. "God, we shouldn't have come this way."

He stood for a moment, face shadowed, regarding the fence and thinking I knew not what bitter thoughts. Bleakly, he said, "I'll try it."

While I cursed myself, he lowered his body to the ground, lay down flat and pushed himself under, dragging the lifeless leg. Then, holding onto the wire, he pulled himself erect. The leg slid on a patch of ice and he fell with a grunt.

I squirmed under quickly and tried to put an arm around

him to help. Savagely, he jerked away. I could see the tears of frustration glinting on his eyelids. He hauled himself up again and went on ahead.

And then, abruptly, we were in the clearing around the cottage. It was outlined against the sky, even more sinister at this time of night, bent in on itself, a hunched evil being with a nonhuman intelligence.

"Is this what you were coming out to when I forced my company on you?" he asked.

"What?"

"It was the cottage you wanted to see, wasn't it, Norma? Daisy told us you've been poking around it."

Faintly I said, "You know Daisy. She makes a big deal out of everything."

"Crippled."

This time I was silent, but he went on without encouragement. "One on the outside, one on the inside."

"No need to expound. I get the message."

"Tell me about it, Norma."

"What makes you think it's any of your business?"

With an exclamation, he withdrew his hand from a tree trunk he'd just grabbed for support. Before I could ask him what he'd come into contact with, he went on. "Four years ago a little boy was killed, and you interviewed the one who found the body. The body was discovered not far from the Barker cottage. I don't understand the part about the state hospital. Where does that come in? But anyway, it's clear that you've decided to solve the case. So you came to Freetown and moved into Daisy's boardinghouse. Why? Do you *really* think Daisy or Johnny or me or Verity or Strandy or Mrs. Webster is a murderer?"

We stood there, facing each other, neither able to see the other's features clearly. In the distance were the lights of the big house, glinting through the bare branches to show us the way. But they weren't beckoning. They made me afraid.

"What makes you so sure the murderer lives in the Barker house, Norma?"

Reluctantly I began to walk toward the lights. He had to do a quick hop to keep up with me. "As Strandy would say," he panted, "silence is best. That's what lawyers always tell their clients. Why are you so interested in that little boy, Norma?"

I stopped so suddenly I nearly made him fall again. We were only a foot apart. "All right, Wesley. I think the murderer is one of the people in the Barker house because the little boy saw a strange sight the day before he was murdered. He was looking into one of the cottage windows and saw a person hunched over what seemed to be a body. The person caught sight of him just before he ran away. The next day he was dead. It just seems logical to me that the person was someone who knew the cottage well."

He was silent, waiting for more, but when I appeared to be finished, he asked softly, "And why are you so interested, Norma?"

I looked upward, asking for help, but the stars told me nothing. "That little boy was my son, and if I have to, I'm going to spend the rest of my life looking for his murderer."

Gradually his breathing slowed down. Around us the woods seemed to come alive with small rustlings and patterings of night creatures. Then a plane went by overhead and drowned the other sounds out. After an eternity, he said tiredly, "I'm sorry, Norma."

We resumed walking. The words "I'm going to spend the rest of my life" buzzed in my mind prophetically. If I weren't careful, the rest of my life could be over tomorrow or next week. I wanted to tell Wesley about what I considered to be attacks on my life, but I didn't. I had already told him too much. If he were the murderer—but the thought stopped there. I wasn't going to be able to survive another blow. If he were the murderer, it wouldn't matter what happened.

Head lowered, I trudged silently. I was praying to Teddy, asking him again if he would mind if I gave it up, if I went back to living. And like a moth, I continued toward the unbeckoning lights.

Fifteen

In the before-deadline mayhem, I felt, not like an island of peace, but like the contagion ward in a hospital. Rewrite men were taking down their stories on the telephone, reporters were dropping their yellow sheets of typed paper on the copy desk, the men around the rim were reading and penciling rapidly, someone yelled, "Where the hell is the jump on 'spray'?" Chris stood behind the political reporter, almost tearing the sheets from the machine.

Only I was working on a feature which had nothing to do with the day's deadline. It wasn't just the excitement around me which made me feel isolated. Hostility emanated from Chris in almost physical waves. He hadn't joked, made a pass or addressed a nonbusiness remark to me in two days.

I finished the pollution feature, checked my watch and saw it was too early for the next assignment. I wanted to talk to Chris, but I had to wait for the lull.

Following my usual trail when I had nothing better to do, I stalked the stories like someone tracing a stream from its source in the mountains to its final destination at sea. I meandered past the girls typing the yellow tapes, past the galley machines, past the composing room where Chris was working on the front page. I didn't go any further. Not to be too obvious about waiting for him, I pretended to be watching the man I knew only as Danny making the wax cake for gluing the galleys.

"Miss Boyd!"

It was George Van Fleet, calling from the news room. I took

a deep breath and went back. For a moment he ignored me, letting me stand there and stabbing at the copy with his pencil as though he hated it. Finally he said, "You spelled this name two different ways. Which is the correct one?"

Looking at the bald spot on top of his head, I wondered how much time he'd spent trying to find me in error. I got my notes, found the correct spelling and told him. He flipped the sheet at me and I bent to do it myself, face flushing and hands trembling faintly.

When I straightened up, I saw that Chris was back at his desk. I didn't give myself a chance to change my mind. Going up to him, I asked, "Chris, what's the matter?"

It was my day for being ignored. A long moment passed while Chris pretended I didn't exist. Demoralized, I wanted to tell him what he could do with his job, but instead I turned away. He didn't let me get very far. "What makes you think anything is the matter?"

"Oh, gee. Why do you want to play games?"

For the first time since I had known him, Chris looked at me with dislike. He stared, wringing the maximum mileage out of my discomfort.

"I don't usually go around asking people for explanations when they're unfriendly," I continued, "but a lot of odd things have been happening lately, and I'd like to know what you think I've done."

Something flickered in his eyes. "Odd things happening lately?"

No one was looking at us directly, but the room had quieted down, and anyone could hear the conversation without trying. "Could I see you for a few minutes after work?"

Indecision teetered on his face. I wasn't sure on which side of the fence he would fall until he leaned back, laced his hands behind his neck and said, "Okay. Meet me at Max's at five."

I nodded, relieved.

The afternoon dragged interminably. Every time the moderator at the League of Women Voters annual luncheon asked for more questions, I felt murderous toward the inevitable woman who couldn't resist the sound of her own voice.

Finally I leaned forward and whispered to the publicity

chairman. "I can't stay any longer. I'll call you when I get back to the office and see if—"

"Oh, please don't go yet. I'm sure that they're going to take a vote soon."

"I'd like to, but I have another assignment. If you could take notes, I'll call you later and get the whole thing in tomorrow's edition."

I slipped out, went to see a local politician, and then returned to the office. When I finished that story, I telephoned the league publicity chairman, got the additional information, and wrote it up. I made Max's by five-fifteen.

Since it was not Friday, the only one from the office at the bar was Chris. He was sitting alone, nursing a martini. I slipped onto the stool beside him and ordered a daiquiri. In answer to his raised eyebrow, I said dreamily, "I always order daiquiris this time of the year. Or anything with rum in it. It reminds me of a trip we took to Hawaii once just about now—" I stopped abruptly and fished in my shoulder bag for a cigarette.

"Who is 'we'?"

"My mother, father and I," I lied.

"You have a mother and a father? No kidding. I thought you materialized out of the air that first day you showed up at the office."

"Okay, Chris. Tell me why you're mad at me."

The bartender placed a plate of nuts in front of us and we both began munching. When he was gone, Chris said, "Why did you telephone my wife and tell her I was annoying you with propositions all the time?"

I choked on a nut and took a sip of the drink. "Would you repeat that? No, never mind. Tell me about it."

Keeping his eyes on my face, he said, enunciating carefully as though I were deaf or a foreigner, "Grace told me that Norma called and said I was making a pest of myself chasing after her."

It was so stupid I felt relieved. Almost let down. "Is that all?"

"Is that *all*? Grace is very insecure and that telephone call upset her."

"Chris, how can you possibly believe that I'd do a thing like that?"

130

Near us a woman was fascinated by the conversation. When I glanced at her, she turned away guiltily.

"The person who called said she was Norma." He was beginning to look doubtful. "And in a way it's true. I mean, I *do* ask you to have a drink with me—"

"Anyone could say she was Norma. How often have I spoken to Grace on the telephone? Never. How often have I spoken to her in my entire life? Maybe two or three times. Once at the pool party and a couple of times when she's picked you up at the office."

Hostility had definitely seeped out of him. "Why would someone do a thing like that?"

I shook my head. "What a spider web."

"What's a spider web? And that reminds me, what did you mean when you said odd things have been happening lately?"

Wishing I could control my impulses, I tried to distract him from that question. "Do you realize that if I hadn't swallowed my pride and asked you what was wrong, you'd have gone on thinking that I could do a thing like that? Don't you know me at all? That isn't my kind of thing."

"Whose thing is it?"

Two couples entered and noisily ordered a round of drinks, so that Chris had difficulty hearing my, "Would Grace recognize Daisy's voice on the telephone?"

He craned his neck so that he could look at my bent face. "Did you say what I think you said?"

I nodded.

"Why in hell would Daisy do a thing like that?"

I was conscious of the woman again, not looking at us but sitting stiffly in a listening position. Watching her in the mirror behind the bar, I saw her casually flicking ashes on the floor.

"My husband and I used to listen to conversation in restaurants all the time," I said without thinking. "It was fascinating. People would think we were a bored long-married couple the way we'd sit at the table without talking. Once we heard this older man telling this young girl that he didn't mind how she felt about him as long—" I had disappeared into another time and when I looked up at Chris' face, I was surprised at the expression on it. It was shocked.

"Your *husband?* You're *married?*"

Awareness surged back like blood to a numbed limb, stinging me. I picked up the small cocktail napkin and brought it to my mouth, not because I needed it but because I wanted to hide behind it. "I *was* married. I'm divorced."

"Well, well. Little Norma. Every minute you're rounding out to more and more of a human being."

"Will you ask Grace if it could have been Daisy on the telephone?"

"I think she would have recognized Daisy's voice."

"Not if Daisy were disguising it."

"Anyway, what the hell are we talking about? Why would Daisy do a thing like that?"

"To get you to fire me."

"Why would she want me to fire you?"

I kept running full steam ahead into brick walls. Within the last few minutes I'd mentioned both the trip to Hawaii and Lawford as though I were doing everything I could to be found out and prevented from executing whatever plan was simmering beneath the surface of my mind. "I—well, I'm not sure."

He wanted to order another round, but I refused. "What other things have been happening lately?" he asked.

"I hate to tell you. You'll think I'm paranoid." Reflectively, I added, "I bet more people have been done away with because they were afraid to reveal their suspicions and be labeled paranoid."

"Yeah. Go on. What else?"

"Well, remember when I was on the weekend shift and sprained my ankle?"

"Are you telling me someone pushed you?"

"Wait, will you. Just as I was leaving, the telephone on the reception desk rang and that's when I fell. You see, someone put grease on the top of the stairs and then telephoned to make me run—"

It sounded incredible even to me. He stared at me a moment and then looked toward heaven as though asking for help. "Okay. What else?"

"If you think that one is bad, wait'll you hear the next."

"I have a strong constitution."

"One night after eating at the house, I had the worst stomach ache of my life."

"Which means, of course, that someone tried to poison you."

"The only thing I had which the others didn't was instant coffee. The next day, the jar disappeared."

"What do you mean, disappeared?"

"It was gone. Vanished."

"Maybe someone borrowed it."

"Why didn't they tell me?"

"They forgot to."

The outer door opened and a middle-aged man entered. After glancing around speculatively, he chose the stool beside the woman who had been listening to us. It was obvious he didn't know her yet, but I had a feeling that he would shortly. Her attention slid away from us and I felt freer.

"Chris, do you remember the time we all went swimming together?" I continued. "Verity was dragged under water and held so long she nearly drowned."

"Verity? Are they after her too?"

"Did you notice something odd about her and me?"

"I don't know about her, but yes, I've noticed something odd about you. Of course, I'd like to do a little more research—"

"We're roughly the same height, not too different in build, and we both have long straight hair—"

"Ah ha. Don't tell me. 'They' thought it was you."

Reaching up, the bartender turned on the six o'clock news on TV. We watched for a moment. Corruption in national politics, a local strike, another money crisis, two teenagers arrested for rape. When the commercial came on, Chris turned his attention back to me. "Now there's only one thing to clear up. Why are 'they' after you?"

"Why do you keep saying 'they' when I mentioned Daisy?"

"Okay, why is Daisy after you? I admit that she's a little kooky, but not malicious—" His voice trailed off indecisively and he looked thoughtful.

"Have you ever watched Daisy's face when someone has crossed her?" I asked proddingly.

Pretending that the nuts were marbles, he set them up and

tried to hit them. After a moment, he said, "Once George Van Fleet was nasty to her. I never paid any attention to the bastard myself. He's a good copy chief, and that's all that matters. But he told Daisy that she managed to get all the office free passes. I happened to be looking at her. It's hard to explain, but she almost scared me. Then the next minute she was smiling and I thought it was my imagination."

Evidently Chris had ordered another round when I wasn't looking. The bartender placed the glasses in front of us. Softly, I said, "So you've noticed it too."

"There's only one thing you haven't explained. How did *you* annoy Daisy, Norma?"

I was silent, filling the pause with a sip from my drink. I'd gone this far, why not tell him the rest? But I remembered how irritated I had felt with myself after confiding in Wesley. At this rate, everyone in town would know what I was after, and there could only be one of two results. Either the murderer would become so careful it would be impossible to trap him. Or he would get me first.

Instead of answering, I said, "You could argue that I slipped down the stairs accidentally. You could attribute my stomach ache to a virus. You could believe that someone would grab Verity's ankle as a joke. But at last I have something concrete. You *know* someone called Grace and pretended it was me."

"Other people have had to face tragedy."

How many times would I hear those words? (And, in time, repeat them.) On this occasion they came from the mouth of my mother. Still wearing the blue suit she'd flown east in, her suitcase on the floor beside her, she was sitting on the edge of the couch, back straight, feet together. To me she had seemed the same as always, still chubby, red-cheeked and pretty. I'd been too self-absorbed to notice how drawn her face was, how her skin sagged. It was already within her, cells gone berserk.

"You look awful," she was telling me. "You remind me of those stories of derelicts found dead in their rooms. When was the last time you took a bath? Your hair's a mess. You need some fresh air." She continued scolding and I never found out if

she was already aware of death's proximity and was making a superhuman effort to save me before it overtook her.

I remained where I'd been when she arrived, lying on the couch, doing nothing, thinking nothing, like the vegetable I'd become ever since Lawford had walked out. The days were blanked out as though I'd been on a drunken spree. I couldn't remember when I'd washed or changed my clothing or had anything to eat. I didn't find out until much later that the reason she had come was that Lawford had called her.

"We have a lot to do, so we'd better get started. We have to call real estate agents and start packing—"

"Packing! I just unpacked."

"—and get some food in you and get hold of a lawyer. You're coming home with me."

I tried to sit up but dizziness overcame me and I rested my head on the back of the couch and shut my eyes. "Home with you?"

"Of course. What else? You don't think I'm leaving you like this and I can't stay away too long. The Heckelmanns are looking after the cat and the dog—"

Home. I'd left to marry a handsome, rising young executive, carry on a career, have a baby. I'd driven away the husband, no longer had a career, and killed the son. I was nothing. I was disappearing, losing my identity. "What will I do at home? Watch TV? Knit shawls for the church bazaar? Do volunteer work for the hospital?"

"Norma, I don't care what you do, but anything will be better than this." She surveyed the disorder. A dirty dish on the coffee table, gray spirals of dust in the corners, ashtrays heaped with cigarette butts. "Have you done anything aside from smoking?"

"Why should I?"

Folding her jacket neatly on a chair, she began picking up newspapers, straightening books and emptying ashtrays. I watched her through half-shut lids. "Listen, Norma, when your father died, I felt the same way. I went completely to pieces. I wanted to give up. For weeks I did nothing to help myself. I let other people take care of you and the house and the lawyers and the banks, and every time a friend came over, I sobbed on her shoulders. I was a jellyfish. But someone made me go to a psychiatrist—"

"And you lived happily ever after. At least you had me."

"You're a lot younger than I was. You have a whole life in front of you. And the psychiatrist did help. He—"

"You don't know me very well if you think I'm going to some perfect stranger and tell him that when I was two years old I lost a doll and so that's why I mind losing Teddy—"

"Keep quiet, Norma. You're getting hysterical. I'm certainly not leaving you here alone."

"How are you going to make me leave?"

It wasn't that I didn't want to go. The last thing I wanted was to remain in this house in this town. But some contrary impulse made me force her to leave me with no choice.

As always, she came through. "I'll get a court order and have you declared incompetent."

"I see. You'll hide me away somewhere in an institution where I can't bother anyone." It sounded attractive. No work to do, no decisions to make, nothing to cope with.

"If I have to. Now start packing."

I walked out on her. Taking off, I left her to struggle with the books and the silver and the dishes, to contact a moving company, to search the yellow pages for real estate agents, to telephone her lawyer, while I roamed through the woods.

The sky was a strong clear blue, more like spring than fall, and high above I watched a buzzard hawk, wheeling closer and closer to the earth. I knew nothing about hawks, but all I could think of was vultures searching for carrion, and if Teddy hadn't been found, perhaps he would have been seen by just such a bird—

That was when I came upon the cottage in the woods for the first time. Suddenly it materialized. Teddy's supposedly imaginary witch's house. Even in the brilliant sunshine, it was strangely unpleasant. A house associated with death.

So he'd been telling the truth. And if he'd told the truth about the house, it was possible he'd told the truth about seeing someone dragging a heavy object across the floor. And about the person's anger at him for spying.

136

The Invisible Boarder

Standing there in the dappled sunshine filtering through the leaves of the trees, I made no move to approach. I couldn't make myself search it then. I listened to a crow cawing, a robin chirping, flies buzzing, and I made a resolution. I wasn't ready for it yet, but some day I would come back. I would return to the cottage and find the reason for Teddy's murder. And the murderer.

Hours later my mother found me fast asleep on the grass.

Sixteen

I was nine years old again, lying in bed back home. Hearing a cat meowing, I jumped up and found a kitten the size of my hand in a gift box. Wild with delight, I started to pet it, but it scrambled out of my hand and disappeared. Then I was running home from school, panting and afraid. I flew through the house, calling for my mother, but she was gone. Again the scene changed. Now I was in a poorly lit corridor trying to see numbers on doors. I search frantically, late for a test for which I had never studied.

"I know I'm going to fail."

The words, evidently said aloud, woke me up. I lay still, every nerve tingling, my heart pumping with fear. Bits of the dream came back gradually, but they weren't what was making me afraid. It was something else, the same nightmare which had descended upon me for years.

The familiar misery washed over me, the pain tonight greater than usual. Tears poured down my face and my chest felt as though it were going to burst. Turning on the bedside lamp, I glanced at my watch, hoping it would be close to morning. Two A.M.

I couldn't stay in bed. Shivering, I put on my robe and slippers. I considered going downstairs to watch the late late show, but the icy cold and the thought of the huge shadowy rooms stopped me. Besides, it wasn't what I wanted. Like a wounded animal needing the comfort and the warmth of another of its kind, I pattered down the hall. To delude myself that any human being would do, I stopped at Verity's door and listened. I could hear her deep regular breathing. Continuing down the hall, I went to the door I had had in mind all along. For a time I heard nothing, and then, faintly, came the creaking of the bedsprings as he turned over. I tapped, hard enough for him to hear if he was awake, gentle enough not to awaken him if he was asleep. Or anyone else, I hoped.

His voice came back instantly. "Yes?"

"It's me. Norma."

There was a brief silence. Then the springs creaked again, and after that there was a thud. I heard him swear.

"May I come in?"

"Yes. Come on in."

The door was unlocked. The curtains weren't drawn and I could see the outline of his body on the bed. Still swearing, he was trying to reach the fallen crutch. The artificial leg was on a chair.

"Just stay where you are," I whispered, afraid someone would hear. "And don't put on the light. I don't want it."

I put the leg on the floor and sat down on the chair.

"You'll freeze if you sit there."

Obediently, I rose, went to the bed and, gingerly, crawled in on the side opposite him. He threw me a pillow. Although I was miserably cold, I was careful not to touch him. As he didn't ask me what I wanted, and as I was content to be there, the moments passed silently. But gradually I became conscious of something other than the warmth of human companionship. My despair was seeping out, and filling the vacuum was another emotion, just as painful in its own way.

Suddenly I heard a strangled noise from the other end of the bed.

"What's the matter?" I gasped.

He was laughing.

"Stop that. Someone will hear you."

"What if they do? When I was a little kid I used to crawl into my brother's bed whenever I was afraid. And now I'm thirty-two, and you're—what are you, Norma? Twenty-seven? Twenty-eight? And you're not my brother, for sure. But you know something? It's just as innocent as it was with my brother. Even Mrs. Webster couldn't object."

"Mrs. Webster would say isn't it nice that you're a Presbyterian and I'm a Methodist and you let me share your bed."

He began to choke again, filling the room with an eerie gurgling sound, but finally he quieted down. The seconds ticked by, and I no longer felt comfortable. When the silence had built up to such a degree it threatened to explode like steam, I said, "You don't think—I mean, you aren't assuming that I'm making a pass at you, are you?"

"Hell, no. That would be too normal, Norma, baby. The obvious thing wouldn't occur to you at all."

He didn't know how wrong he was. "I felt so—lousy, I just had to talk to someone. I went to Verity's room, but she was asleep—"

"And so was Mrs. Webster and Daisy, so you picked me. Okay, talk."

I sat up and pulled my legs close to my body to make sure I didn't touch him. "I can't."

"You felt so lousy that you had to talk to someone, but now that you're here, you can't. It figures. I mean it figures to *me*. Someone who didn't know you might feel confused."

"I—it isn't as illogical as it sounds. I mean, I just had to be near another human being."

"So you chose someone who presented no threat."

"Oh, God."

"The thought didn't occur to you?"

"Actually, no. What choices do I have? Johnny has a wife. And Strandy—"

"—is a black."

"And Strandy has a girl friend, I was going to say. And Mrs. Webster turns me off. And when it comes right down to it, *you* give me one big fat pain in the ass. What the hell has the loss of a leg to do with—" I broke off. All the thoughts I was trying to suppress kept popping out.

"Okay. Prove it."

Sharp and desolate in the night air came the scream of an animal in pain and terror. It was hideous—protracted and agonized. For a moment we were both rigid, and then the shriek was cut off sharply. The silence was even uglier. "And we didn't even try to help it," I said.

"Help it?" he asked slowly. "Help a wild animal in the woods? We couldn't have gotten there in time." He was about to expound, but then, determined not to be sidetracked, he repeated, "Prove it, Norma, baby."

"Prove what?"

"You know damned well what. Prove that you're not disgusted by a man with a stump."

I tried to shrink into nothing. My knees were against my chest, my forehead against my knees. Softly, I said, "Why do people have to be so ugly to each other? Why must we try so hard to hurt each other?"

"You're evading the issue."

I thought of the desolate room awaiting me, of the ghost who haunted it, of the long hours before morning. To hell with it, I thought. Why not? If he had been tender, if he had shown any feeling at all, it would have been easy. Because it was what I wanted more than anything else, it was what had been at the back of my mind all along.

But then, without a conflicting conscious thought, I threw off the covers, tumbled out of the bed and turned on the light all in one movement. He blinked, pupils contracting.

"I'm not evading any issues, you stinking, sniveling blackmailer. I can't stand your self-pity. And I don't have to hop into bed with you to prove that I have no prejudice against stumps. Any more than I have to hop into bed with Strandy to prove that I have no prejudice against blacks. Or hop into bed with Johnny to prove that I have no prejudice against married men. I'm so sick and tired—"

He caught hold of my hand in a grip so painful I gasped. I struggled to free myself, but he held on effortlessly, as though I were a child. In the sudden silence, I realized how much noise we had been making and I wondered if anyone was listening.

Gently he said, "Get out, Norma, baby. Get lost. I didn't go crawling to you. You came to me. I didn't need you. You needed me. I can handle my nightmares. You can't." With a flick of his wrist, he sent me spinning. I caught hold of the bed post to keep from falling and whirled around. And then I saw what was on the bedside table. A jar of vaseline.

141

For a moment I forgot everything else—my fear, his words, my pride. Staring, I said, "What's that for?"

He turned, confused. Evidently, he saw nothing unusual. "What's what for?"

"The vaseline."

He looked back and forth between the jar and me. Then he leaned back and put his hands under his head, watching me from half-shut eyes. "That contraption over there"—he pointed with his chin at the artificial limb—"occasionally chafes. *Now* what's going on in that head of yours, Norma, baby?"

I turned blindly and went out into the hall, leaving his door open.

"What's going on?" Daisy called out. "Who's there?"

"It's me, Norma. I went to the bathroom."

Back in my room, I rolled into a tight ball to keep from freezing. At first all I could think about was how I had fouled it up. If there'd been any chance for something to develop between Wesley and me, I had ruined it tonight. And then other thoughts began crowding that one out. Visions were forming and disintegrating in my head: a deserted building, a spot of grease at the top of a flight of stairs, a body bouncing from step to step before reaching the bottom. A girl's ankle caught in a murderous grip and the girl going down, down to the bottom of a crowded pool. A shadow, a featureless form sneaking into a bedroom and dropping something into a jar of coffee.

The fourth vision was still amorphous, still in the realm of the yet-to-happen.

Seventeen

On Sunday morning I ensconced myself in a chair in the study from which I could watch the traffic on the stairs. A book open on my lap, I saw Mrs. Webster leave first. She was dressed for church and lunch with her daughter. Nearly an hour afterward, Daisy and Johnny departed for brunch at a neighbor's house. After that, time dragged. It was after twelve before Strandy's girl appeared, waited languidly in the car, and then the two of them drove off.

I was still at it when Verity appeared in the doorway, looking pretty in a beige pants suit, her coat over her arm. "Norma? I've been looking for you. A friend of mine and I are going to a matinée and then out to dinner. Would you like to join us?"

I wavered, contrasting the dreariness of what I had in mind with the cheerfulness of what Verity offered. But as usual, duty won. "Verity, I'd love to, but I'm expecting a call."

Not asking any questions, she said briskly, "If you change your mind, or if the call comes early, join us. We'll be at the Playhouse, and afterwards, the Shanghai Garden."

"Thank you, Verity. Maybe I will be able to join you later on."

Only Wesley was left in the house.

Finally I decided to take a chance that he would continue doing whatever he was doing up in his room. Sometimes, I knew, he would spend an entire day reading the Sunday newspapers. I got my jacket and gloves and went out. In case he

143

happened to glance out of his window, I followed the driveway instead of the path. When I was no longer visible from any of the windows, I changed direction.

Although the sun had appeared briefly early in the morning, it was gone now. It was chilly, with a threat of snow in the air. A thin layer of ice crackled underfoot when I reached the low swampy ground. Following a stone wall, I arrived at an open field and realized that I'd lost my way. From the other side of the field came the clomp of horses' hooves, and a man on a chestnut Morgan and a little girl on a white Connemara appeared. I had stumbled onto the local horse trail.

Walking briskly, like someone out for exercise, I nodded at the man and he nodded back. The little girl turned away. By the time they were out of sight, I had reached a thicket of pine trees so evenly planted they looked artificial. The branches closed overhead, forming a dark, dank cavern. To get my bearings, I headed downhill, knowing I'd find a road.

Hanging onto tree trunks to steady myself, I couldn't fight off the sensation that someone was following me. Ever since I had left the house, I'd had the unreasonable impression that I wasn't alone, that I was being watched, that every movement was being anticipated. A faceless, formless being seemed to know where I was going, what I was thinking. But whenever I stopped abruptly, I could see nothing, hear nothing.

A dog began to bark when I came to a white clapboard house with the beige ribbon of road just beyond it. A collie, he stood on the front porch to make sure I didn't get any closer. I continued downward, realizing that I had by-passed the cottage completely.

A car was approaching, and I edged back to the shoulder to get out of the way. But the car slowed down and I saw Wesley behind the wheel.

Remembering the elaborate precautions I had taken to evade his attention, I felt like a fool. We had scarcely exchanged a word since the night I had gone to his room, but nevertheless, he asked, "Do you want a lift?"

I approached the car but didn't meet his eyes. "No thank you, Wesley. I'm out for the fresh air." I saw that he was wearing a heavy pullover and that there was a paddle racquet on the seat beside him. Startled, I asked, "You're going to play paddle tennis?"

He was grinning. "All the helpful little lectures I've been listening to recently are beginning to take hold."

Leaning my elbows on the door, I grinned back. "I'm meeting Verity and a friend at the Shanghai Garden later. If you're planning on getting back early, perhaps we can both go."

"I'm planning on it now."

I took my arms off the door and watched him drive off. Exhilarated, my heart churning pleasantly, I turned back to the woods. I wanted to get it over with as quickly as possible, and this time I tried to stay alert. Catching sight of the roof of the big house, I used it as a guidepost.

And finally I reached the familiar clearing.

No matter what part of the year or what part of the day I came upon it, the cottage always looked oppressive. On its bare strip of ground, it was secretive, each window an empty eye socket.

Quickly, before I could change my mind, I went to the front door. It was locked.

I felt shocked, as though I had found footprints on the beach of a deserted island. The sensation of being watched and anticipated increased.

I tugged at each of the ground-floor windows and found them all sealed. There were no lattices or vines leading to the upper windows.

I looked behind me at the tangled woods, a close-ranked phalanx hemming me in to prevent escape, hiding the enemy who constantly eluded me. Somewhere, watching me, was that faceless entity, unseen but omnipresent, a being who laughed at my poor groping attempts to discover his identity, who made casual, almost contemptuous stabs at my life. But if he had gone to so much trouble to keep me out, there was something to hide. I found a sizable rock and smashed one of the windows.

The sound of shattering glass was like an explosion in the quiet of the woods. I expected repercussions, and waited fearfully, but all that happened was the rustle of wings as a jay left its perch. The hush of winter descended again.

Using my gloved hands to remove the glass, I unlocked the

window and raised it. It was easy to climb in, and as for the damage, perhaps Daisy would attribute it to children.

The smell of decay was stronger than ever. It was overwhelming—the mustiness of putrescent waste, necrotic tissue of small animals, the moldering artifacts of ancient life.

As I advanced into the room, glass crunched underfoot. I examined the bottom of my shoe, wondering if Daisy would detect the splinters.

Beginning at the top, I did a more systematic search than I had the first time. The bat was evidently asleep, and I took about fifteen minutes, moving the mattress, getting on my hands and knees and peering into corners, opening the trap door to the attic. Nothing.

Back downstairs, I examined the kitchen again: porcelain-topped table, the rotting cabinets, the greasy stove. The bathroom, depressingly ugly, was too small to conceal anything. The living room had one closet, and all it contained were rusted hangers. And then, in the harsh, early afternoon light I saw something which had escaped me the last time. A hairline-thin square crack under the kitchen table.

My breath coming more quickly, I bent down to examine the linoleum. It was a trap door to the cellar. I ran my finger around the crack, searching for a ring or a knob, but there wasn't any. Getting up, I looked for a tool. Among the broken remnants of kitchen equipment, I found a rusted blade. I pushed the table to one side and began prying at the crack. The blade broke.

Swearing, I glanced at my watch and saw that it was still a little before two. I tried a piece of broken glass, and this time I felt some movement, but before I could lift the trap door, the glass broke also.

In spite of the cold, I was sweating with frustration. If I had to go back to the house to get a good tool, I would never be able to make myself return to the cottage. At that moment I heard my keys rattling in my pocket. Muttering at my stupidity, I took out the ring and inserted one under the crack. Then I heaved. In a moment, three sides of the square began to lift.

The trap door was heavy. I nearly dropped it, but grabbing it in time, I got my weight under it and lifted, breaking off a fingernail. I remember worrying fleetingly about the fingernail as I got the door upright and allowed it to smash backward on the floor.

Below me was a flight of stairs leading to an old-fashioned root cellar.

"Just like Aladdin's cave," I said aloud and was startled by the sound of my own voice. It took a great deal of effort, but reminding myself it was daylight, I forced myself to descend.

Aladdin's cave had glowed with shimmering light from jeweled fruit. This filthy cavern was shrouded with spiderwebs, the walls encrusted with slime. Something small and black scurried away from the stairs. I couldn't find an electric switch, and the daylight filtering down from above scarcely helped. Waiting for my eyes to adjust to the gloom, I began to discern a small room, the periphery lined with cardboard boxes and worm-eaten suitcases.

Again I had to steel myself, but I began to search the boxes. The first one contained clothing so old I could tell nothing about the original style, fabric or color. Thrown in with the fabrics were mold-coated shoes, crushed hats, unmatched gloves, even stockings. I dumped the contents on the floor and left them there. The first suitcase was crammed with tattered books, letters, ancient school notebooks. I had neither the time, the inclination nor the light to read the letters, so I left them for later and went on. More of the same. One trunk was filled with broken toys, games, cracked dishes, rusted brass and silver knickknacks, old paintings, the makings of a rummage sale.

And then I came to the rakes, shovels and shears.

For a moment I considered. Then, bending, I ran my finger along the uneven edge of one of the shovels. Dry crumbling earth still clung to it. Naturally. Shovels were used for digging in gardens. Or for burying bodies.

Feeling like an ass, I began to circle the dirt floor, peering closely at the consistency of the earth. And almost immediately I saw it. The outer rim of the cellar floor was hard-packed, but the center was softer.

Picking up the nearest shovel, and muttering derisively to myself, I began to dig. Fortunately, the part of the floor that was softest was also the best-lit, since it was closest to the trap door. I dug half-heartedly, not really believing in what I was doing.

Neatly, I piled the dirt to one side so I could throw it back in. My arms began to ache from the unaccustomed exercise, and I stopped to rest, glancing upward. The light didn't seem so bright. Nearly three o'clock.

I went back to digging. I was sure I would discover nothing, but at least I would have the satisfaction of knowing that I had done all I could. And then the shovel struck something.

I nearly dropped it. For a moment I stared in horror at the hole.

I could see nothing. Whatever the shovel had contacted was still covered with dirt.

Breathing erratically, I began to imagine that the air was growing more corrupt with the effluvia flowing from the floor. Each breath I took was spreading contamination throughout my body.

Finally I moved. Carefully, like an archaeologist afraid he might destroy a valuable find, I worked around the object. My eyes needed constant rubbing to keep them from glazing, and each shovelful of dirt required a tremendous effort.

Reluctance and determination were still warring when I saw it. The clawlike remains of a human hand, bleached and fleshless.

I made a strangled sound. Rooted, like someone in a nightmare, I couldn't run. I had a sensation that the bone would become animated and the connected parts would appear, forearm, shoulder, neck, and finally the skull with its sightless eyes and soundless aperture of a mouth.

After a moment I backed away. For some reason I tiptoed, as though I could awaken whatever was down there. Something touched my neck, and before I realized that it was a spiderweb, I flung the shovel at it. And then, from above I heard a sound, a whisper, a footfall, something.

I looked up. I was just in time to see the trap door crash down.

Eighteen

I remained where I was, eyes uplifted, arms outstretched, as though I expected the trap door to reverse itself and swing back again. Now there wasn't the faintest sound from above. And not the faintest glimmer of light below. Not a crack anywhere.

An eternity passed while I refused to believe what had happened. It was a dream, a story I was reading, it wasn't real. It was the absolute blackness, my worst nightmare come true, that did it.

Inflamed, horrified, I lost all control. I flailed out wildly, smacked the staircase with my wrist, and then scrambled up the steps, falling and slipping before I found the trap door and hurled myself against it. It was solid, unyielding. Bloodcurdling screams blended with the smashing of my fists. My hands became raw and bloodied with the senseless beating, and my throat burned with the senseless shrieking. No tiger run amok, no alcoholic suffering from delirium tremens, no rabid dog gone berserk, no maniac on a rampage could have behaved more irrationally. Without any thought except to stop whoever had done this from leaving me here alone, I erupted like a volcano, spewing rage and bubbling entreaties.

I don't know how long I kept it up. It seemed to me that I was out of my head for hours, screaming epithets, begging, praying. Time wasn't measurable below ground the way it was above. Time didn't exist in hell.

And then, gradually, the ache in my throat and the pain in my hands began to impinge on the panic, and sheer exhaustion diminished the paroxysms. I slid backward to the foot of the stairs and lay there, hiccuping and quivering, my nails digging into the dirt. I didn't want to think, preferring madness to a rational appraisal of what I faced.

But slowly, inexorably, as the turmoil died down, the more quiet terror began to creep up around me like vaporous fumes. I lay on the ground, curled up like a fetus, dread seeping into the marrow of my bones, my nerve endings, my brain cells. The immediate horror of the blackness was being superseded by a growing awareness that I was in an abyss with no exit.

Tentatively, I opened my eyes. There was nothingness, not the slightest gossamer of luminousness. This was what it was like to be blind. I rubbed my eyes, trying to force them to see, but the ebony dark refused to be rubbed away.

Thoughts shaped themselves, melted and re-formed. They ebbed and flowed. First came all the stories I had read of people bricked up in walls, buried alive, chained in dungeons. What was worse, the thirst or the hunger? How long did it take to die of thirst? Of hunger? Would I go out of my mind or would I remain rational, conscious of each moment of agony? Then I remembered the sensation I had had in the woods of being watched every step of the way. It hadn't been an illusion. Whether it was due to some perception beyond my ordinary senses, or whether I had glimpsed or heard evidence of another human being without taking full cognizance of it, I had known all along that I wasn't alone. But, like a hunter tracking a lion, I hadn't been aware of the moment when the lion had moved stealthily behind me, reversing our positions, changing from the stalked into the stalker. After that came the realization that this was the worst thing that had ever happened to me. When Teddy had been murdered, I had had the option of killing myself. But how did one kill oneself locked in the dark with no weapon but a shovel?

The seconds ticked by into eternity. For some reason I was desperate to know how much time had passed, as though the information were vital. But there was no phosphorescent dial on my watch.

At that point I remembered something which, incredibly, I had forgotten during my panic. The thing with which I was sharing the cellar. Very near, within reaching distance, its or mine, were the remains of what had been a human being. In the blackness, I could picture the bleached claw, the decayed, rotting, putrefying flesh.

I pressed down the bubbling hysteria and crouched closer to the stairs. A hope, a delusion, made me keep my eyes shut so that I could cling to the belief that when I opened them I would be able to pierce the dark. See if the thing was still in its grave. Make sure it hadn't moved, crawled closer.

Abruptly, I thought of Verity. She was sitting in a movie house, perhaps laughing at a horror film. Or it was later than I thought and she was in a candlelit, cozy restaurant, ordering exotic delicacies. And if I hadn't been obsessed, I could have been with her.

Then I thought of the others. When would they return home? Mrs. Webster might decide to spend the night at her daughter's house. Strandy could show up any time or not at all. But Daisy, Johnny and Wesley would all be back early. Would Wesley be alarmed by my absence, or in his prickly way, would he think I had stood him up?

Now I regretted my lack of warmth toward them. There wasn't one of them I'd been really intimate with, no one I had to account to, no one to worry about me. They could easily assume I was spending the night with an acquaintance at the office.

Besides, it was one of them who had dropped the trap door over my head.

How well would the murderer sleep tonight, knowing where I was, what I was going through?

I retreated from that thought. Tomorrow morning when I didn't show up at the office, Chris would check the house. When time passed, would they assume that I was strange enough to take off without any of my belongings, without informing anyone? Or would they call the police? In any case, the smallest number of hours I had to spend here would be twelve. The most would be the rest of my life.

Again I retreated. But only to come up against another thought. Even if the police were alerted, who would think of the cottage in the woods? Few people walked here this time of the year, and of those few, none would be likely to hear a scream from a closed cellar. Even if I had the strength to keep screaming.

The iciness seemed to be draining the blood from my veins, making me numb. I wanted to go to sleep, save my strength for when they might begin searching. But I knew I would have to be nine-tenths dead before I would allow myself to fall asleep. Because waking up here, having no idea of the passage of time, confused and in darkness, would drive me out of my last remnant of sanity. Occasionally I lifted my wrist as though I could see my watch. Suddenly, without even knowing I was going to do it, I took a deep breath and expelled it in a thundering "Help!"

In the pulsating quiet that followed, I began to cry. Quietly, without hope, I wept into my hands. No one would hear me. No one, with the possible exception of the murderer. Perhaps whoever it was, was still up there, listening, waiting to see what I would do.

I folded my arms on the lowest step and burrowed deeper. Why was God punishing me? What had I done to deserve this?

"Aren't you going to tell me what the doctor said?"

Lawford was at the kitchen table of the tiny apartment, working on papers. As I walked in from the bus stop, he looked up.

"He asked me if I was married."

He put down his pen and leaned back. "He asked you if you were married?"

"I looked so shocked when he told me I was pregnant he assumed that I was unmarried."

"Oh. So it's definite. Well, what did we expect? Throwing up. Nausea."

"I expected it was an ulcer. Lawford, what are we going to do?"

"Nothing, I guess. Relax and enjoy it."

"Enjoy it! I want to finish college. We had it all arranged. We were both going to work and save up a lot of money and travel—and then we were going to have a baby."

I went to the refrigerator, looked at the almost empty shelves and chose half a grapefruit. Morosely, I began to eat.

The Invisible Boarder

"We'll have to reverse it. Have a baby and then save up a lot of money and travel."

"I can't have a baby right now. It isn't fair."

"Tell it to the baby."

"Lawford, maybe we can find someone who will help us. Some doctor—"

"Forget it. It's too chancy."

"There are reputable doctors who—"

"Yes, but we don't know who they are."

"How am I going to finish college?"

"You can go to classes for a long time—probably until your eighth month. Then afterwards we'll find a sitter and you can go back."

"Why me? Why did it have to happen to me?"

Why me? Why did it have to happen to me?

The words echoed in the dank cold and I realized that I had said them aloud. Me because I hadn't wanted Teddy. Me because I'd gone back to school and left him with indifferent sitters. Me because, as the saying went, I'd insisted it wasn't the quantity of time one spent with a child. It was the quality.

That was why God was punishing me.

In the end it was hatred, a desire for revenge that finally hauled me from bovine inactivity to a human level again. The best thing that could happen from the point of view of the murderer would be for me to sink into mindlessness. My body wouldn't be found for years, if ever. And by then no one would know enough about the circumstances to punish the perpetrator.

I uncurled my legs, and holding onto the stairs, pulled myself erect. My muscles ached, and I swayed and nearly buckled. Waiting for sensation to return, I tried to picture the room as it had been when I could see.

The stairs were the focal point, my way of orienting myself. Wishing I had string, I felt in my pockets and found the gloves. On all fours, I inched along, dropping one glove and then the other, and in spite of the cold, first one shoe and then the second, forming a tactile pathway. I had to find the shovel. It was a small room, hard to get lost in, but I wasn't taking chances. Avoiding the thing in the center, I tried to edge toward where, it seemed to me, the shovel had dropped. I was beginning to worry about how long it was taking when I touched something solid. Instinctively I recoiled, and then I realized it was only the shovel. I picked it up and felt for the shoe. The inky sightlessness was so intense it seemed to be pressing down on me as though my chest were weighted with rocks. I couldn't find the shoe and I had to fight down an impulse to start running in circles.

The thought I'd been trying to smother most kept pulsating to the surface. The blackness, the creeping cold, the thing in the grave, the possibility of dying of thirst—even those weren't the worst I had to face. Like steps leading into an inferno, each new fear arrived in an orderly progression.

And now it was air.

I didn't know how tightly sealed this crypt was. If it was light-proof, it could also be air-proof.

It was too much. I opened my mouth to howl with despair when my fingers touched the shoe. It was only my marker back to the stairs, but I pounced on it as though it were a lifeline, a sign from heaven. Still groping, I found the second shoe and then the gloves. As I retrieved each item, I put it on again so as not to lose it. Clutching the shovel, I reached the staircase.

I held on a moment. I was breathing hard, and each lungful of air seemed to be more tainted than the last. The atmosphere was growing foul. I climbed cautiously, afraid of breaking a leg, which would finish me off altogether. Then I turned around so that I could sit. I hooked my legs under the steps below me, grasped the shovel in both hands and smashed as hard as I could against the trap door. I beat rhythmically, using every ounce of strength.

The trap door remained firm. Because there was nothing else to do, I kept it up. What was the murderer doing at this moment? Breathing fresh air, satisfying his thirst and hunger, reading a book or sitting in a movie, taking a bath, chatting with friends. The possibilities were infinite, and they all struck me as precious.

Perhaps the kitchen table had been placed over the trap door. Perhaps it had even been nailed down. No, I would have heard that. I continued to pound. If nothing else, it was possible someone would hear it.

When my arms were so sore that I couldn't keep them lifted a moment longer, I started down the steps. I had to rest. Either I was too tired to keep the shovel out of my way or I was too confused to judge correctly, but the shovel tangled with my feet, I gasped, grabbed at the empty air, lost control and crashed over backward.

I cracked down hard. For a moment, fear of having broken my back, together with the pain, kept me stunned. And then I became aware of soft earth and something else. Something sharp and cold touching my neck.

As I realized where it was that I had fallen, I was swamped with the image of the bleached bones moving, brushing away the dirt, slithering out of the tomb, weaving toward me, reaching out rotted claws—

I screamed and screamed, with such tearing ferocity my head felt it was blowing apart. What I had been guarding against, frenzied panic, took over, and I ran in circles, a deranged lunatic.

The screams blotted out everything else, so that I nearly didn't hear it. Someone was lifting the trap door.

Nineteen

I gushed relief like a broken dam. Not knowing what I wanted to do most, I sobbed on Wesley's chest, gulped in lungful after lungful of sweet icy night air, looked rapturously at the star-studded sky. Since these various activities weren't compatible, I had to do each in turn. He asked no questions, but held me loosely and patted my back. Once I felt his lips brush my hair.

It wasn't until I was completely run down and the front of his jacket was soaked that he said, "Let's go back."

For a moment I didn't move. I had forgotten his leg and I leaned heavily against him. Then I shuddered and clung tighter. "But someone in that house tried to kill me."

"What do you want to do?"

"Can't we go somewhere else?"

"Where?" he asked practically. He looked down at my dirt-streaked jacket, filthy slacks. "Come on. They'll have to shoot you right through me."

He tried to take my hand, but I withdrew it with a gasp. It was bloodied and raw. As we threaded our way, I tried to see my watch. It wasn't even six o'clock and I'd thought I'd spent a lifetime in that cell. Far ahead, past the snapping, whipping branches of maples, we could see the lights of the house.

I kept breathing deeply, as though I could store up air for the future. Walking ahead to push twigs and branches out of the way, Wesley didn't notice my shivering. I no longer felt the alien presence in the woods. Whoever had left me to die was gone.

Either he or she assumed that no one was ever going to find me, or else he had fled at the sight of Wesley.

It had gotten beyond me. What had seemed like a straight-forward quest had become a maze with the murderer watching from a vantage point always a step ahead of me. I wondered what he would do when he found out that I was safe. Perhaps, once I contacted the police, he wouldn't take any more chances.

I watched Wesley weaving around the birches ahead of me. The slight limp, the set of his shoulders, the shape of his head, the unfashionable clean line at the nape of his neck—they were all becoming more familiar to me than Lawford. Or even Teddy. As my awareness of one increased, my memories of the other two kept fading.

The house loomed above us, forbidding under the cold stars. As we approached the back clearing, the cat jumped from the garbage can with a clatter of metal, and I clutched Wesley's jacket.

He turned at the tug and started to say, "What's the matter? It's only a cat—" and then his voice died. In the light spilling from the kitchen window, I could see his hooded eyes, the muscle twitching in his cheek. I wanted to turn away but I couldn't.

He reached out, caught the fingers of the hand I had tried to clutch him with, and pulled me toward him. Or perhaps he didn't have to pull because I started toward him almost the instant before I felt the pressure. I was still shivering when we came together, and I wasn't sure if it was fear, cold, or excitement. His lips felt as icy as mine at first, but they warmed up as our faces pressed closer, and his arms circled me so tightly they went past each other. Then his mouth began to move over my cheek and neck. Every part of me tingling with remembered sensations, I nearly forgot the past few hours.

And then abruptly he let go and I stood there blinking, swaying, feeling bruised and resentful, let down. I didn't move until he tugged my hand. "Come on, Norma. We've got to get this over with."

The words hardly registered. I followed him to the kitchen door, and as we entered, we heard a rumble of voices from the direction of the living room.

"I'll call the police," he said, turning on the dismal light. Every corner was lost in shadow.

"No, Wesley, wait." He looked at me inquiringly. "I mean, once they're here, they might question me for hours. I want to wash up, you know, pull myself together—"

He nodded. "Okay. I'll give you half an hour. Wait, I'll take you upstairs to make sure everything is all right."

We went up the narrow, winding back staircase, flicking on lights wherever there was a switch. All that happened was that the blackness turned gray. He checked my room and then the bathroom, grinning at his own suspicions. For a moment we stared at one another, and then he spun around and went downstairs.

Half expecting that my hair had turned gray during my incarceration, I examined myself in the mirror. My hair was its normal light-brown, but the rest of me wasn't normal. My eyes were bloodshot, my face haggard, and every inch of me was streaked with dirt.

As I undressed and put everything I had worn in a corner of the closet for the cleaners, I wished I had told Wesley not to mention what had happened. It might have been useful to watch their faces as I walked in. Now it was too late.

I was exhausted as I got ready for the bath. I wanted to go to sleep, not face the police, the hours of questioning, the long explanations. What had begun as a vague fishing expedition had led to an ugly catch, and I almost wished that I had never started any of it: come to Freetown, gone to see Bobby Oppenheim, visited the hospital, and most of all, gone to the cottage.

But then, I reminded myself, I wouldn't have found Wesley.

I washed my hands gently and then put on a pair of Daisy's rubber gloves before soaking myself in the tub. I scrubbed every part of me, even my hair, trying to wash the ugliness as well as the dirt down the drain. It was beginning to recede, a nightmare which had happened to someone else. Disjointed sounds and images flickered through my mind, the screams, the crash of the trap door, the blackness, but it was as though they were appearing on a screen.

Finally, when the water began to cool, I got out and dressed. Leaving my room was like going out of the wings to the center of the stage, in full view of a hostile audience, and without a line memorized.

I could hear the buzz of voices as I started downstairs, muffled, questioning, exclamatory. Hesitating a moment, I put an invisible curtain between them and me, blurring my vision and my hearing. Then I entered the living room.

I had a confused impression of firelight, hazy blurred colors, shadowy faces all turned toward me. Someone handed me a drink and I accepted it gratefully. Someone else lit a cigarette for me and led me to the couch. Only a short time ago I had thought I would never be warm again, never drink again, never smoke again.

"I think she's in a state of shock." It was Daisy's voice. "Poor thing. She really should be left alone after such an *appalling* experience. Do you feel up to talking, Norma? I can't believe anyone would do such an ugly thing. Murder is one thing, but burying a person *alive*—"

As she rattled on, she held out a plate of small sandwiches. I hesitated, examining her expressionless face. Almost as though she knew what was in my mind, she reached down, picked one up and began eating. Ravenously, I did the same.

"Okay, Miss Boyd, do you mind telling us why you went to that shack and started digging up the floors?"

For the first time I realized that there were two strangers present. Wesley had called the police without waiting for me. One was middle-aged, grizzled and heavy. The other was a little younger, dark-haired and thin.

They all seemed unnaturally quiet and unnaturally motionless as they waited for me to answer. A log in the fireplace broke in two and the flames sputtered.

"I'd like to know about the body," I said, my voice cracking. "Whose is it?"

"We might not know that for days. Weeks, even. We have men digging it up right now and they'll take it to the lab. Let's hear it, Miss Boyd. Start at the beginning."

Start at the beginning. What was the beginning? The day the red-faced policeman came to tell me they had found Teddy's strangled little body in the woods? Or was it the day I had been chatting with Beth Threlkeld and then painted a wall instead of taking Teddy to town? Or the day I had dismissed his story about the cottage in the woods? Or perhaps it had been the day he was born, arriving before he was wanted? Or the day he was accidentally conceived? Or maybe even the day that *I* was conceived, lacking some basic ingredient having to do with maternal instinct?

I looked at the circle of faces—Daisy, avidly interested; Johnny, his mind elsewhere; Wesley, tense and keyed up; Verity, shocked, fascinated; Strandy, alert, looking as though he were preparing the case for court; and Mrs. Webster. Ordinarily my mind slid over Mrs. Webster as though she were a familiar piece of furniture. But this time I noticed an unusual restlessness in her. She was a person trying to make up her mind about something.

Abruptly, I asked, "When did everyone get back?"

They looked puzzled, all except Daisy, who suddenly burst out laughing. "Do you know what she's doing? She's checking our alibis!"

"Miss Boyd," the heavy-set man said impatiently. "Let's hear your story first."

"Oh, wait," Daisy bubbled. "I think Norma is right. We ought to have charts and things to show where we all were when the trap door was dropped. Let's see, Johnny and I got back from our brunch around three and Johnny went upstairs to sleep and I went to the kitchen to iron—actually we don't have any alibis, do we?" She laughed.

"I had a fight with my girl and came back early and went to my room," Strandy said promptly. "No alibi."

"*I* have a perfect alibi," Verity said. "I was with a friend all afternoon. We went to a movie, had an early dinner and I came home only a short time ago."

Everyone was looking at Wesley. Biting the skin around his nails, he only became aware of the scrutiny gradually. He blinked. "What?"

"Come on, Wes," Daisy said with inappropriate gaiety. "You're stalling. Do you have an alibi or don't you?"

"What alibi?"

"For when Norma was trapped."

He looked from one to the other. "I played paddle with a friend for an hour and then drove around for a while."

"Ah ha. Suspicious. Very suspicious. Why?"

"I was thinking."

She was about to ask another question but changed her mind and looked inquiringly at Mrs. Webster. Composedly, her hands folded on her lap, Mrs. Webster said, "I was with Ruth—my daughter," she added for the benefit of the detective, "most of the afternoon." Hesitating a moment, she added, "I was wondering. It has nothing to do with what we're talking about, but if a person notices something odd—"

"What's that?" the policeman asked sharply.

"—and promised not to mention it to anyone—"

"Ma'am—"

"Of course I've read somewhere that anything unusual must be mentioned in the case of murder—and this must be attempted murder—"

"What are you talking about, ma'am?"

"I'm not sure there's a connection."

"Ma'am, if you have any information, it's your duty—"

"That's it. I don't know if I do. I'll have to think about it."

The detective, looking choleric, was about to persist, but then dismissing Mrs. Webster as unimportant, he turned to me. "Okay Miss Boyd. Let's have it."

Avoiding everyone's eyes, I stood. "I'd like to speak to you in private."

Daisy laughed.

Lumberingly, the policeman rose and said, "All right. Where can we go?"

"Oh oh. I wonder what vile secret our little Norma is going to divulge to the law. How *thrilling!* You must use the library and the rest of us will give you our solemn promise that we'll sit in a circle holding hands so that no one can eavesdrop. I *abhor* snoopers, don't you?"

I didn't want to but I turned to look at her. She was smiling with a gaiety that never reached her eyes.

The thin, younger detective remained behind, and the heavy, older one followed me to the study. I lit the lamp, and when we were both seated, he said again, "Let's have it."

"My name is actually Norma Garretson." I watched to see if it meant anything to him. It didn't.

"You mean you're using a false name?"

"No, I mean my married name is Garretson. My maiden name was Boyd and I went back to it when I got my divorce."

"Miss Boyd or Mrs. Garretson or whatever your name is, what's going on around here?"

"I'm telling you. My husband and I moved to Freetown a little less than five years ago. My son was four years old at the time." It wasn't hard to keep my voice flat and expressionless. My eyes kept glazing with exhaustion and every few minutes I pulled myself erect in the chair to keep from going to sleep. "My husband, that is, my ex-husband, was with IBM and we'd moved three times in the five years we'd been married. Anyway, I was busy getting settled in the new house and didn't have much time for my son. I didn't have much time for socializing either, which is why I didn't expect to be recognized when I came back. Although one woman did recognize me."

I noticed the expression on his face. It was a mass of conflicting emotions: irritation, confusion, suspicion. I decided to get the worst of it over with. "My son was murdered."

That nearly brought him out of his chair. Evidently Wesley had told him nothing except for the bare facts of the afternoon. He started to exclaim, and then, perhaps remembering a tenet of his training, sank back again silently.

"Perhaps you weren't in Freetown when it happened. His name was Teddy Garretson."

"I've only been here two and a half years."

"The house we bought was on Old Dam Road. If you look at a local map, you'll see it's parallel to this road, and the cottage in the woods is about halfway between the Barker house and the one we bought. Anyway, while I was busy getting unpacked, Teddy played outdoors alone a lot of the time. It seemed safe. Not like a city street. I mean, you know, no traffic, no drug addicts, no muggers. Only murderers."

"Take it easy, miss. Here, I'll get you another drink." He took my glass and disappeared. Thinking I had sounded completely dispassionate, I was surprised at his uneasiness. In a moment he was back with the refilled glass. "Listen, I know

162

you've gone through a lot, locked in that cellar all afternoon and what not. Do you want me to come back in the morning?"

This time the conglomerate of emotions on his face covered the gamut from sympathy to embarrassment. I swallowed. "No. I want to get it over with. The afternoon before—before it happened, Teddy came home with a weird story. I didn't pay any attention to it because he had a tremendous imagination. Also, since we moved so much, he didn't have friends and he was alone a lot. He tended to make up things. So I didn't believe him." I stared at the bookshelves a moment and then repeated, "I didn't believe him."

Finally the policeman said, "Go on."

"What? Oh, yes. Well, Teddy told me he'd found a little house in the woods. I'd been reading 'Hansel and Gretel' to him the week before and I assumed that was what inspired the story. He told me he peered into one of the windows—the cottage has very low windows—and saw someone dragging a large, heavy object across the floor. Evidently he made a sound, and the person looked up. Whoever it was had seemed so angry that Teddy had gotten frightened and run home."

"Was it a man or a woman?"

"Teddy never told me. He used the word 'somebody' and I never thought of asking him. Until it was too late."

In spite of my weariness, in spite of the thousands of times that I'd gone over it, it was coming back in all its horror. The warmth of the September sun on my neck, the balminess of the air, the sweet fragrance of apples, the colorful phlox and zinnias. There'd been a fly buzzing on the screen door, and far off, the plaintive coo of a mourning dove mingling with Teddy's voice. *"All you do is be busy."* I'd continued unpacking books, paying more attention to dead words than to the one human being who meant more to me than anything else in the world. If it had been raining, he might have remained indoors and watched television. If I'd been less obsessed with orderliness, I might have taken a walk with him. If Beth Threlkeld hadn't arrived, I would have finished early and gone to town with him. *"Mommy, I saw Hansel and Gretel's house." "How about that? Where?" "They was dragging something on the floor and they got awful mad when they saw me."*

"Go on, Miss Boyd." He popped gum into his mouth.

I'd nearly forgotten him. I looked at him blindly for a moment. "Sorry. Well, Teddy's story made no impression on me. The next afternoon I was busy painting a wall. I'd promised to take him to town but a neighbor dropped in to say hello. We got to talking, and the afternoon slipped by. When she left, it was too late for me to do anything but finish painting. I saw him playing at the edge of the woods and then I forgot about him."

"We won't go. I know." "Just wait a little longer." "You always say wait. We never do anything." "I know how you feel, honey, but I simply have to finish this one wall." "You don't even read." I'd stopped working for the neighbor but not for Teddy.

"You forgot about him," he prompted.

"Suddenly I noticed that it was getting dark and Teddy was still outdoors. I started searching, but I wasn't really alarmed, not at first. But it got later and later and finally I went back to get my husband." *"What were you doing all afternoon?" "Well, this neighbor dropped in. A very nice woman. A Mrs. Threlkeld." "So you forgot all about Teddy."* The alternating currents of optimism and dread. The assurances that children were frequently found days after they disappeared. The flashlights blinking in the woods. The icy chill growing with each passing hour. And finally, "Mrs. Garretson, I'm sorry I have to tell you—"

"Miss Boyd, do you want to go on?"

"That's all."

"That's all?"

Drained, depleted, I couldn't understand his surprise. "Teddy was dead."

"You haven't even started telling me what you were doing in the house in the woods."

"Oh. Well, the police never discovered who murdered Teddy. I came back to find out. The house in the woods was a logical place to start, wasn't it?"

"You came back to find out," he repeated. He nodded his head at some private thought. "Okay, let that go. What made you wait such a long time?"

"It took me that long to, well, pull myself together. I was

sick for a while. And then, my husband never forgave me. There was the long ugly business of the divorce. Anyway, when I was finally able to function, I wrote to the *Gazette*. I had worked on a newspaper after Teddy was born and they were looking for someone with experience. So I came east."

"To solve a murder the police couldn't."

I caught something in his voice and looked at him with more attention. "Well, you know, the police had other things on their mind."

"Tell me if I have it straight. You figure your son witnessed a murder—that someone was burying a body in that cottage in the woods and your son caught them at it and they had to kill him. Right?"

"Yes."

"How was your son killed?"

I took a long swallow of whiskey. "Strangled."

"Have you got any ideas about who did it?"

"No." Putting the empty glass carefully on the table beside me, I said, "But since the murderer knew about the cottage in the woods and that there was a dirt floor in the cellar, well, I'm assuming that it was someone who—uh—"

"Is living in this house?"

I didn't meet his eyes. I began pushing back the cuticle on my nails. "It seems logical."

"And the murderer knows what you're up to and dropped the trap door over your head to stop you."

"It isn't the first thing that happened to me since I'm here."

He'd been discarding the first stick of gum and was popping another into his mouth, but that stopped him. "What?"

I went through it again, the fall, the stomach pains, the incident in the pool. He listened noncommittally and then asked, "Who knew you were in the woods?"

I wasn't going to strain his credulity with any vague sensation of being followed. Instead I said, "Well, Wesley for one. But it couldn't have been he. He was the one who rescued me."

"How did he know where to look?"

"When he drove off this afternoon, he passed me on the road. Then, when he returned, and he saw I wasn't in the house and that my car was out in front, he got worried. I'd forgotten about that. They would know something was wrong when they saw my car. Anyway, he thought of the cottage because we'd gone walking once before and come upon it. And I told him, well, more or less what I told you."

"Who else could've known where you were?"

"Anyone, I suppose. I thought they'd all gone out, but maybe one was watching, or got back early or guessed—" I took a deep breath and began tracing the pattern on the rug with my toe. "Mrs. Barker once found me at the cottage. She was quite annoyed. So annoyed she locked the door after that."

He was silent for so long I had to look up. He was watching me speculatively. Dropping my eyes, I felt in my pockets for cigarettes but couldn't find any.

"How long have all the other people in the house been living here?"

"What? Oh, I see. I'm not sure." I brushed my hair back from my sweating forehead. "The Barkers have owned the house a long time, at least ten years. And Mrs. Webster is their oldest boarder. I think she's lived here at least six or seven years. But somehow I can't picture her killing little boys and dragging bodies across floors. Verity's been here about four years, maybe five. However, she's not organized enough to plan a murder. Besides, she might kill someone in anger. But a four-year-old? I can't see it. And Strandy's been here only three years. So that let's him out."

"Which leaves Mr. and Mrs. Barker."

"Oh, Johnny couldn't—he's the sweetest, kindest, gentlest—" I broke off. For a moment we were both motionless and silent. Then I got up and tucked my shirt into the slacks. "If you're finished with me, I think I'll get something to eat and go to bed. I don't know which I'm more of. Tired or hungry."

Paying no attention to what I was saying, he ran his hand over the back of his head and then examined his palm. "In other words, Miss Boyd, that leaves Mrs. Barker."

Twenty

During our stay in Hawaii, I'd been wading at Makapuu one day when a monstrous colossus of water had come hurling down upon me. I had watched its approach numbly, not expecting such fury, but the titan had swallowed me and I hadn't been able to surface. It was a half a minute before I'd come up gasping, sputtering and staggering under the impact.

Entering the office the following morning, I was reminded of Makapuu. Every face turned to watch me as I came in, and I nearly keeled over under the barrage of questions.

"You sure you aren't murdering people just for a story, Norma?" Chris asked. He was reclining on his spine as usual, with the inevitable pencil resting on his ear. "What in hell made you dig in that basement?"

"You remember the little boy who was murdered. The one the boy scout found? It was right near the Barker cottage. I thought I'd poke around and see what I could unearth."

"Unearth. Ha ha. That still doesn't explain what made you dig up the floor in the cellar."

"I heard a rumor that the kid had seen someone pulling a heavy object across the floor of the cottage the day before he was killed. So I figured he was murdered so he couldn't identify—"

"I never heard that rumor."

"Hello, everybody."

I turned around. Grace Upham had just entered the office. She was noticeably different from the women who worked at the *Gazette*. It had something to do with her clothing, which was dull, her figure, which was ample, and her hair, which was too coiffed. And perhaps with her expression, which was relaxed.

"What are *you* doing here?" Chris asked. "I thought I gave you my pound of flesh Friday."

She smiled around the news room at people she knew. "June Van Fleet called a little while ago and asked me if I were going into town and could bring some papers George took home. He won't be in today because he was hit by a car—"

"Hit by a car!" Chris glanced at me in surprise, wondering at the consternation in my voice.

"It wasn't serious. He stepped off the curb without looking and was knocked down. He's just shook up. But he took home some weekend features to look over last night and was worried about getting them back."

Vaguely I was aware of Chris saying something to Grace about, "Meet my second wife," indicating me, and Grace replying, "I'm always happy to meet Chris' second wives," but what I was thinking about was what Chris had told me when we'd been discussing the telephone call Grace had received. Something to do with George Van Fleet insulting Daisy. And now he'd been knocked down by a car.

"Oh, that's absurd," I told myself aloud.

"No, it isn't," Chris protested. "Twenty years is enough of my life to give to just one woman. I have to spread myself around more before it's too late."

Grace and I smiled at one another. Evidently the incident of the telephone call had been smoothed over. "What's on for me today?" I asked Chris.

"Elope with the boss."

"And after that?"

"If you don't know, forget it. Do a first-hand account of your discovery of the body, and after that you have a Planned Parenthood meeting to cover. Although with all these murders, we might not need it."

"A first-hand account? I don't have any facts. I don't even know whose body it is."

"Since when do you need facts? Write a two-column spread in your own words about—"

"Spondigaliscoreuareous."

"What?"

"Those are my own words."

"You know something? This used to be a quiet town before you arrived. Now we have accidents every other day and bodies in basements and people falling down stairs. What I don't understand is why that person whose body is in the Barker basement was never reported missing."

"How do we know he or she wasn't? There *could* have been an alarm out. Or maybe—" My voice trailed off.

"Maybe what? Okay, Grace. Thanks. See you later."

"Maybe it was someone no one would report missing. I mean, well, a derelict, for instance. Or a foreigner who didn't know anyone in this country. Or—" I took a deep breath and watched him for a reaction. "Or suppose, just suppose someone had a relative he wanted to get rid of. He could say the relative left town. Or maybe it was an elderly person no one knew about. Or, let's say, a defective child or an insane person—"

"You mean like the wife in *Jane Eyre*? Hey, Johnny, come here a minute."

Looking more tired than usual, with dark smudges under his eyes, Johnny joined us at the news desk.

"Norma says that the body in your basement belongs to some relative you wanted to get rid of—"

"I didn't say that Johnny wanted to get rid of a relative. Just someone."

"Anyway, do you have any aged relations you've been disposing of lately?"

"I have a youngish relation I wouldn't mind disposing of sometimes. Listen, you two. That cottage is acres from the house. Anyone could bury an army there and we wouldn't know about it."

"But who slammed the trap door on Norma?"

"Maybe a vibration made it fall."

"A vibration! I had it turned back on the floor. Besides, Wesley said the kitchen table had been placed over it."

"Well, maybe it was one of the world's increasing number of nuts who just like to kill people. Period. Like the guy with the nurses. Or the one in the tower in Texas. Or—"

I heard it all from a distance. They both seemed bright and clear, but surrealistic and far away. Flat, deformed figures on canvas, painted with precision in primary colors but in a demented manner. I was thinking it was going to be like last time. The whole investigation would fritter away into nothing.

Finally I returned to my desk and wrote up the feature, and then I went out to the Planned Parenthood meeting. I was going back to the office when I decided, on the spur of the moment, to take a detour.

The red-brick town house was bright and new-looking in the cold winter sunshine. I walked across terrazzo floors to the office which said TOWN CLERK and found a pleasant-faced woman behind a desk. She smiled and asked if she could help me.

I didn't know of any subtle way to do it, so I asked bluntly, "Could you check something for me? I'm a reporter from the *Gazette* and I'd like to know if a family named Barker, Daisy and John, ever had a child."

The woman's face remained pleasant, but a hint of reserve shaded it. "I don't understand."

"I need some information for a story I'm writing."

"I'm afraid that all information about births, deaths and marriages must be obtained by the persons involved, or by an authorized—"

"Suppose I'm related to the Barkers, may I get the information?"

"Only if you proved it. And in any case you would need their permission."

"I don't necessarily want to see the birth certificate. I only want to know if a birth occurred."

"Why not ask the Barkers?"

"Well—it's hard to explain. It's all part of this story. It's rather involved."

"There's one thing you could do. If you know approximately the time of birth, you could check the newspaper birth announcements. They're public property."

I took a deep breath. "Not only don't I know the approximate time of birth, I don't know *if* the child was born at all."

"Then I wouldn't be able to help you anyway. I'd have to know the year. In any case you'd have to get a court order or some legal agency like an adoption service or the veterans' administration to ask for it."

I tried to analyze my own persistence. After my latest brush with death, I had decided to leave it all to the police. Yet, back and forth, the opposing forces warred—the need to pay my debt of guilt to the little son I'd allowed to die, and the need to put it behind me and start fresh. "Surely just knowing if a child was born isn't violating anyone's privacy."

"It goes back to the time when anyone could get birth information on demand. People could find out if a baby was legitimate by checking the birth certificate. Although today they only list the name and the date of birth, even schools have to get the birth certificate from the individual or the parents. As I said, you'll have to get a court order or ask the family."

"How about the police?"

"Well, yes, the police could get it. All births are recorded in the state capital. Are you sure the baby was born in this state?"

That rocked me. The baby could have been born in China for all I knew. "I see. Well, thank you anyway."

I went outside and stood on the steps, considering. Then I walked to the sweet shop, bought a pack of cigarettes and asked for the change in dimes. Choosing the telephone booth at the gas station, I dialed the number the detective had given me. The sergeant who answered got him immediately.

Without giving him a chance to speak, I said, "This is Norma Boyd. Please don't think I'm trying to tell you how to run this investigation. Or that I'm crazy. But I've got these ideas or leads or whatever you want to call them. They're far-fetched, I know."

"Sure, Miss Boyd. Go ahead." He sounded curious.

"Well, when I was searching the Barker cottage, I found an old baby rattle. I know—it could have been there for twenty years, but I was wondering if there was some way you could check on whether the Barkers ever had a child."

"A child? What has that got to do with anything?"

Desperately, I said, "I told you it's far-fetched. I mean,

suppose the child were defective in some manner. Daisy has very rigid standards, and her self-image would be utterly shaken if she had a retarded child."

"So?"

I gave up the roundabout route and plunged. "If Daisy were hiding a child in the cottage for one reason or another, she could have killed it in a fit of rage, and when my son caught her at it, she killed him too."

There was a pause. Then, "That's the damnedest thing I ever heard in my whole life."

"You never heard of a mother killing her own child?"

"Yeah, I've heard of mothers killing their own children, but that's pretty complicated, you've got to admit."

"So's life," I said sententiously. "Could you find out if they ever had a child?"

"I could ask them."

"But if they were hiding it—"

"If they had a kid in this state it wouldn't be hard. But as for the rest of the country or another country, it could be a real shemozzle."

I hesitated. "Another thing."

"*More?*"

"The Barkers once made out a check to the state mental hospital—"

"How do you know?"

"I went through their checks."

This time he whistled. "You could be in real trouble one of these days."

"Could you find out what it was for? I went to the state hospital, but they wouldn't tell me a thing. All I could get was some gossip. One of the nurses told me that there was once a Margaret Barker there. But I don't know if they're related."

"Maybe you ought to join the police force when you get tired of being a reporter. Okay, I'll check it."

"Wait. Don't hang up. Have you identified the body in the basement?" The operator interrupted and I deposited another dime.

"You're in a phone booth?"

"Well, I can hardly call from the house, can I? Or even the office."

"Do you want me to call back?"

"No, I've got a supply of dimes. Do you know to whom the body belongs?"

"I was going to tell you but you didn't give me a chance. We don't know who the guy is—"

"Guy?"

"—but we have a description. The boys in the lab say he's been dead about four years—"

"That fits in! That's when Teddy saw someone dragging something across the floor."

"Yeah. And he was in his thirties—which lets out the retarded kid theory—"

"Oh. Why did you let me run on like that?"

"I was curious. And he was about five feet ten inches tall and he once broke his ankle and that's about all we know so far."

"What about his clothing?"

"He was buried naked."

"But aren't there all kinds of ways of identifying bodies from teeth and that sort of thing?"

"Only if we have records to compare them with. We're checking to see if there were any missing-person reports about four years ago."

"I see. Well, thank you."

"I'll call you as soon as we have any information, Miss Boyd."

It was cloudy and cold outside. I went through the rest of the day automatically, finishing my assignments and even working on a feature which wasn't due until the following weekend.

Afterward I hesitated, wondering whether to eat before returning home or to take a chance on Wesley being there and asking me out. We hadn't had a chance to speak to each other since the night before. Then I remembered that this was one of the numerous occasions he had to catch an early plane to Detroit and wouldn't be back until the following evening, or at the earliest, late tonight. Depressed, I ate at a diner. When I'd wasted all the time I could, I headed back.

As I opened the door, Daisy came bounding out of the study. There was no way of telling what Daisy was thinking. She might have decided to attribute my snooping to an eager-beaver desire to get a scoop, or she might have been planning my next accident. On the surface she was as pleasant-faced and as friendly as though nothing unusual had happened. Then I saw that she had a new sensation on her mind.

"Norma! Where've you been? You're late. How do you feel? You look like death. I told you not to go to work after that *awful*—"

"I'm all right. Just tired."

"I'm not surprised. I have to speak to you. The *strangest* thing has happened."

At that I became motionless. I didn't know if it was Daisy's usual exaggerated hyperbole or if there was a factual basis for her excitement.

"I promised Ruth I'd speak to each one of you as soon as you came in. She's terribly worried. It isn't like her mother—"

"Who's Ruth?"

"—to stay out late and not tell—Ruth is Mrs. Webster's daughter. Did Mrs. Webster say anything to you about staying out late this evening?"

A nerve began to throb in my throat. For a minute I didn't know why, and then I remembered. Mrs. Webster had said something to the policeman. *"If a person notices something odd and promised not to mention it to anyone—"*

What odd thing had she noticed and to whom had she made the promise?

And afterward, *"I'm not sure there's a connection. I'll have to think about it."*

Perhaps Mrs. Webster had thought too long.

I was being ridiculous. Lightly I said, "Mrs. Webster and I never discuss our social schedules."

"This is serious, Norma. I've known Mrs. Webster for *years* and she's never done anything like this before. You know how precise she is about everything. She never does *anything* on the

174

spur of the moment. She always tells me or Ruth if she's going to be out."

I waited. It was just another attention-getting ploy on Daisy's part, I told myself.

"Well, Ruth just happened to telephone this evening to speak to her mother and was surprised she wasn't here. And *I* was surprised because I thought she was *there*. Ruth's been calling every fifteen minutes since. She's absolutely *frantic*."

"She's a big girl, Daisy. She can take care of herself."

"She always comes home and fixes herself a light supper in the kitchen. If she isn't coming home, she tells me."

"I know what," I said, pressing down the fluttering of my stomach. "She decided to have a mad fling and go to the movies." I went up the stairs like a sleepwalker. If anything happened to Mrs. Webster, it would be another thing I was responsible for. I was the one who had reopened this mare's nest.

Twenty-one

Mrs. Webster's married daughter was exactly the kind of daughter Mrs. Webster would have. Pleasantly dull. She wasn't stocky like Mrs. Webster, but in a few years she would be; she wasn't wrinkled like Mrs. Webster, but in a few years she would be; she wasn't gray-haired like Mrs. Webster, but in a few years she would be. And all this in spite of the fact that she was only in her early thirties. She wasn't one to work on improving what God had given her. Two small children, whom I tried to ignore, clung to her.

In a sweet, educated voice, she said, "I can't really tell if anything is missing. And I see her suitcase is here."

She had come over so early we were all still in our robes. Daisy, Verity and I stood around watching her examine the closet and chest of drawers.

"*Something* must be missing," Daisy said. "She didn't go to work yesterday naked." She and Ruth were an interesting contrast. One had never been young, the other would never be old.

"We had an argument at lunch Sunday," Ruth continued as she stared helplessly at the neat dresses. "We almost never argue, but she was apt to, well, give us too much advice, and well, I—wasn't very nice, and she left in a huff. That's why I called last night. To apologize. Can't *you* tell me if anything is missing, Mrs. Barker? You probably know her wardrobe better than I do."

176

Daisy laughed but her eyes were chilly. "I never go into my guests' rooms. Everyone cleans his or her own, you know."

"I don't mean—you know, seeing her every day." Half shielding the contents of the drawers from profane eyes, Ruth went on speaking more to herself than to us. "Her coat and purse are missing. But I'm not sure—I don't know how many nightgowns she had. Maybe she went to visit someone without telling me because of the argument we had. Or maybe, well, she can't stand grubbiness, and the thought of being interviewed by the police could have—" Her eyes clouded, and she looked at us as though we'd been guilty of bad taste. Then her inherent good manners took over and she added, "Of course it must have been painful for all of you."

"I've had worse experiences," I said.

She glanced at me, and then quickly away, afraid of being soiled.

"Let's go, Mommy," the little boy whispered.

"Stop it, Billy. You're tearing my slacks." She looked down as though noticing for the first time how they were all dressed. I was sure that ordinarily she was a neat person, but her short hair was uncombed and her slacks and jacket paint-streaked. I wondered if she'd been painting a wall when her mother disappeared. Both children were wearing a haphazard miscellany of un-ironed shirts and pants. "I'm afraid that I came out in an awful hurry when I called this morning and found out she hadn't come back."

"I'm sure she's visiting someone," Daisy said. "A friend or a relative."

"Our nearest relative lives in Washington. The state, that is."

"You'll see. She'll show up at work this morning."

"I certainly hope so. The store doesn't open until ten. If she isn't there, I'm calling the police."

I wanted to point out something about the grubbiness of the police, but Daisy was exclaiming, "Not again! She'll be terribly embarrassed if she's visiting a friend and you made a big fuss. Heavens, we've had enough of the police around here to last us for years."

"Mommy." Again the little boy tugged at her slacks and looked up with an unspoken appeal in his eyes. The slightly older girl sat, composed, with her knees crossed, watching us with detached interest. She was six or seven.

"All right, darling, we're going."

"Listen," Daisy said. "If she isn't at the store, check her friends."

"Why is her suitcase here?"

"Maybe it was a spur of the moment thing. Besides, her handbag is so large, she could carry a *dozen* changes in it. The only reason I can't tell you what's missing is that it's hard to picture what isn't there. If I opened my *own* closet, I couldn't tell you if anything was missing, and I have *nothing* in the way of clothes. Let's go downstairs and have some coffee. I fixed some muffins as soon as you called."

Ruth allowed herself to be drawn into the hall and toward the stairs. Speaking for the first time, Verity said, "Well, I'd better get dressed for work," and disappeared.

Ever since she had arrived, I'd been waiting for an opportunity to speak to Ruth alone, but so far none had presented itself. Still hoping, I said, "I'm going straight to my ten o'clock assignment from home. I'll join you."

Looking faintly surprised, Daisy said, "Oh, good."

Downstairs, I helped Daisy with the cups, sugar and cream. Then I poured milk for the children and gave them each a muffin. The little boy cheered up. When we were finally seated with our steaming cups of coffee, I realized that I wasn't going to get rid of Daisy. Turning to Ruth, I said, "Mrs. Uh—, did your mother ever—"

"Andrist. But call me Ruth."

"Did your mother ever hint that she had information, or knew a damaging fact about anyone—"

I became aware of what I was doing when I looked up and caught sight of her face. She didn't spill her coffee, or make a sound, but she put the cup down carefully, touched a napkin to her lips, and stared at me with stricken eyes. Her face, innocent of make-up, had turned a no-color between green and gray. She was still speechless when Daisy laughed. For no particular reason I remembered that when Ruth left I would be alone in the house with my landlady.

Finally Ruth said, "Are you hinting that my mother found out something damaging and was—harmed because of this knowledge?"

"I'm sure your mother is fine," Daisy said before I could answer. "Pay no attention to our little Norma. She has a remarkably well developed paranoid complex."

"If anything happened to her," Ruth said in her little-girl voice, "it will be my fault. I should never have allowed her to leave the house angry. In fact she should have been living with me no matter what Roy said. If she'd been with us, she would never have become mixed up—" Remembering Daisy's presence, she faltered. "I don't mean I object to *you*, Mrs. Barker. It's just that it was wrong for her to be with other people when her own daughter could have taken her in. And I don't like the idea of her living with colored people. I'm not prejudiced. My cleaning woman is colored, and she's a close friend of mine. Some of my friends won't allow colored people in their houses because, after all, they might use the same cups and glasses." She looked down at her cup. "Of course Mother was always careful to use only her own utensils and a different bathroom— oh, dear, I don't know what I'm saying. It's this worry—" Distractedly she stood up. Both children were now playing a game with toothpicks on the floor while munching muffins. She pulled them to their feet and began adjusting arms into sleeves. "If anything happened to her, I'll never forgive myself."

"Is Grandma sick?" the little boy whispered.

"After all, she took care of *me* when I needed it. Why wouldn't I take care of her when *she* needed it?"

"Are you crying, Mommy?"

"No, where's your hat?"

"I don't have any."

I got up to help with the little boy. He looked at me warily but cooperated.

"Look," Daisy said. "This is a tempest in a teapot, a mountain out of a molehill, a—what's another one? If Norma hadn't found a body in the cottage, I bet you'd never have thought twice about your mother spending a night with a friend, would you?"

"Oh, I would. She never does things like that. You know."

I finished buttoning the little boy's jacket and held on a moment longer than I had to. He drew away. A child flanking her on either side, Ruth headed for the back door. And then, abruptly, she stopped. When she turned I saw her eyes widen and I knew that she had remembered something. I looked at Daisy, trying to will her out of the room, but of course she stayed.

"I don't know if it means anything—it's probably nothing. But there *was* something Mother mentioned once. I nearly forgot. Actually I hardly paid any attention to it, because, well, because sometimes I don't pay attention to what she's saying."

"What was it?"

"It was a practical joke, she said. Someone was playing a practical joke on Norma Boyd, and for some reason it bothered her."

I was painfully aware of Daisy beside me, not because of anything she did, but because she was so still. She had almost stopped breathing. "What kind of a joke?" I asked.

"I'm not sure. She saw someone coming out of your room—"

"Out of *my* room?"

"Yes, and the reason Mother was troubled was that the person had no business being there. That's the way she described it. This particular person had no business being there."

"Who was it?"

"She didn't say."

"Was it a man or a woman?"

"I don't know. If she mentioned it at the time, I don't remember. Anyway, this practical joker, whoever it was, made Mother promise not to mention the incident to you."

"Yes?"

"That's all there was."

"I see." I heard Daisy let out her breath, but I wasn't sure whether it was in relief or disappointment. *"No business being there."* Then it couldn't have been Daisy. If there was one person who could be said to have any business being in my

180

room, it was my landlady. Of course the whole thing could be completely unconnected with Teddy. And Mrs. Webster might show up in the evening not knowing what the fuss was about. On the other hand, if someone *was* in my room, that could account for the incident of the coffee jar.

So immersed was I in my calculations that I didn't hear Ruth say goodbye, or realize until afterward that the little boy had waved at me.

Twenty-two

I stood on the catwalk, holding the railing and watching the presses spinning in their inexorable orbit. The day's edition was being ground out.

A boy plucked a folded newspaper from the chute, checked the margins and called out directions. Eddie Beinecke, the head man, came up to stand beside me. "Thinking of taking over my job, Norma?"

"It's too complicated for me. I'd better stick to writing."

"And I couldn't write a story to save my life."

"It's differences like that that make the presses go round."

"You know something? You're the only reporter who ever comes up here. And not just once, but a couple of times a week."

"It's fascinating," I said almost to myself. "I never get tired of watching. It starts so slowly, but once it gets going, it's nearly impossible to stop."

"You can say that again. Once in my life—more than twenty years ago—I saw a man slip off the catwalk and go into the presses. They couldn't stop them in time. I was sick for a week."

"Eddie, come here a minute." He darted off, but I remained where I was. Crews moved around me, pulling papers off the feed-out, binding them for the trucks, adjusting levers. I watched the saw-toothed blades swallowing and digesting the raw paper. The noise was deafening as each moment the cylinders seemed to pick up more speed.

Below, I caught sight of one of the school groups being

given the tour by a man from the composing room. A troop of about twenty fifth- or sixth-graders were loosely assembled, watching the presses.

And then I noticed the two mothers accompanying them. One was a stranger. The other was Beth Threlkeld.

"Hey, Norma, watch your step," Eddie shouted.

Trying to move out of her line of vision, I nearly tripped. I clutched the railing, my heart pounding. Damn the woman, I muttered. Damn, damn, damn. She was hounding me, haunting me with her avid curiosity, her determination to prove that I was Norma Garretson.

Just then she looked up and saw me.

As she lifted her hand to wave, her face was a curious mixture of pleasure at seeing an acquaintance, and a kind of slyness, the expression of someone who has the blackmail information.

I walked down slowly. Pointing to the control panel, the *Gazette* man was trying to explain the hodgepodge of switches —black for the ink-fed roller, blue to throw rollers in or out of contact with plate cylinders, brown to throw blanket cylinders on or off, yellow to engage or disengage the infeed roller. I couldn't understand a word of the lecture.

After a while Beth joined me and shouted in my ear, "Fascinating, isn't it?"

I nodded.

"I think I'll give up dress designing and go in for newspaper work."

I smiled politely.

"Listen, I'm going to drop the children off at school after this. How about joining me for lunch?"

"I'm sorry. I have an assignment in a few minutes."

"We ought to get together soon. Since you're new in town, you probably don't know too many people, and since I'm on my own—"

"Yes, we really should. I'll call you one of these days." From the corner of my eye, I caught sight of Chris coming in from the composing room. Nodding to Beth Threlkeld, I hurried to Chris, took his arm and led him from the room, asking him a question about one of my assignments.

That evening, when I returned home, there were no cars parked out front. Other times I had welcomed the privacy, but now I was reluctant to enter the deserted house.

I stood in the cold hallway, leaving the door open behind me as though I might need a quick escape route. The house hummed with small noises: the water pump, the refrigerator, the furnace, a clock, a dripping faucet.

As though Daisy had materialized on a screen in front of me, I could almost see her face, almost hear her voice. *"Shut the door, Norma. I don't mind heating the house, but I do object to heating the entire town."*

Obediently, I closed the door and leaned against it. For a moment I tried to picture the huge entranceway the way it should have been: walls glittering with mirrors and oil paintings, a sixteenth-century rose-and-blue Kashan carpet on the floor, refectory tables and chairs, a Mycenaean krater in a Caffieri commode, and crowning it all, a crystal chandelier. Glancing up at the invisible chandelier, I became aware of the dark gallery and the row of closed doors, each one concealing its own miseries, its own secrets.

I turned on the low-voltage lights as I went past the gloomy ballroom, behind the staircase, through the butler's pantry to the kitchen. Looking behind me constantly, I consulted the slip of paper in my purse and dialed the detective's number.

"It's Norma Boyd again. Did you find out whose body it was?"

"No, Miss Boyd. The funny thing is we have no record of anyone reported missing at about that time who fits the description."

"I guess you've heard. Mrs. Webster is missing."

"Yeah. Her daughter called in. We're checking the hospitals, but you'd be surprised how many people go off for a few days or even weeks without telling their relatives. Besides, the woman who owns the store where she works said she called in this morning to say she didn't feel well."

"She did!" I tried to sort that out. "But if she was sick, she'd be with her daughter or here at the Barkers'. Where did she say she was?"

"She didn't."

"Are they sure it was Mrs. Webster who called? It might have been someone pretending to be Mrs. Webster."

"We thought of that. Her daughter said that you think something happened to Mrs. Webster."

I spun around so quickly I nearly knocked a chair over. From the corner of my eye I'd thought I'd caught a movement at the window. How many times in recent weeks had I been conscious of being observed, even followed? And how much of it was real and how much imagination?

"Miss Boyd?"

"What?"

"You okay?"

I hesitated. What was I going to do? Ask him to come over and hold my hand every time I felt nervous? "Yes."

"What makes you so sure that something happened to Mrs. Webster?"

"I'm not sure of anything." Even of the evidence of my own senses. "Mrs. Webster hinted that she knew something—you heard her—and, then, I guess her daughter told you about that other conversation."

"Yeah. Was this Mrs. Webster a good friend of yours?"

"No, of course not." Why of course not? I'd ignored her, dismissed her from my mind, and mainly because of her age. And now she could be dead because of my activities. "Did you ever find out if the Barkers had a child?"

"What's the difference? The body in the basement belonged to a man in his thirties."

Again my attention was distracted. The small murmurs and vibrations in the house appeared to have changed subtly in pitch; either a sound had been added or subtracted, I couldn't tell which. But there had been a shift. I was still trying to analyze it when I thought of another question. "Did you find out if there's a connection between the Margaret Barker in the state hospital and the Barkers here?"

"We have a man going up there tomorrow."

"Well—thank you. I hope—that is, if you hear anything about Mrs. Webster, you'll let us know, won't you?"

"Sure thing, Miss Boyd."

I remained where I was for a while, reluctant to leave the

security of the kitchen. I was waiting, but I didn't know what for. It was as though I had sent out invitations and was biding my time until the replies came in.

Finally I rose and went into the study, automatically turning on the television set. Occasionally I peered into the hidden corners behind me. The advantage of the study was that it was comparatively small and I could pick a chair that faced the hall.

The six o'clock news came on, and from the comfort of my chair I watched a war, a strike, a prison break and a hijacking. Afterward, an old Disney film came on, and I remembered the last time I had seen that same film. Then I had been accompanied by a three-and-a-half-year-old, and I could almost smell the popcorn again, almost hear the children's shrieks of laughter. He had laughed too, although he hadn't understood it, and he'd stood up on the seat to see better. Behind him, another child had shouted for him to sit down. He had obliged, and then, almost immediately, popped up again.

I didn't want to watch, to be flooded with the bittersweet memories, but I was under a spell and couldn't move. I was still waiting for something to happen. And then the film stopped for a commercial, and sandwiched between the two of them, I heard music from above.

I froze. The music was ethereal, light and airy, wafting down the staircase from the supposedly deserted rooms above. I was rooted to the chair, and only my eyes swiveled to the ceiling, trying to pierce it. The eerie tune seemed to be emerging from a source beyond reality.

The television sound came on again, blotting everything else out. Seconds ticked by as I continued sitting. The presence I'd been aware of for weeks was close by, in the house. And this time Wesley might not appear to save me. When I finally forced myself out of the chair and turned off the set, the music still drifted downward, wraithlike.

Something snapped, and coatless, oblivious to the cold, I flew out of the study, across the specter-filled ballroom to the front door. I grabbed the knob and turned frantically. It was locked.

Again I froze. I couldn't remember if I had locked the door when I'd arrived. I didn't generally, but this time nervousness

186

might have made me do it. In any case, my keys were in my purse and I had no idea where I had dropped it.

Slowly I turned my back to the door so that I could face the entire expanse of hall, doors, stairs and gallery. Cavernous, filled with recesses, it kept its secrets. It wasn't as bad as the cellar, I kept telling myself. Not nearly as bad. I could make a dash for the back door, and if it was unlocked, I could run around the house, slip into my car and drive away. Once, however, I was past the staircase, I would be beyond the point of no return, and if the kitchen door was locked, instead of merely bolted on the inside, there was no way out. Unless I broke a window. Which would take time. On the other hand, if I did get out, there was the dark expanse in back of the house where anyone might be lurking. Or the car keys might have been removed. Or someone might be huddled in back of the Volkswagen ready to reach out gnarled claws and curl them around my neck.

Which left the other choice. To make a dash for my room, hope the key was there, and lock myself in until the others returned.

There were only two telephones in the house. One was in the kitchen. The other in Daisy's bedroom.

All the time I wavered, the haunted melody continued its floating descent.

"Verity?" I quavered futilely. "Wesley?" I tried to peer out of the window beside the door to see if there was a car out front. But the gloom was too thick.

There was no answer. Only the ghostly strain.

And then it too was gone.

The silence was as terrifying as the music. Afraid to move in case I made the wrong one, I remained glued to the door.

And then I thought, whoever it was had just turned off the music. So he had to be upstairs. So I could make the dash to the kitchen.

I sprinted across the hall, past the stairs, without glancing upward, and smashed open the door of the butler's pantry. To my horror, the kitchen, which I had left with the lights on, was pitch-black. I lost my bearings, hit something with my hip and doubled up with pain.

In the subsequent silence, I heard the sound of breathing.

I spun around. Whoever had turned off the music was behind the door to the back staircase. In a moment the door would open, and I would see a sight so monstrous, so ghastly, so frightening, I would be mindless forever.

I opened my mouth to scream, and through the darkness, from behind the door to the back staircase, someone laughed.

Twenty-three

I was sitting on a chair, my whole body shaking, and Daisy was saying, "What in the world is the matter with you?"

Her calm, pleasant voice, punctuated by the mocking laugh, brought a bitter bile up to my throat. Blinking in the light, I tried to read her rocklike features, but she was indecipherable as always. I waited until I had control of my voice, and asked, "What were you trying to do, Daisy?"

Her back to me, she had begun taking lettuce, cucumbers and peppers out of the refrigerator. "I hope I bought enough greens. What was I trying to do? What do you mean?"

"Why didn't you let me know when you came home?" Although of all the people who lived in the Barker house, I most feared Daisy, now that I knew it had been she all along, all fear inexplicably died. I wasn't afraid of Daisy when I confronted her, only when she was an invisible force creating malicious mischief.

"I didn't even know you were home, Norma. I saw your car out front but I thought you'd probably gone out to dinner with one of the others. Isn't it funny? It will make a marvelous story. There we were—both of us groping in the dark, terrified of each other. Honestly, Norma, your paranoia is beginning to infect me too. I jump at every little thing these days—"

I felt entangled in a gossamer web, not tight enough to strangle, but impossible to shake off. Her story was plausible enough on the surface, and yet it didn't ring true. Why should she assume I'd gone out when she saw my car? Why not call out when she came in? And most important, why hadn't she heard the TV set?

"Didn't you hear the TV?" I asked.

She was peeling carrots, face concentrated. "I wonder if I have enough celery. I'll borrow some of yours. I'm going to fix a *yummy* vegetable salad tonight. I hope Johnny won't be unpleasant about it. I keep telling him meat's bad for him—"

"Didn't you hear the TV going?"

"No. Should I have? I was talking to Tolstoy and—"

"Did you lock the front door after you came in?"

"Yes, of course. I was rather annoyed when I found it unlocked. You read these *hideous* stories about spaced-out weirdos who pick an innocent family and carve them up just for the hell of it. I wonder if Verity would mind if I borrow some of her cheese and ham. She probably won't. Particularly if it's for her *beloved* Johnny—"

"You went straight upstairs and turned on the radio?"

"Yes, of course. I feel as though I'm being grilled by the Russian secret police. What's with you, Norma? I went upstairs and then when I turned off the radio, I thought I heard these mysterious sounds from below, and naturally I got worried. I sneaked downstairs—darn. No lemons." She became aware of my scrutiny. "Why are you staring at me like that?"

My eyes dropped and I shook my head. "I didn't know that I was staring. I was thinking. Why did you laugh?"

"I laughed because you thought *I* was the prowler, and I thought *you* were the prowler. What a couple of ninnies we are. Norma, your nerves are shot. Have you ever considered seeing a doctor? I sometimes think you're about to topple over the edge. Okay, the salad is ready. I hope Johnny doesn't get stewed and stay out late again. I'll be *furious* if he does. Let's have a drink and go in the living room. Are you going to dinner tonight, you lucky thing?"

"I don't know."

As she spoke, she got out the glasses and ice, and I followed her to the other room. I watched her as she poured drinks from the same bottle into both glasses. Then she stuffed newspapers, twigs and logs into the fireplace and lit the paper.

The fire began to crackle cheerfully, the warm orange glow

lighting up the old stone chimney. But in spite of the fire, the drink, Daisy's soothing monologue, I felt stiff and unrelaxed. I watched her mouth until I was hypnotized into a comatose state. She hopped from subject to subject like a fly.

And then, finally, the others began arriving. I heard Strandy and Verity first, arguing about the origin of the word "honky." Shortly afterward, Johnny came in, and as I listened to their voices and laughter as they hung up their coats and washed in the downstairs lavatory, I began to uncoil, the tension leaving the back of my neck.

They drifted into the living room, Johnny rubbing his hands to bring back the circulation, Verity winding her hair around her finger in a familiar gesture, Strandy acting the clown with a soft-shoe routine.

I caught snatches of conversation about my panic, about next year's skiing, about Daisy's imminent birthday, about staying home and having a potluck supper. I listened sluggishly until I heard Mrs. Webster's name mentioned.

"I'm sure she's all right," Verity said. "People often do that—disappear for a few days and then show up acting surprised because anyone was worried."

"That doesn't sound like Mrs. Webster," Strandy said.

"Maybe she has a boyfriend," Daisy said, laughing. "Anyway if she doesn't show up we're all going to have to have alibis again."

"I wonder what she meant when she hinted she knew something," I said.

"Oh, Norma, the mystery fiend." Daisy jumped up to get a pencil and paper. "She probably meant she saw someone having dinner with someone else's wife. Okay, I'll start with my movements. We all saw her go up to her room Sunday night. No one noticed her Monday morning, right?"

"I did," Verity said unexpectedly. "I saw her leave for work Monday morning."

"Good. Then we know it happened—if it did happen—somewhere between Monday morning and seven in the evening when she generally gets home. Now I got up six-thirty Monday morning—"

"You never got up at six-thirty in your life," Johnny said.

"And fixed Johnny's breakfast—"

"You never fixed Johnny's breakfast in your life."

"And took a bath. And don't tell me I never took a bath in my life. And got dressed and had coffee and went to town—" As she continued describing her movements on Monday, I noticed what a good mood she was in. She hadn't even resented Johnny's needling.

"I knew a girl once," Verity said, putting down the crossword puzzle she was working on and lifting her glass, "who kept a diary of everything she did since she was eleven years old. If someone asked her, 'Where were you on the night of June 16, 1965,' she could tell you."

"And what were *your* movements on Monday, Norma?" Daisy asked.

The front door opened and uneven footsteps sounded in the hallway. Instantly the atmosphere of the house changed for me again, and far more radically than it had when Strandy, Verity and Johnny had returned. Then it had become warmer, but now a magic ingredient had been added, an extra dimension, a current which titillated every nerve in my body. When he entered the room, I moved slightly and he sat down beside me. He didn't pay any special attention to me, but it didn't matter. He didn't have to.

"We were just discussing Norma's movements on Monday," Daisy explained. "You know, when Mrs. Webster disappeared."

Evenly, I said, "I don't need an alibi. I was the one who began this whole investigation."

"Obviously that makes you the guilty party. Because you're the least likely. Tell us every move you made on Monday, what your assignments were, what routes you took."

They were all watching me, even Wesley. Verity was scratching her forehead absently with her pencil, Daisy was sitting upright, hands clasped on her lap, Strandy and Johnny were both unusually attentive. There was a curious tension in the air which confused me. As though holding a precious chalice, I placed my glass on the table unsteadily. But the unsteadiness didn't come from the drink. Looking down, I saw that my knuckles were white, and I unclenched my fists slowly. "I'm getting awfully hungry," I said.

"No, you don't," Daisy said gaily. "You can't get out of it that easily. I'm going to start a pot of spaghetti soon. Okay, begin."

"Ask me about *my* movements," Strandy interposed.

"Okay, Strandy," Johnny said. "Tell us about *your* movements."

Clapping a hand over his heart, Strandy said, "I refuse to answer on the grounds that it might besmirch the name of the woman I love. Wild horses won't make me tell you where I was between the hours of two and four on Monday afternoon. It is a far, far better thing that I do, than I have ever done; it is a far, far better place I was than I have ever known. Like Carton I will go to the gallows with face uplifted—"

"If it's like Carton, you won't be going to the gallows at all," Johnny said. "I don't have an alibi either. And not because of fear of besmirching anyone's name. Reporters can claim they were anywhere as they flit from one assignment to the next."

Gradually the tension seeped out of the air. Verity went back to her crossword puzzle, Wesley put on the record player and Daisy and I went to the kitchen to start the spaghetti. We used two unopened cans of clams I had for the sauce and added more vegetables to the salad. Then we collected plates, silver, and paper napkins, and returned to the living room to set up a buffet on the long table. Still chatting, Daisy said, "We can pretend that this is my birthday party. Actually my birthday is tomorrow, but that unspeakable Johnny is going to a perfectly *gorgeous* Republican dinner tomorrow night on an assignment, and he claims that I wouldn't be allowed to join him without paying. I'm so furious that I'm going to get dressed to the teeth and find a bar and pick up the best-looking man I can find."

As her voice trilled on, I found myself forming a vague plan. Perhaps I could make her so drunk she would come up with a damaging admission. "I tell you what, Daisy. Since Johnny can't take you out, I will."

"Oh, Norma!" Daisy was so rapturous she grabbed me and kissed my stiff cheek. "How *divine!* I haven't been to a really superlative restaurant for years—"

"Wait a minute, Daisy," Johnny protested. "Norma didn't say anything about a superlative restaurant."

"Where will we go? What will I wear? Oh, I wish I could afford to splurge on something *sensational* and upstage you completely, Norma. Maybe we can pick up *two* good-looking men."

"Would you like to borrow something of mine?"

Daisy was convulsed. "I'm about six inches shorter than you and twenty pounds lighter. No, I'll get something together. Maybe Verity has something I can shorten. She's smaller than you and thinner. Oh, I'm so excited. I knew when I accepted your application to join us, I was doing the right thing."

"You don't have to borrow anything of mine, Daisy," Verity said. "You know that printed pants outfit you've always admired? I'll give it to you as a birthday present."

"Verity! I love you all. You're all marvelous. See, Johnny? *Someone* cares about my birthday."

"*I* care, Daisy, but I have to work. Or you don't get those luxuries you're so fond of—like food and mortgage payments."

"I'll supply the champagne tomorrow night," Wesley said, watching Daisy's enthusiasm with amusement. I was beginning to feel a faint twinge of conscience.

"Wesley, you angel! I simply *adore* champagne. You're all so wonderful I can't bear it."

"What shall I get you?" Strandy asked.

"How about a guillotine?" Johnny suggested. "Since you admire Carton so much."

Daisy's gaiety vanished as though wiped off with a cloth. The familiar stillness came over her, every muscle in her face motionless. But before she could say anything, Verity jumped to her feet and took her arm. "Come on, Daisy. Let's try on the pants outfit while the spaghetti is boiling. You'll have to shorten it before tomorrow." She pulled Daisy out of the room and toward the stairs while the rest of us remained. It was peaceful and quiet.

After a moment Strandy said, "We seem to have lost sight of the fact that Mrs. Webster is missing."

"She's probably visiting a cousin in Podunk," Johnny said. "If there actually is a Podunk."

"If there is," Wesley said, "you can be sure Mrs. Webster would have a cousin living there. Anyway," he continued to Strandy, "why should *you* care? She never addressed a remark to you the whole time you've lived here."

Grinning, Strandy said, "She can't help it if she's prejudiced against Unitarians."

Coming back downstairs, Verity sat down beside Johnny and lit a cigarette. Like Wesley and me, they didn't touch or even look at one another, but the air between them crackled.

The silence was broken by Daisy bounding down the stairs with the outfit Verity had given her and an old sewing basket. "All I have to do is cut a couple of inches off the bottom. Otherwise they'll be nifty. Maybe not quite as snug around some of the strategic areas"—she blasted the air—"but sexy enough."

"You haven't told me what you want for your birthday," Strandy reminded her.

"How about a grand piano?" Johnny suggested.

"Strandy, there's a new book I'm dying for, and it won't cost quite as much as a piano."

"Too bad Mrs. Webster split. She could buy you a Picasso."

"Johnny, if you don't stop—"

Again Verity intervened. She had picked up the crossword puzzle again as soon as Daisy had reentered the room, and now she asked, "What's a palm civet?"

"How many letters?" Strandy asked promptly.

"Eight. It's plural."

"Well, that makes a difference. Let's see. We know a civet is a cat. Now all we have to do is find out what a palm is."

"It's a tree cat," said Wesley. "Obviously."

Contemplatively, talking to no one in particular, I said, "Do you recall the scene in *Remembrance of Things Past* where he's telling his friends he's dying of a fatal disease? They're all anxious to go off to a party, so they pretend they think he's joking. That way they can leave without appearing to be callous." Shutting my eyes, I nearly put my head on Wesley's shoulder, but I stopped myself in time.

They all stared at me, puzzled.

"What I mean is, here we are, acting silly, concerned with

trivial matters, while Mrs. Webster might be a captive somewhere, the way I was, or in pain or afraid, or even dead."

"Let's not get sloppy," Verity said briskly. "She's probably
watching TV at a friend's house. In any case, there's nothing
that we can do. The police are looking for her. What kind of
flower is the French name Marguerite?"

"A marguerite is a daisy, stupid," Johnny said.

I sat up so suddenly I jostled Daisy's arm and made her drop
the scissors. "What's the matter?"

"Is your real name Margaret?"

"Of course. Why? What's so interesting about that?"

I shook my head and pretended to peer at the crossword
puzzle over Verity's shoulder so that I wouldn't have to meet
Daisy's eyes. I was furious at myself for the lack of discipline.
So it had been Daisy at the state hospital.

I was still pretending not to notice Daisy's scrutiny when
the telephone rang. For some reason everyone suspended
activity, listening. Finally Johnny got up to answer it.

No one said anything while he was out of the room. We
couldn't hear anything, but we waited tensely. The moment he
reappeared in the archway, I felt like a soldier's wife seeing the
army officer and the blue staff car pulling up in front of the
house.

But I had already lived through a far worse moment than
this. "It's Mrs. Webster, isn't it?" I asked.

His face gray, Johnny nodded. "She was found strangled in
the woods."

Twenty-four

Daisy was waiting for me in the living room. For once she was subdued. Although Wesley was in the room with her, she wasn't chatting. She had tentatively suggested that we postpone her birthday celebration, but I had convinced her that it wouldn't do Mrs. Webster any good if we sat at home and did nothing. She didn't know that the party was more in honor of Mrs. Webster than it was in honor of Daisy. The latest death had obliterated the last twinge of conscience I had about getting Daisy drunk and trying to shake the truth out of her.

Pointing to a magnum of champagne on the table, she said, "Wesley brought that home."

Wesley was standing, still wearing his overcoat. "Why don't we all go?" he said. "I know *I* don't want to hang around here."

Not meeting his eyes, I pulled on my gloves and smoothed the fingers carefully. "Some other time. This is my treat for Daisy."

"Why?" Daisy asked. "I'd like the others to come. It will be more cheerful."

"I've already made the reservations," I said dully. "We can all go out together some night when Johnny can join us. It wouldn't be the same without Johnny." I glanced around. Just as the room wasn't the same without Mrs. Webster. Damn it, I reminded myself, I hadn't even liked the woman.

I buttoned my jacket, and finally, reluctantly, met Wesley's eyes. He was puzzled, not hurt or angry. It was as though we'd come to a silent understanding which made him certain that the reason I didn't want him to accompany us wasn't personal. But it bothered him just the same. He studied my face for a moment, shrugged and said, "Have a good time." Still wearing his coat, he waited for us to leave.

"Get that look out of your eyes, Norma," Daisy said when we were outdoors. "After all, *you* were the one who said that he couldn't join us."

Daisy made only sporadic conversation as we drove into town. It was strange being with a silent Daisy.

Chez Jean was a small restaurant I had found while out on a story, and the food showed more initiative than the name. Through the dimly lit interior, the headwaiter led us to a banquette behind a small table decorated with candles and a fresh flower arrangement. A fire crackled in the fireplace cheerfully. Since it was the middle of the week, it wasn't crowded, and no one was seated too close to us. The other tables were taken by a few couples, a family group evidently celebrating an important occasion, and a young couple engaged in an earnest, low-voiced conversation. They paid no attention to us.

I ordered double bourbons for us, and Daisy said, "Wow. We really are celebrating, aren't we?"

Pushing my cigarettes at her, I said, "Birthdays come but once a year."

"Praise the lord. Anyway, you were right. It's much better being here than sitting around gloomily at home. This is a lovely place. How did you ever find it?" Gradually her natural ebullience was bubbling to the surface again.

When the waiter brought the basket of French bread and the relish tray, I pulled them toward my end of the table so that it would be difficult for Daisy to reach them. I didn't want her dissipating the effect of the drinks. "I like the atmosphere of this place, Norma. It's full of intrigue. Look at those two over there. They *have* to be spies. And I bet the family group is part of the Mafia with the Don at the head of the table. But the couple next to us is *absolutely* darling. My guess is that it's an assignation and she has a husband and small baby at home, and he's urging her to abandon them and fly to Greece with him." She continued her running commentary about the other occupants of the room—their clothing, economic backgrounds, probable ages, reasons for being here in the middle of the week—her words buzzing like flies against a screen. After a while I ordered another double round of drinks, but I didn't touch mine.

"Norma, if you were a man I'd think you were trying to get me drunk. Wow. I feel better every minute."

We ordered the *escargots* to start with and then the *Médaillon de Veau du Chef*. Since I knew nothing about wines, I left it to the waiter. He brought us a white Bordeaux which I dutifully tasted and pronounced fine.

"The last thing we need is another book," Daisy was saying, "but I asked Strandy for Pynchon's *Gravity's Rainbow*. I really wanted one of those coffee-table art books, but I couldn't ask him to spend upwards of twenty-five dollars. What's wrong, Norma?"

I was staring over Daisy's head at a latecomer whom the headwaiter was leading to a table. I couldn't believe it. Not again.

Her hair was coiffed differently this time, pulled back in a severe knot, and she was inappropriately dressed in tweed skirt and pullover.

"What? Oh, nothing, Daisy. What were you saying?" Leaning my chin on the palm of my hand, I half shielded my face. But Daisy's voice carried, and the woman glanced in our direction.

Instantly, she looked enormously pleased. Veering off course, she came straight to us. "Well! Well! We meet again. It must be fate."

I felt the hot flush rising to my face, but I hoped that they wouldn't notice it in the dimness. "Hello, Mrs. Threlkeld. Uh—do you know Mrs. Barker?"

"Are you Mrs. Barker? We had a telephone conversation once." She laughed easily, without embarrassment. "I have a confession to make to you, Miss Boyd. I was so amazed at your resemblance to the Mrs. Garretson I met once that I called Mrs. Barker to check on you. The resemblance is really uncanny."

"Oh?" I said.

Peering around behind the dress designer, Daisy asked, "Are you alone?"

"Yes, I am. I was simply dying for French food this evening, and well, you know, a divorced woman doesn't get invited out too frequently, and so I decided to go out for dinner on the spur of the moment. My eldest baby-sits now, so I came straight from work."

"Join us," Daisy said expansively. She motioned to the waiter to set another place.

"Are you sure it's all right?"

I murmured something inaudible.

The two of them began to chat as though they'd known one another for years. Daisy said that the fact that I resembled the Garretson woman so closely supported a theory of hers that everyone in the world had a double. The dress designer said that the Garretson case had been very sad and the poor woman had gone out of her head afterward. Daisy said that Norma was interested in the case and was trying to solve it. The dress designer said that she thought it was a hopeless project, trying to solve a four-year-old murder.

And I had discouraged Wesley from joining us.

"What will you have to drink, Mrs. Threlkeld?"

"Martini. Please call me Beth."

Sipping the second double bourbon I had meant for Daisy, I decided to enjoy myself. There was no way that I was going to get information from Daisy with the other woman around. And in a short time we'd go back to the house and Wesley would be there.

Aloud I said suddenly, " 'Jenny kissed me when we met. La ta te da de da de da. Say I'm weary, say I'm sad. Say that health and wealth have missed me. Say I'm growing old, but add, Jenny kissed me.' "

Daisy, a snail suspended at the end of her fork, stared at me. Then she began to chew thoughtfully. "Johnny's always telling me that *I'm* a kook. But I think you surpass me. You've been behaving oddly all evening. You were definitely nervous when we started out, and now suddenly you're relaxed. Although, as a matter of fact, you've been more or less nervous since I met you."

The waiter, arriving with our dinners and the dress designer's Tournedos Rossini, saved me from answering. Someone ordered a third round of drinks, and the conversation began to get hazy. Although I was aware of the fact that I was talking too much and laughing too much, I couldn't stop myself. As the evening progressed, Daisy seemed to become more and more harmless, eccentric rather than dangerous.

"At least she's a happy drunk," Daisy said.

I found myself having an after-dinner brandy although the other two abstained. When the waiter brought the check, the cloud around me was so murky the numbers were indecipherable. Handing the slip of paper to Daisy, I said, "Here's my purse. Could you take care of it?"

Their faces were blurs without features, their voices sounds without meaning. I tried to get up and nearly fell down again. "Whew. I feel dizzy." Dimly, I heard them discussing me. Daisy, they decided, would drive my Volkswagen home, and the dress designer would take me home in her station wagon. Apparently Daisy had invited her back to the house for champagne. Sluggishly, I watched Daisy leave and then Beth Threlkeld was helping me to my feet. "Upsy Daisy," I said and laughed.

"You'll feel better outdoors."

My head whirling, I felt myself guided toward the door. It seemed to me that people stared at us and conversation stopped. I made a resolution never to return to this particular restaurant.

Cold air hit my face but I didn't feel better. I stretched out in the back, and then an interminable stretch of time passed before I heard the driver's door slam and the motor start up. The car reversed and then jerked forward, almost sending me off the seat. Although my shivering stopped when she turned on the heat, my nausea increased. I could hear her talking, the words indistinct, as though coming through a door. Once I tried answering, but only blurred syllables emerged.

I remembered hearing that it was better not to lie down and shut one's eyes when drunk, but I couldn't make it to a sitting position. Another bit of remembered advice was to keep one foot on the floor. I tried that, and oddly, it helped. Finally the nausea was so pronounced, I dragged myself up enough so that I could lean against the door.

The dark streets were deserted and I couldn't see one pedestrian. All of a sudden I narrowed my eyes in a vain attempt to clear my vision. It seemed to me that we were taking the long way home. I glanced at my driver, and as I did so, I caught a glimpse of her profile as she turned slightly to the right. Her neat features were emphasized by the severe hairstyle. For a reason I couldn't understand, her face began to wave like a fish viewed under water, and her countenance began to blend with Daisy's.

"Didn't we pass this before?" I asked suddenly.

Now I could see only the back of her head. "No, of course not."

"Wow. I feel like we're going in circles. Where are we going?"

"To your house, of course. Daisy invited me over for a glass of her birthday champagne."

Daisy. At the beginning of the evening it had been Mrs. Barker.

"I've never felt so drunk before. I don't know what hit me."

It hadn't hit me completely until the brandy. Well, it was logical. Brandy on top of bourbon and wine.

Unless Daisy had dropped a pill into my brandy.

But I was getting confused. It wasn't Daisy who was with me. It was Beth. Not Mrs. Threlkeld. Beth.

Again I tried concentrating on the streets, but my brain wasn't functioning. Nothing was familiar. No, that wasn't it. It *was* familiar, but in the wrong way. Anomalous. That was it. It was the wrong time of day for what we were passing.

"Funny," I said. "Funny. I can't seem to—"

"Yes?"

"Shouldn't we—aren't we—"

"Why don't you take a nap? That way you'll feel fresh for the party. The champagne party."

But I had to stay awake. I was sure that if I didn't stay awake—what? I rubbed my head and then turned ponderously to open the window beside me. It was automatic, but when I pressed the button, nothing happened. "Would you—I'd like some air—could you adjust the control button—"

"Sorry. It's broken."

"Then could you turn off the heat?"

"Sure thing." She leaned forward. Oddly I felt no relief.

"Where are we?" I asked after a moment.

"Don't you recognize the road?"

"No, that is—I think—" It was too much for me. The heat, the rocking motion, all that I'd had to drink. The more I tried to concentrate, the more addled I became. Why fight it? Why not take a nap as she had suggested?

By now we should have been passing the house where I'd seen the woman and the small children getting out of the station wagon. I remembered the stabbing envy I'd felt. I was no longer envious. I was going home to Wesley.

At the thought of Wesley, I relaxed. Any moment now I'd be walking into the living room and he'd be sitting there, reading or listening to music. He would look up with his familiar grin, half derisive, half something better, and I'd sit down beside him. Perhaps hold his hand.

I was nine-tenths asleep. Eyes shut, I felt the car slow down and turn up what I presumed was the driveway. No longer did I think of the trees as forbidding, the shrubbery overgrown, the lights depressing. It was a graceful curving driveway, the woods were natural, the lights welcoming.

I was only partially conscious of the fact that the car had come to a stop. I wanted to open my eyes, but the lids seemed glued. I heard the car door open and shut, the back door open.

What was Wesley doing? What an odd way to carry me. Not in his arms, but over his shoulder like a sack of potatoes. The fireman's carry. Not very romantic. It was damned uncomfortable. I muttered something, but I knew it made no sense. My tongue was thick, and there was something wrong with my hands and feet.

I felt a hard bump as my head hit something concrete.

Making a supreme effort, I unglued my lids. My head wobbled and I caught odd swaying glimpses of gray-black walls, a railing, monstrous shapes like dinosaurs. Moonlight, filtering through dusty windows, penciled the walls with spidery patterns, made the long-tailed reptiles appear to be stirring out of their endless sleep.

What was this place?

Memory stirred sluggishly. I could picture men hurrying along catwalks, boys taking folded newspapers from chutes, a foreman calling out instructions which echoed hollowly against the walls. And beneath it, around it, encompassing it, that inexorable hum as of machinery grinding out something unspeakable.

There were no men, no boys, no foremen. But there was a hum. A droning which would increase slowly, relentlessly until it grew into a clangorous polyphony that would hurl itself against my nerves, tear at my sanity.

Presses. At night. But the *Gazette* never printed at night.

Why did I hurt so much? What was wrong with my wrists, my ankles, my tongue? For no reason I remembered Lawford beating a rat once with the handle of a broom. He mashed at it and ground at it, but it wouldn't die.

A hard object was pressing into my back. Reaching behind me to make my position less painful, I found I couldn't move my hands. I struggled in panic, but they were absolutely immobile.

The knowledge crept along slowly, an inch at a time, as I fought to keep it at bay. My hands were tied. My ankles were tied. I couldn't move my tongue or make any meaningful sound because there was something in my mouth.

My brain took in each detail, but without meshing them together into a pattern. As though I'd been lobotomized, I could observe, but I couldn't conclude.

Then I caught sight of her. She was standing slightly behind me, looming over me as though from a great distance. I thought at first that she'd stretched in some peculiar manner, and then I realized that she was standing and I was on the ground. She was talking.

"I've telephoned Daisy," she was saying conversationally. Evidently she had been speaking for some time. "I told her that I left you in the car a moment in order to go the ladies' room, and when I came out again, you were gone." She paused. "When they find you, they'll assume you were crazed by brooding, grief and liquor, and you chose this method of suicide. I've heard of weirder suicides."

I stared at her like an idiot. I couldn't see her face. Only the outline of her head.

"We're only three blocks from the restaurant. Easy for a grief-crazed woman to make it, don't you think?"

She turned to look downward. "The presses will be picking

up enough speed any moment now. It's fortunate I went on that
Gazette tour and found out how they work. It's better than the
other ideas I had. I kept following you, trying to think of ways to
warn you off, but you wouldn't be warned. You never even
noticed me watching you."

She was wrong. I had noticed. How many times had I been
aware of a spectre, a presence, a being who didn't belong? And
how many times had I dismissed the sensation as imagination?

"Why didn't you leave it alone, Norma? I never meant to kill
your little boy. He looked through the window and saw me
trying to bury my husband. I couldn't tell how much he
understood. I was afraid it would percolate in his mind and he'd
remember some day. I went to your house to see what his
reaction would be. When I left, he was playing at the edge of the
woods and he kept watching me from the corner of his eye. I
couldn't chance it."

She might have been explaining again why speech-making
upset her. Her voice was sincere, honestly interested in making
me understand.

"You were so stupid, Norma. Almost as stupid as that older
woman—what's-her-name. She saw me coming out of your
room the day I mixed the rat poison with your coffee, and I told
her I was a friend of yours playing a joke on you. Then the idiot
called to say she felt it was her duty to inform the police."

Her voice droned beneath the quickening rhythm of the
monoliths whirling in their orbit. A scrap of metal far below,
caught by a moonbeam, glinted like a jewel. Soon there would
be something else on the floor. Something that had once been
me. *"Once in my life I saw a man slip off the catwalk and go
into the presses. They couldn't stop them in time. I was sick for a
week."* I could almost hear Eddie Beinecke again, telling me
about the accident he'd witnessed years before. His voice had
been filled with emotion. Beth Threlkeld's voice was as flat as
though she were reciting the alphabet.

The spell snapped and I tried to scream. The dry cotton gag
in my mouth absorbed all the moisture in me and made my
tongue feel as though it had been grated raw. I couldn't take
my eyes off the presses. I was like a driver who, seeing an
approaching car, accelerates helplessly.

I felt her hands under my arms and then she was hauling me to my feet. I thrashed and pulled and tore at the ropes on my wrists. From behind, I grabbed hold of the railing and held on, feeling the sores opening on my hands and the blood trickling between my fingers as she tried to drag me free. The world turned and spun as I kicked out at her with my bound feet, butted at her with my head. The thundering below roared in my ears, meshing with the silent scream in my throat. Moonlight, presses, struggling bodies all fused in a cataclysmic horror of movement and sound. She was unexpectedly strong, stronger than I would have believed possible, as she beat at my clinging fingers with her closed fists, and the pain shot through every nerve in my body.

Then the chaos changed texture. From below, I caught sight of something that hadn't been there before. A white oval, a face, staring upward, the mouth a black hole in the center.

It was bobbing closer, like an erratic balloon, the uniform below it catching on the railing, a hand tearing buttons loose, the shout just reaching us above the roar of the colossus.

At the sound of the watchman's shout, she turned to look down. For a moment she faltered, eyes gaping, grip loosening.

It was all I needed. With the remaining strength left in my body, I butted her in the chest. I could hear the breath leave her lungs in a whoosh of air. She opened her mouth, clutched at me, and then while I watched in unbelieving horror, she lost her grip, her arms flailed wildly, and almost in slow motion, she went over backward into the presses.

Her screams of abject terror thundered all around me as I sank down on the catwalk.

Twenty-five

Like a mole burrowing underground, like an ostrich covering his head with sand, like a baby refusing to be born, I wanted to stay in my room forever, huddled under the blankets and never emerging.

Three deaths. Teddy, Mrs. Webster and Beth Threlkeld. All, in a sense, traceable to me.

As though I were a junkie without a fix, my skin was prickly with irritating stimuli, and every nerve was open to unpleasant sensations. I didn't want to have to see, listen to, or talk to another human being for the rest of my life. What I did want was to get into my car and drive and drive until an ocean stopped me. Or get into a plane and fly forever. Escape was what I wanted, but most of all, escape from myself. And no earthly vehicle was designed for that.

Over. Over. The tune wouldn't stop weaving through my head. The sustaining hatred, the need for revenge, were over. I couldn't remember Teddy's face no matter how hard I tried to whip my sluggish memory. I knew the shape of each of his features, the color of his hair and eyes, the texture of his skin, but they wouldn't fuse into an entity. I couldn't recall the sensation of holding him in my arms, or of kissing him, of or feeling his hands on the back of my neck. It was over. Gone. Evaporated. I had nothing to stiffen me and I was shapeless, like washed-out finery.

Someone knocked.

Shrinking further under the bed covers, I tried to make

myself disappear. I wished now that I had torn up bed sheets, knotted them together and escaped into the night. Except that it was no longer night. Objects were becoming faintly visible in the shadowed room.

"Go away," I said. "Leave me alone."

"Norma. It's me."

"Go away."

"Come on, Norma. I want to talk to you." I heard him rattling the knob. "I'll wake up Daisy and get the other key if you don't open this. Hurry. We'll do your favorite thing. We'll go for a walk in the woods."

I didn't want him to get Daisy and I didn't want him to see me like this. Getting out of bed, I staggered dizzily and steadied myself by holding onto the table. "Wait downstairs. I'll get dressed."

· Listening to his retreating footsteps, I stared at myself in the mirror. Then, shuddering, I turned away. I took a two-minute shower, dressed and went down.

As I stepped outside the back door, I felt like an artifact dug up after a thousand years. The world resembled the inside of a pearl. Even the dead leaves on the ground shimmered with rosy iridescence. A pink light from the east was reflected on top of the maple tree, and the sun was a brilliant red sliver coming over the crest of the horizon. In the west, the yellow orb of the moon was still visible.

The universe erupted into sound as I emerged from the house. The air was filled with a myriad of twitterings, and as I squinted upward, I could see starlings and sparrows wheeling across the sky. Even the temperature had broken the thirty mark, and the fragrance of impending growth seemed to saturate the air. I saw him, a black cutout against the sky, and I started toward the leaf-striped birches.

We began walking the familiar path, Wesley falling behind when trailing branches and low bushes made it impossible to keep abreast. Occasionally he sniffed the air or stooped to pick up a pine cone as though we were on a nature walk. The tapping of a woodpecker made him stop to search the surrounding woods, but he couldn't find it.

He didn't start speaking until we were nearly at the dry stream bed, but I hardly heard him. My brain was a mirror of the sky, misted with hazy vapors. His voice blended with the peepings of the birds and the rustling of the leaves, and I was content to tramp along and sniff the air and watch the clambering squirrels.

Until I caught the words "state hospital."

"What?" I said.

He drew back his arm and threw a pine cone so high it sailed over the tops of the birches and disappeared on the other side of the stream. In the silence that followed we could hear a crow cawing.

"Weren't you listening?"

"No."

For a moment it was a tossup whether he was going to get angry or shrug it off. He shrugged it off. "Daisy had a baby years ago, apparently the only child she was able to have, and it died—of perfectly natural causes—and it got her so depressed she committed herself to the hospital for a short time. You really thought Daisy killed Teddy?"

My mind was beginning to fill again with an unwanted kaleidoscope of images, words, colors, memories, sounds, voices, and I walked more quickly to outdistance them.

"Hold it. I can't keep up."

"Sorry."

"Norma, you're going to have to learn to walk more slowly."

"Why?"

He watched a hawk wheeling in the distant sky. By now the sun was high, a blurry white, and the moon had disappeared. Instead of answering me, he asked, "Norma, since you were so sure someone was trying to kill you, why didn't you run away? Leave Freetown?"

"I wanted to find Teddy's murderer."

"Was that the only reason you stayed?"

"No. I had another reason."

"What?"

I could hear the sound of dripping water as we reached the

lowest part of the Barker property where a stone wall ran along the demarcation line. Here the air was protected by overhanging trees, and the iciness of winter was beginning to melt.

"You have to have everything done for you, don't you, Wesley. You never give a little ground."

When he didn't say anything, I glanced up and saw that he was grinning. "Please be kind to me. I come from a broken body."

"You're the other reason, Wesley. Does that satisfy you?" I had a picture of our future together, now that I'd set the pattern. Wesley stubborn, never giving in, and I taking the subservient role. The Barkers in reverse. Aloud I said, "I bet the Barkers are really happy. Daisy needs to dominate and Johnny needs to be dominated. And Verity had better accept it."

"Who brought them into this? Let's get back to us—" His words were drowned out by a plane droning overhead.

"Damned civilization," I muttered. I felt something brushing the back of my neck, and I lifted my hand to flick it off. The next minute he'd spun me around unexpectedly, and I forgot civilization and murder and the Barkers.

Then he was muttering, "Idiot. Damned idiot. If that watchman hadn't come in—"

When we started walking again, I tried to bottle and package the moment, keep it airtight so I could never lose it. It would be something I could bring out for the rest of my life whenever I needed the fragrance of happiness. I would be able to inhale the memory and it would be as fresh as it was now.

On the path in front of us a fawn appeared. We both froze in order not to startle it. It hesitated a moment, and then, lifting its head, it caught our scent. In a flash it disappeared.

Without having to discuss it, we'd been heading for the cottage in the woods. We stopped at the edge of the clearing and examined the dark windows. I was no longer afraid. I had no sense of blind eyes watching me, unseen hands reaching for me. The restless spirit which had inhabited the house had been exorcised.

"Why do you think no one ever missed Beth Threlkeld's husband?" I asked. "Why wasn't he reported missing?"

Wesley shrugged. "Right now I know two women whose

husbands walked out on them. Simply packed up and departed for points unknown. If a wife doesn't try to get the police to trace her husband, I guess no one does. Especially if he has no other close relatives."

"Do you suppose that those two women you know could have killed their husbands also?"

He took my hand and started to lead me away from the cottage. "At least you don't have to worry about *that* problem."

"I wonder what will become of her children."

"Whose?"

"Beth Threlkeld's."

"Why? You planning on adopting them?"

"It would be poetic justice. I'd get hers to make up for mine."

"Listen, they probably have a grandmother or aunt or something. Besides, we're going to have enough problems with our own children. A father obsessed about his leg and a mother obsessed about one lapse of attention."

"I'll never have another lapse."

"Sure you will. But next time there won't be a woman around who's just murdered her husband. You must admit it was an unusual set of circumstances."

"There could be other circumstances."

"Norma, I refuse to allow the mother of my children to act over-possessive."

"Wesley, I refuse to be yelled at for being possessive about children who aren't even conceived yet."

Not watching where I was going, I tripped over a trailing vine and went down on all fours. I was rubbing a smear of blood off my ankle when I noticed that he'd put out a hand to help me up. I hesitated and he grinned again. "It's all right. You can take a chance."

Grabbing my hand, he hauled me erect. We continued on our way, twigs snapping beneath our shoes, prickly branches scratching our hands. Once I didn't hear him behind me and I turned to see what he was doing. He was bending over a rotted log, digging at the dead wood with a stick. "Time to rise and shine, you guys," he told whatever dormant life he was disturbing.

"Come on, Wesley. We've got to get to work."

He glanced at me swiftly under lowered lids and then straightened. "You're going to work today?" he asked after a moment.

"It won't be any easier tomorrow or the next day."

He nodded, more to himself than to me, but said nothing. And finally we emerged on the lawn in back of the big house.

I stopped to examine it. It was the same large stucco monstrosity, the paint faded, the trim corroded, some of the windows cracked. Moreover, in the back were none of the attempts to soften the aging process with myrtle and azaleas and a pink door. It was nothing but an old house. What I'd felt had been in my own head.

Except for the fact that I'd sensed that it was tenanted, if only occasionally, by more than the legitimate inhabitants. An unseen presence, an unknown quality had roamed the halls, added something to a coffee jar, waited for an elderly woman to be alone, watched for a girl who took walks through the woods. An invisible boarder.

Taking a deep breath, I followed Wesley in.

I made myself meet their eyes as they suspended conversation and looked at us. For a moment we were all silent and then Strandy said, "Here comes Detective Boyd." They had heard the entire story the night before when the police had brought me home.

Sitting down beside him, I poked him in the ribs. "At least I never suspected *you*." Daisy handed me a cup of coffee and I stared at it uneasily a moment before I remembered that I had nothing to fear. "Daisy," I said suddenly, "what were you doing outside of my window the first night I arrived here? I saw you crouching on the ground under the moon."

Unlike the house and the cottage, Daisy still hadn't metamorphosed. Her face was as smooth and as unfathomable as always. "What?"

"I saw you doing something under my window the first night I was here."

For a moment there was no comprehension in her eyes and then she burst out laughing. "Oh, Norma. You're *marvelous*.

212

'Under the moon.' How romantic that sounds. What did you think? That I was concocting a witch's brew?"

It was exactly what I had thought.

"I'll never understand," she continued, "why I was your favorite suspect. Why not Johnny? He may seem sweet on the surface, but underneath—you can never tell. Or baby-faced Verity. Or Strandy, with the inscrutability of Africa—"

"It's the Orient that's inscrutable, stupid."

"Or Wesley."

"You haven't told me what you were doing that night."

"Actually, I was searching for a gold pin Johnny once gave me. I thought I might have dropped it outdoors."

"Gold pin," I echoed blankly. I was remembering the glint of metal in the front hall and the broach I had dropped into a pocket. "Oh. I found it. It had an *M* on it, didn't it?"

"Found it! Why didn't you give it to me?"

"I forgot all about it." I kept watching them, Strandy and Johnny resembling an all-American poster for racial integration, Verity slumped like an abandoned doll, Wesley appearing whole and unmarred beside me. And Daisy, the ageless sphinx.

"Daisy, were you once dark-haired and heavy?" I asked bluntly.

This time she didn't laugh. Her face even more rocklike, she said, "Norma, you take a lot of getting used to. I once did weigh a lot, and yes, I've lightened my hair. I was miserable—as you've probably heard—and let myself go. But when I recovered, I lost the weight again and did things to my hair."

I lit a cigarette, and then out of habit, shoved the pack at Daisy. I was thinking about Mrs. Webster's daughter and wondering if I ought to call her and tell her how sorry I was. Another brick in the edifice of my guilt. Another weight to carry for the rest of my life.

Gradually the others began to drift out of the room to get dressed, and finally only Wesley and I were left. We continued sitting, watching one another. Sighing, I said, "I've got to get ready for work."

He covered my hand with his. "Now, aren't you sorry you mistrusted Daisy so much?"

I thought about it for a while. Then, slowly, I said, "All right. Daisy did not kill Teddy or Mrs. Webster or Mr. Threlkeld." I tried to organize my instincts, my intuitions about Daisy. "But there's something about her. I feel that it's possible that sometime in the future—she's a latent, a potential—" I floundered, not able to use the word blatantly.

It was Daisy who used it for me. Standing in the doorway, she smiled pleasantly. "Murderer, Norma?"

About the Author

MILDRED DAVIS lives in Bedford, New York. She is married and has four daughters. Her first mystery novel, *The Room Upstairs*, won the Mystery Writers of America Edgar for best first mystery of the year of its publication.